SHADOWS
OF STEEL

By the Author

Shadow Series

Moon Shadow

Shadows of Steel

Visit us at www.boldstrokesbooks.com

SHADOWS
OF STEEL

by
Suzie Clarke

2021

SHADOWS OF STEEL

ISBN 13: 978-1-63555-810-4

This Trade Paperback Original Is Published By
Bold Strokes Books, Inc.
P.O. Box 249
Valley Falls, NY 12185

First Edition: January 2021

CREDITS
Editor: Ruth Sternglantz
Production Design: Stacia Seaman
Cover Design by Tammy Seidick

Acknowledgments

Writing can be a very lonely process and I know of no author who can write a manuscript without some type of encouragement. Thank you to all those who helped make this book possible. Bold Strokes Books and their professional staff. My beta readers—I'm forever in your debt. Thank you to my mother-in-law, Cappy, who never faltered in her support and encouragement. Thank you all for standing by me and encouraging me. You are the best.

To Carol,
Who walked me home in the dark when we were kids so the
Alcum Stretcher wouldn't get me, stood by me when I was alone,
and cheered me on to the finish line—forever a friend,
forever a sister, and forever in my heart.

CHAPTER ONE

The mixture of mottled-gray clouds covered the early morning Cleveland sky, contrasting the scant orange, yellow, and faded green leaves left on the maple trees. Rachel Portola watched out the bedroom window as the cold, moist November wind blew the fallen dead leaves across the yard, forcing them into deep rustling piles along the wooden fence line. She looked down and watched Claire as she woke and rolled over, looking up at her.

"Bad dreams again?"

Rachel slid down, the warmth of the bed around Claire beckoning her to move closer. She wrapped her arm around her waist and nestled next to her. It had been months since Justin tried to kill her to steal the computer program, months since their survival, but the memories lingered, haunting her in the night, long after the scars were healed.

"Sometimes when the dreams come, I can't get the feelings out of my head. It's like we're right there again."

Claire slid her arm around her. "We're safe, rest."

She blinked and stretched when the sun's full light flooded the bedroom, feeling Claire's soft full breasts press against her as her hand slid over her stomach and then up. She put her hand over Claire's. "I am never going to get enough of the joy of waking up next to you."

Claire leaned into her ear and kissed it, her breath sending a shudder down into her core.

"What time do you have to be downtown at the Federal Building?" Claire asked.

"Ten o'clock."

"You've already met with them and the MI6 agent a couple of times about the program Justin stole. It's going to be okay, isn't it?"

Rachel turned over toward her when she heard the concern in her voice. She kissed her shoulder and then looked up into her face, seeing the pout Claire always got when she wanted to say something but didn't quite know how to say it. "They just need some more information about the program—don't worry."

She waited, but Claire didn't respond. She reached up and gently ran her hands through her long wheat-colored hair, tracing the scar on her temple with the tip of her finger, seeing the muscles in her face tighten. "You shouldn't be this stressed in the morning. It's not good for you."

"Did it really help you to talk with a psychologist?" Claire asked.

She slipped her arm around Claire's waist and kissed her face, brushing her lips against the side of her neck, catching the familiar scent of the cocoa butter and vanilla body wash she used. She lifted her leg over Claire's thighs and slid onto her. "Yes, it did. We went through a lot in Alaska, trying to survive the plane crash, and then here in Cleveland, surviving Justin." She hesitated. She didn't want to think about it. It made her sick to her stomach to even say his name. "If you feel you need to talk to someone about it, then you should. Betsy's really good. She doesn't judge." She moved against Claire, felt her nipples harden, the friction sending tingling surges of heated want down through her body. She caressed the sensuous curve of her hip, then down onto her thigh. "Do you think you'd like to talk with her?"

"Mm, I don't know. I just…I don't know. I can't think right now."

She kissed Claire's neck, moving up. "There's a lot of good therapists out there. If you don't feel comfortable talking with Betsy, I'm sure she can recommend someone…You feel so good…I'll leave her number on your desk in case you'd like to call her."

Their breathing increased. Rachel spread Claire's legs with her thigh and pressed against her center, feeling her heat and wet. She looked into Claire's sea-green eyes, seeing the flush of color around the iris, the sex blush on her cheeks, feeling her own body react to her want, the need pulsing down into her—her own nipples aching to feel Claire's mouth surround them. She felt Claire move against her thigh and thrust slowly.

"Did you talk to her about us?" Claire asked.

"What? Yes, I did. I talked about how I felt and what was causing me pain."

Claire's hand went over her back and moved down, pressing her fingertips into her spine, pulling her into her. "I should feel sorry I trapped you, but I can't."

"You didn't trap me. I had a choice. Claire, that feels so good."

"Yes, but I didn't give you much of a choice—it was either choose me or leave."

She felt Claire's hand move up the inside of her thigh.

"I fought so hard not to love you," Rachel said. "I don't care what course our lives take us—nothing I do will ever be as glorious as being with you." She reached down and took her hand from Claire's thigh, interlocking their fingers, moving her hand up and pressing it into the bed, thrusting into her. She slid down and took a hard erect nipple into her mouth, tasting and feeling its beauty.

Claire arched and reached down, moving her free hand over the side of Rachel's neck and shoulder.

Rachel moaned as she withdrew from Claire's breasts and moved down, licking her stomach, feeling the surges of ravenous pulsating want.

❖

Eshee Yumiko, CEO of SeaBridge, stood motionless, watching through the conference window, her arms folded tightly against her chest. The operations chief, down below on the production floor, instructed his staff how to adjust the machinery to clean and bag the rice. A thin film of dust covered his light green shirt, the protective mask he wore, once white, now a cloudy gray.

Most of the employees had no idea the production was a distraction from illegal operations, and those who knew didn't care—they were only concerned about their next paycheck. Eshee knew labor was cheap in the Philippines, benefits were nonexistent, and everyone waited in line for the opportunity to work. She pushed the button and the window darkened, shutting out what she didn't want to see. She turned and looked at her stepfather, Bayoni Bautista.

"How close is MI6 to finding out our operations, Father?"

The muscles in Bayoni's gaunt face tightened. He moved toward the dark conference table, running his bony fingers over its smooth mirrored surface, then sat down at its head.

Eshee could see the outward effects of the liver cancer more clearly as she looked deeper into his face. The skin was darker with a yellowish tinge, the elasticity gone, the lines around the eyes and mouth deeper, and the sclera of his eyes now a ghostly white.

Bayoni casually brushed a smudge of light discolor from the pants leg of his tailored gray silk suit, the coat, once crisp and form fitting, now hanging loosely over his drooping shoulders. "Our sources are quite clear they suspect, and the traitor is giving them accurate information, but they are looking at their own interests, not toward the United States. I do not believe they suspect we are skimming insurance funds there. We have positioned ourselves perfectly in the health insurance system in the US, and it will eventually prove to be our greatest asset. All things come to those who wait, Eshee." His face grew darker. "But the program you purchased for our computer systems has caused more damage than we originally thought. How close are we to getting it corrected and out of our financial system?"

Eshee shifted her weight. She didn't have an answer. The security program that was intended to protect their confidential financial data had embedded itself into a critical part of their systems, and she knew he held her responsible as the one who approved the illegal purchase of the program from Justin McKinney. She held her hand close to her side, making a fist and squeezing tightly. "Our best programmers are working to correct it." She could feel his wrath underneath his calm demeanor and knew she needed to redirect him. "Who is the traitor who gave MI6 the information, Father?"

Bayoni looked toward his trusted aide. Eshee watched the aide leave, then looked back at her stepfather, seeing his facial muscles tighten, his eyes narrow, the look of domination sweep over his face—the look she had seen many times.

"Daughter, we must do what we must."

Eshee nodded and took her seat beside him.

The aide returned with Gian Fujiyama, who entered the room and bowed politely toward Eshee and stepfather. Bayoni motioned for the man to sit. Gian nodded and took a seat at the end of the table, hands folded, head slightly lowered.

"How long?" Bayoni solemnly asked him.

The man kept silent, eyes fixed on the table.

Eshee rose slowly, the same look of dominance reflecting back from her stepfather's face.

"How long have you betrayed us?" She watched as beads of sweat formed on Gian's forehead.

He swallowed, continuing to look down, his hands shaking slightly. "Six months."

Eshee watched as Bayoni stood slowly and left the room. She got up and walked behind Gian, taking the gun with the silencer from the aide's hand. She pointed it at the back of Gian's head and fired, watching as the body slumped forward onto the table.

"Clean it up," she said, handing the gun back to the aide as she left the room.

She went into the lavatory of her private office, glancing only briefly into the mirror, refusing to see, merely checking her face. She knew how to detach her emotions from her actions. This was not the first time she had killed, and she knew it wouldn't be the last. She began to wash the blood spatter from her arms and hands. She raised her head. The motionless face looked back, the eyes narrowed, revealing a momentary flash of the repressed conflict within. She immediately looked down at her blood-smeared arm, refusing to see. To see what? The wrath of her father-in-law—the pain of her stolen innocence? He had made her what she was, and now he and everyone else would pay. She looked back up to the faceless ghost in the mirror. *I am not a monster.*

She put on a clean white lace blouse, went into her stepfather's office, and sat down in the large cushioned chair in front of his ornately carved wooden desk, calmly crossing her legs.

Bayoni reached out with his perfectly manicured hands and gently touched the intricately hand-carved black mahogany carabao figure on his desk. "Protect our operations in the United States at any cost. Operations there must not be compromised. We will extract the finances from them like a dodder plant feeding on its prey."

Eshee faintly smiled. "Yes, Father."

She looked out the office window as the wind beat against it. She could see the white-foaming waves rising from the beginnings of a Philippine typhoon, hurling up, trying to get to her, but she would defy it like she defied everything that opposed her. Eshee Yumiko was going to get what she wanted, no matter what obstacles were in her way, no matter who she had to kill, maim, or remove from her path. She turned and looked at her stepfather, remembering how he forced himself on her when she was twelve, remembering his wrath when she tried to fight him off.

Yes, all things will come to those who wait—I assure you, old man.

She went to the bar and lifted the stopper from the decanter of lambanog, the faint scent of fermented coconut escaping into the air as the raging storm reflected back into her eyes.

Rachel reached out and placed her arm over Claire's lap while Claire sat up in the bed and opened a card.

"Aw, it's a birthday card from Derrick."

"What does it say?"

"Wishing you the best birthday ever. Looking forward to you two coming for a visit soon, Derrick. He's been a great friend to us, don't you think?"

"Yes, he has. I don't know what we would have done without him in Alaska. He's a great surgeon, that's for sure."

She handed the embossed card to Rachel, who admired it and then placed it on the nightstand.

"That's very thoughtful, considering how busy he is." Rachel rolled over and reached into the nightstand beside her. She brought out a dark purple velvet jewelry case wrapped with a white ribbon and handed it to her.

Claire eagerly untied the ribbon and opened the case. Her eyes lit up. "It's gorgeous. Put it on me, please?"

Rachel took the delicate diamond and jade necklace out of the case and placed it around Claire's neck, kissing her nape as she fastened the gold clasp. "Happy birthday."

Claire turned and kissed her, wrapping her arms around her. "Thank you, it's beautiful. I love it so much, but my birthday isn't for another couple of days."

"I know, but I couldn't wait. I wanted to get you something and surprise you."

"It's beautiful, Rachel, thank you so much." Claire began to caress her, her hands gliding over her body.

Rachel forced herself to look at the clock. "I'm going to be so late."

She reluctantly left her, showered, and began to get ready for her meeting.

Claire rolled over onto her stomach and watched her while she dressed. "I know I say it a lot, but you're so beautiful."

She never heard it enough, not from Claire. She buttoned the last button on her blouse, went to the bed, and kissed her.

Claire's firm delicate fingers made their way up her thigh. "Don't go—stay with me?"

"You never make it easy for me, do you?" She felt the familiar twinge of separation anxiety creep in from the dark pathways of the past. She forced it back and looked into Claire's eyes, longing to stay with her. "You are the one who's beautiful. I'll be back as soon as I can. Do you want to go riding later when I'm done? Ash needs a good workout. I haven't ridden him in almost a week."

"I can't—did you forget? Tilly is flying in from Las Vegas today for a long weekend, and I told her I'd pick her up at Cleveland Hopkins, and I have an order I need to finish up in the studio."

"Tell her I said hello and that I'll see her later this weekend. Be careful driving—it's supposed to snow today."

❖

Derrick slipped out of bed and took off his Patek Philippe wristwatch, placing it on the nightstand. He showered and dressed, then packed the three new individually wrapped sets of surgical scrubs inside the leather overnight bag. He never used the hospital-provided scrubs—someone else had touched them and put them on their body.

He was scheduled to perform the first of two knee replacements in an hour. He stared at his cell phone. He wanted to call Claire. He wanted to cancel his surgery schedule for the next three days and fly to Cleveland. He wanted to take her out to dinner, or go dancing, or take her to a show. Yes, he knew she wasn't ready, of course he did, but he would help her get ready. The only thing he really needed to do was get Rachel out of the way. He knew Claire didn't really want to be with her. He knew that in Alaska. She told him she was with Rachel, and he knew it was only because she had been traumatized. Who wouldn't be after what she went through? So he would bide his time, carefully plan, and then she would be his. Until then he would be their friend because Claire felt comfortable when he included Rachel, and he wanted her to be comfortable and happy. He would make her happy—he knew it.

❖

Claire parked the car on the top level of the airport parking deck. She hurried to the elevator, wrapping her heavy coat around herself, shivering as the chilling wind assaulted her. When she descended the escalators, she could see Tilly standing near the baggage carousel, waving, luggage surrounding her like brightly colored piles of oversized building blocks. Her once red hair was now blond, she had lost weight, and she looked tired.

"Tilly, I love that coat—is that the one?"

She hugged her and watched as Tilly smiled and stroked the front of the luxurious coat, the muted colored fur moving softly against the touch of her fingers.

"Yes, isn't it fabulous? I like it almost as much as the other one." She crossed herself. "May it rest in peace."

Claire bowed her head and smiled, remembering how Tilly had cut up her beautiful fur coat so she would have something to put on her bleeding blistered feet when they were surviving in the rugged Alaskan mountains. "May it rest in peace."

They both laughed as she helped her with her luggage.

"Good grief, Tilly. You're only staying for a long weekend. My back is going to be out from carrying all this."

"Be thankful we're not going somewhere else, and I'm only coming home. Sarah said she gets off work at the hospital about seven thirty tonight."

Claire flashed back to the of day of the plane crash, to watching Sarah, their childhood friend, her hands soaked in their blood, stitching Tilly's slashed thigh with a needle and dental floss. And then she saw her kneeling beside *her* to stitch the side of her face. They would have all died if Sarah hadn't known how to put them back together.

"Claire?"

She forced herself back into the moment. "Yes, that's what she told me. I'm sure she'll want to see you as soon as she can. You at your mom and dad's or downtown?"

"At home. God, I never learn."

"I wish I could stay and visit with you at the house, but I have an order I have to get done immediately, my last one for the year. I'm so glad I decided not to take any more orders after October. I love closing the pottery business from November through January. It frees me up to really work on special pieces. What's going on with the show?"

"We're dark until Tuesday, which gives me time to rest my voice."

Claire watched her shiver as she wrapped her fur coat tightly around herself when they left the elevator. A deep frown crossed Tilly's face when she saw the gray and pale purple colored clouds gathered to the north over Lake Erie as they made their way east on I-480.

"I'm so glad I don't have to drive in this weather anymore. How's Rachel?"

"She's better, but she still has nightmares. Each of us has struggled since the mess with Justin, but I think of all of us, she's struggled the most."

"She sure went through it."

Claire glanced over and saw Tilly's moist eyes.

"Damn, I'm such a crybaby when it comes to all that crap we went through."

"How's your back?"

"It's a mess. The Caprice Organization is so good about doing what they can to help me protect it while I perform, but I don't think it will ever be like it was before the plane crash. I have to wear the brace almost all the time now."

Claire reached over and took her hand. "I'm so sorry, Till."

"Don't worry—I have drugs." She smiled. "What's Rachel been doing to help herself? How's her leg?"

"She's been done for a while now with her psychologist and physical therapy. Her leg's good. She bought a gorgeous quarter horse and has it out near Kirtland at one of the big farms out there. She named him Ash. She said it means *friend.* I go riding with her once in a while— someone is always looking for riders for their horses—but mostly she goes by herself. I tried to teach her how to use the potter's wheel, but she's not interested."

"Has she had any offers on her computer program yet?"

"She's narrowed it down to two. I think she's just about ready to decide."

"How much do you think she'll get for it?"

"Forty to sixty million."

Tilly looked at her and gasped. "Holy shit, that's a lot of money."

"The program is a game changer for corporations. Justin may have been an asshole, but he wasn't stupid. He knew what it was worth when he stole it from her. Remember, he got twenty-one million for it underground, and from what I heard, that was only half of what he and Henson were supposed to get."

They were almost at Tilly's mom and dad's house when the sleet hit.

"Damn, I hate driving in this crap," Claire said.

"Living in Vegas, I don't miss it in the least."

They turned into the tree-lined driveway of the two-story red brick house. Claire helped her with her luggage as Mrs. Evans met them at the front door, smiling and hugging.

They stepped through the doorway and into the living room.

Mrs. Evans hugged her daughter again. "You two are so beautiful. I just can't understand why you aren't married yet." She walked into the kitchen to get them coffee.

Claire called after her, making sure she heard her. "I'm divorced, remember, Mrs. Evans?"

Tilly rolled her eyes. "Yeah," she mumbled, "I want to get married and have a marriage just like Mom and Dad's. Why shouldn't I be miserable like the both of them."

"Shush." Claire tried not to laugh. "You just haven't met the right man yet."

"Well, I have no desire to get married, right man or not."

"That's not true, and you know it."

Tilly walked her to the door when she was ready to leave, grabbing her arm and holding on. "Don't leave me here."

Claire laughed and hugged her. "Come over when you have time. I know Rachel would love to see you."

CHAPTER TWO

Rachel put the file carefully back into the black folder, zipped it closed, and handed it to Commander Brice Chambers, head of MI6's covert corporate surveillance and cyber operations.

"What do you think?" he asked.

Rachel smiled as she listened to his thick English accent, like butter on a hot freshly baked biscuit. "I think SeaBridge Tech is in a world of trouble, and I'd like to know why you think I can help you, Commander. I gave you all the information I could about my program, which they bought illegally from Justin McKinney, and I'm not sure there's anything more I can do to help you."

Commander Chambers explained, "SeaBridge was only slightly on our radar about a year and a half ago when there was an incident with their Philippines coastal operation, just outside Manila. We have been watching them closely since their ties with China have become lucrative, and they have infiltrated the European markets, but red flags went up recently when their financial accounting program glitched and exposed some of their highly confidential data. Their corporate holdings are vast, but there are several pieces we haven't been able to put together yet. The trigger you placed in your program has given us the opportunity to track their financial activities. We think they had their programmers review your program but did not find your embedded trigger until they initiated the software into their financial program, and your trigger disrupted their systems. Until recently, we had an inside person feeding us information, helping us interpret the data, but we suspect he was compromised and eliminated."

Red flags were going up all around her. Someone was eliminated by SeaBridge or by someone else. Who? Was Commander Chambers being forthright, or did he have a hidden agenda? What did he really want? "But how can I help you?"

"Frankly, we need you to get into their entire system. They are heavily involved in illegal international activities that are affecting the European financial markets, and we would like you to work with our cyber division."

"My program was designed to automatically encase and protect sensitive data in the event of an unauthorized attempt to breach the system, and then trace back to detect the origin of the attempted cyberattack. The trigger I put into the program is designed to break down those protections and disrupt the system so I can trace where it's being used. I suspected Justin McKinney would try to steal it, and I knew I had to protect myself and the program. Where does SeaBridge run their actual mainframe computer operations?"

"Manila."

"Commander, I'm sure you have very capable coders, and I am willing to give you the sequencing for the trigger—for a price, of course—so why me?"

"Because you know your program better than anyone. I can't take a risk of anyone else getting into the program and making mistakes. Our initial meetings with you were to assess, and now that I have done that, I feel strongly you are the only one who can help us."

"What kind of travel are we talking about?"

"England and possibly Manila."

"And all I have to do is help your coders or hack the system myself?"

"Yes."

"How much are you offering for my services?"

"Name your price."

She tried to lower some of the remaining red flags, but they were still waving in the stiff breeze coming from across the pond. "How soon?"

"Within the next four days. I realize that doesn't give you a lot of time, but since we have lost our inside contact, we are pressed to deal with this problem as soon as possible."

She looked directly into the commander's brown eyes. "I'll need a little time to decide. I'll call you tomorrow."

"Rachel, we wouldn't be here unless we thought you could help us. These SeaBridge people are very powerful, and I believe, based on what we know, that they are dangerous and have a lot of financial resources to get what they want. They don't care about international laws or rules, or who or what they destroy. All they want to do is glut themselves on their financial gain. They have to be stopped, and I believe you have the unique skills to help us."

They stood and shook hands, the commander placing his other hand over hers, looking directly into her eyes. She saw the genuine concern in his face as he searched for her answer.

"We need you. Please say you will do this. I have been told you have been through some difficult trauma. I wouldn't ask you to do this unless I felt it was absolutely necessary."

She looked directly into his eyes. "Commander—"

"Please, call me Brice."

"Brice." She nodded. "I'm not the only one who went through that trauma. My companion went through it with me, and she is very stressed right now. I don't think I can leave her and feel comfortable about it."

"Then bring her along. I'm sure she will enjoy London, even if you can't always be with her. I know my wife would love to play tour guide and introduce her to our friends and family. She'll make her feel comfortable and welcome."

He smiled, and she knew he saw the answer in her eyes.

She drove to the park near Claire's house and sat in her car making phone calls. She called Jack Ralston, who had arranged her security in Alaska. They discussed her concerns for Claire's safety and made a backup plan in case things did not go the way she hoped they would in London. She called Tilly, then put in a call to Michael Waverly, her attorney.

"Let's accept the offer from Louisiana. I think it's the better deal currently on the table, and it will free me up. I won't have to deal with other prospective buyers."

"I agree. I'll draw the papers up and have them ready for you to sign by tomorrow afternoon. They're going to be very pleased, and I'm excited for you, congratulations."

Rachel added, "Michael, I'd like you to finalize my will and set up the accounts and trusts we've discussed. I realize the accounts won't be funded for four to six weeks, but I need the paperwork ready within the next three days. Also, I want the power of attorney and durable power of attorney put in Claire's name and ready with the other paperwork."

She stopped at the doorway of Claire's studio, watching her while she worked at the potter's wheel, her graceful hands moving effortlessly as she worked the piece of pottery.

Claire looked up and smiled. "I'll be done in a little while—I can't stop now."

Rachel nodded and went into the kitchen, setting the mail down on the counter by the ceramic lit pumpkin, the two painted china pilgrims, and the Indian. She made herself a sandwich and thought about what she had decided to do, knowing there was a risk, but not knowing how Claire would respond.

Claire came in and kissed her as she sat down beside her. "How'd it go?"

She wasn't ready to tell her. "It went okay. I'm going to change to go riding. You sure you can't go?"

"I want to, but I have to get this piece done."

Rachel kissed her and stood, looking back at the figurines on the counter and then at Claire. "I see my people are outnumbered as usual."

Claire laughed.

Claire was curled up on the sofa, going over her schedule when Rachel got home. She bathed, dressed, and went into the living room, then sat on the leather sofa next to her.

"Did you have a good ride?"

"Ash was full of vinegar, but once he settled down, he did great on the trails." She began to unbutton Claire's blouse and kissed her neck, feeling the warmth of her skin against her lips. "I sold my program today."

"You did? How much did you get for it?"

"Fifty-two million over the next two years."

Claire put her arms around her. "That's wonderful, congratulations. I'm so happy for you. Let's go to bed."

They went into the bedroom and she pulled Claire down onto the bed with her.

"Claire, I want us to be financially comfortable for the rest of our lives."

"You know I'm loaded. I don't want you to ever worry about money." Claire began to kiss her as she started to take her blouse off. "I know you're coming into a lot, but if you didn't have a dime, I'd take care of you." Claire smiled. "The thought of that is such a turn-on to me. I wonder why?"

Rachel laughed, then kissed her neck just under her chin, that sensitive spot she liked. "Thank you, baby, but I just want to make sure you'll be okay, and I want to make sure Tilly and Sarah will also be secure. I owe them my life." She kissed her cheek and then brushed her lips against hers, feeling her mouth open.

Claire broke away and held her by the shoulders, looking at her. "You may feel you owe them your life, but you do not owe them your money. First rule of finance for the rich is that rich people are rich because they're smart with their money. Believe me, you saved their lives and mine."

"I'm *rich*."

Claire hugged her again and laughed. "If anyone deserves it, you do. Yes, you are very rich. I want you to have Michael contact my financial advisor. You're going to have a lot of work to do to handle that much money."

She wanted to tell Claire she was taking her to London, but that news could wait. There were more important things needing her attention.

She eagerly peeled Claire's clothes off.

❖

The temperature dipped below freezing. Claire built a fire in the fireplace and brought blankets out, spreading them on the rug in front of the hearth. Rachel brought out pillows and another blanket, then went into the kitchen and fixed coffee for Claire and herbal tea for herself.

Claire leaned back on the pillows and sipped her coffee, watching her, then abruptly sat the half-finished cup down on the hearth. "What are you not telling me? Other than saying it was okay, you haven't said one word about your meeting with MI6."

Rachel looked at her.

"Oh God, what is it?"

"MI6 wants me to assist their cyber division in London. I can't tell you all the details because it's classified, but I *can* tell you I'll be gone for one to two weeks."

Claire sat upright, rigid, the muscles in her face suddenly tight. "No."

Rachel touched her hand, trying to calm her. "It's going to be okay. It's just consulting."

"It's too soon after everything we've been through. Please don't go."

She pulled Claire to her, kissing the side of her head. "It is not a big deal."

"I don't want you to go. I can't bear it."

She held her tighter. There was no way she was leaving her behind. "You're going with me."

Claire pushed back and looked at her. "What?"

"You're going with me. Your passport's up to date, isn't it?"

Claire grabbed her. "I'm going with you?"

Rachel laughed. "Yes, you're going with me."

Claire wrapped her arms around her and rocked her back and forth. "I'm going with you. Are you sure?"

"Yes. I told Brice I wouldn't go without you."

Claire broke her embrace and looked at her. "You're absolutely sure? You're not going to change your mind at the last minute or something?"

"I'm not changing my mind. I'm not going without you. But first, Michael's going to bring some legal papers by for you to sign."

Claire sat back and reached for her hand, taking in a deep breath and smiling. "What kind of papers?"

"I think the technical term is advanced planning. Actually, I'm leaving everything to you except relatively small gifts to Sarah and Tilly, some to my foster parents, and some to the Tribal Council on the reservation in Arizona."

Claire leaned forward and squinted. "I gather this is a little more serious than you've led me to believe?"

"Claire, I'm leaving the country and working with MI6. This thing with SeaBridge is connected to me because they bought the program from Justin, and my trigger has caused a lot of problems for them. You and I are going to be smart and protect ourselves. If anything goes wrong in London, I want you on the next flight back here. That's the only way you're going to go with me. Do you understand?"

Claire sighed heavily. "Well, what can I say—you've made up your mind, so if that's the only way I get to go with you, then that's the way it has to be, but I think you're being pretty bossy about it."

Rachel smiled. "Them's the terms, sweetheart—take 'em or leave 'em."

Claire threw her head back and laughed. "Take 'em, take 'em, take 'em!"

"I know you probably think it's overdoing it, but if things do go south, and you have to come back early, you're going to have some old friends with you. Jack has arranged for Jacob Locklear and Frank Hawkins to be with you. I want you to promise me you'll do what Jack says. The backup plan is for you to go to Las Vegas and stay at Tilly's under security. It's Jack's home turf, and he can protect you better there than here, and I don't want you alone. Tilly said she would love to have you there with her, and Jack will handle everything."

She could see Claire's hands tremble slightly.

"This all sounds a little dangerous for you. I don't want you to get involved in this."

"Claire, I'm already involved. We need to get on with our lives. I need to do this. It won't be like it was before. It's not the same thing. I'm under MI6 protection, and I'll only be there as a consultant, but I'm not taking any chances when it comes to our safety. It's going to be okay. I sent Jack the money he needs for now, but if you will, I'd like you to cover any other costs until my funds are freed up."

"If I say no, will it stop you from going?"

"I love you so much, but I need to do this. I feel it in my heart."

"Rachel, you're driving me crazy. I feel like my emotions are raw and exposed all the time with you. I just want to take you somewhere and be alone. I don't want to share you with anyone right now."

"I completely understand. I think it's a natural feeling after what we've been through. I don't want to be away from you either and that's why you're coming with me to London. It's selfish of me, Claire, but I can't bear the thought of us being separated, and no matter what, I have to know you're safe. Jacob and Frank know what they're doing, so please, if it comes to that—no going rogue like you did before. I mean it."

"I know. I won't. I promise."

"Because last time, you took off back here to Cleveland and almost got yourself killed." Rachel felt the muscles in her jaw tense and her heart rate increase. She pushed the thoughts back down into the dark places.

"I swear to you, Rachel, I'll do exactly what they say."

"And if you have to go to Tilly's, you'll follow what Jack says, right?"

"Yes, I will. Please don't worry about it. I don't want you to worry about me if I have to come back. I want you to stay focused, so you can be safe. When are we leaving?"

"Saturday morning. We have to be at Cleveland Hopkins early."

"Saturday? Good grief, Rachel, that's not any time. What were you thinking? Will we be on the flight with the commander?"

"Yes."

"Is he good-looking?"

Rachel smiled. "He is, but he certainly can't compare to you. I'll introduce you at the airport if you promise to behave yourself."

Claire leaned in and kissed her. "Rachel, you think you are such a badass, but you're not. Let's not talk about it anymore for now. I just want to be with you and make love."

"I just want to be with you and get warm," Rachel replied with a smile. "Let's go back to your room and put the electric blanket on—I'm freezing."

They picked up their pillows, went back into Claire's room, and got in bed. Claire piled the covers over her and got in next to her.

"I just had a flashback of lying next to you, trying to keep you warm in that cave," Claire said.

"Don't think about it. I've decided to push every thought about that mess out of my mind. Better days are ahead of us. I'm sick of thinking about Justin, Alaska, and everything that happened. Let's not do it anymore." She changed the subject. "This feels so good."

"I'll make it feel even better."

Rachel moaned as Claire touched her, the warmth of her body engulfing her.

Chapter Three

R achel walked the cobblestoned street. The evening London fog and the damp clinging feeling of her hair and clothes grated against her body, but she had enjoyed the days and nights and sharing it all with Claire, even though they didn't get to spend as much time together as they had hoped. She was tired of the meetings and the demands on her time, but the trip had been good for Claire. Brice's wife, Annalee, had taken her under her wing and helped her relax, and the fact that Annalee was a practicing psychologist didn't hurt matters.

She walked up to the entranceway of 727 Albert Bridge Court, pushed the small metal buzzer, and the massive, heavy, dark English oak door swung open. Gladys appeared, greeting her like she had each time for the past eight days, and admitted her to the first level of MI6 cyber ops.

As she passed by the plain cream-colored wall, she knew the MI6 agent on the other side completed a full-body scan once again, her information and passport photo instantly coming up on his computer screen: Rachel Portola, age thirty-four, Cleveland, Ohio, United States, five feet eight inches, one hundred twenty-seven pounds, dark brown hair, brown eyes. Her fingerprints and iris scan would be displayed separately on the split screen, along with the information that she was half Native American, and the name of her tribe and its location in Arizona.

She followed Gladys through the hallway to the heavy, dark wooden double doors. Gladys wished her a good evening and left as Rachel entered the security codes. The elevator doors opened, and she stepped in, placing her hand over the scan. She felt the momentary downward motion, and when the doors opened, she stepped out and was greeted again, but this time by an armed MI6 security guard.

"Ms. Portola, please place your palm on the screen and look into the camera," the guard instructed.

Once again, she was admitted into the MI6 surveillance room.

Brice looked up and smiled as she entered, immediately waving her over to him. She joined him and two other agents who were poring over information and incoming data. She surveyed the interactive three-dimensional computer map on the large screen, noting the target building in the Philippines. The live feed from Manila showed the exact location of the two agents in the downtown corporate office building as they moved through the second floor northwest corner office, where, Rachel knew, they were searching the room for the computer flash drive with detailed information about SeaBridge's operations and the person behind their illegal activities.

Rachel looked up at the six round black clocks mounted on the wall, noting it was two in the morning, Manila time.

The communications officer, standing next to Brice, initiated contact with the two operatives. "Roger that, Redstone, syncing the link now."

A barrage of static came over the line, and then a strained, desperate voice said, "Not here…" Interference cut the remote operative's voice in and out. "…I repeat…not…"

More interference in the communication could be heard throughout the room.

Brice looked intently at Rachel and then back to where the two operatives were located on the map. "Redstone, look again—it has to be there." He shook his head and looked at Rachel once again.

There was a long pause as they watched the heat generated images of the two men within the computer's projected hologram.

Redstone's voice came over clearly as he said, "Negative, repeat negative, it's *not* here."

Suddenly four more heat-generated figures entered the lower part of the building and began to move up the stairwell to the floor where Redstone and his partner were located.

Brice shouted into his microphone, "Get out, get out. Four approaching your location, north stairwell entrance, move."

They watched anxiously as the two operatives quickly left the office and moved down the hallway in the opposite direction of the approaching figures, but they suddenly stopped and collapsed. Rachel clutched the edge of the table, continuing to watch as the heat-generated infrared faded from the two operatives and the four unidentified figures circled them.

Brice slammed his hand down on the heavy wooden tabletop. "Bloody hell." He looked at Rachel. "We have to revise our plans."

❖

The cell phone's harsh tone interrupted what little sleep she had managed to get. She reluctantly lifted her arm from Claire's waist and rolled over and pushed the button. It was Brice. She cleared her throat and greeted him.

"I am so very sorry, Rachel, but we need you to go to Manila with us. You are the only one who has the unique skills to get the information we need. We have to find out who is behind their global operations and stop them, and it starts with SeaBridge—it is the key."

She cleared her throat once more. "What do you need me to do?"

"We need you to hack SeaBridge's computer systems and get the data to expose whoever is behind their operations. If that is not possible, then we need you to initiate your disruption sequencing."

She took the phone down from her ear and looked over at Claire who was now sitting up in the bed watching her, a look of panic on her face, or maybe it was just a reflection of what she herself was feeling deep inside. She looked away, trying to hide her own apprehension. Once she said she would do it, there would be no turning back. She hesitated for a moment when she felt Claire's hand on her shoulder. She brought the phone back up to speak. "All right, but I want to get it done and get out of there as fast as possible. My real concern is the backflash. We have to have their system open and exposed long enough to get the data or disrupt their system, but we will be exposed for as long as we open their system. It's like leaving a trail of breadcrumbs right up to our door and having signs posted all along the way."

"How long do you think you will need once you infiltrate the system?"

"About twelve minutes for the data, twenty-seven to thirty minutes if we have to hack to plant the disruption protocols to destroy the system, and I'll have to be within a half kilometer of their mainframe to do it."

"We will leave at zero-three thirty hours from Heathrow. Pack only the flight bag we gave you. We will be there to pick you up shortly."

"I want Claire on the next flight out of here."

"It's already being arranged. Staff will pick her up at a quarter to the hour."

Rachel ended the call, then turned over and looked at Claire, who was wide-awake, looking at her, an expression of pure panic now on her face.

"I have to go to Manila with Brice. It's time for you to go home like we agreed. Pack your bags. They'll be here in a little while to pick you up."

Claire grabbed her and held on. "Please don't go, Rachel. Lie to them if you have to, but don't go."

Rachel gently placed her hands on her arms. "I'll be all right. There's a team going with us."

They got up and dressed. She packed the black leather bag MI6 had given her as quickly as she could.

Claire walked over and wrapped her arms around her again.

"Don't worry. I'll be with you at Tilly's as soon as I can. It's going to be okay. I promise."

"You can't promise shit, and you know it."

She put her arms around Claire's waist, bringing her closer. "Claire, don't. I have made a commitment, and I have to do this." She paused. "I won't be able to call you until I get back here to London."

There was a deafening silence between them, like no one else in the world existed at that moment and everything had suddenly stopped. There were no traffic sounds, no barking dogs, no noises from the other apartments. Claire broke away from her and walked over to her side of the bed, picked a book up off the nightstand, and threw it across the room, slamming it into the wall.

"Doing that won't change anything. This is exactly why I didn't want you to come to London with me. Every single time something important doesn't go the way you think it should, you throw a tantrum. I can't deal with this, Claire."

"I'm sorry. I can't help it."

Rachel walked over to her and held her. "I know. I feel it too. I don't want to go, but I need to do this. I'm sorry."

"How long will you be away?"

"I don't know, hopefully just a few more days, but I promise I'll be back as soon as I can."

"I want you back with me at Tilly's as soon as possible."

"Call Jack. Tell him to initiate the backup plan."

"I'll do it as soon as you leave. Don't worry about me—take good care of yourself, and focus on you. I'll be fine. Please be careful."

Rachel placed her hands on her shoulders, looking into her eyes. "Do everything Jack tells you to do. You promised." At that moment she felt the full force of the dread and anxiety of leaving Claire. Her mind filled with apprehension, and she could feel her heart pounding in her chest. She didn't want to tell her any more because it would make the situation worse, and she couldn't tell her because it was classified—two operatives were already dead, and she knew she could be the next one.

Brice's aide took her leather carry bag and left for the car. She turned to Claire and held her, whispering in her ear, "I'll be with you in just a few days. I promise." She kissed her and forced herself to break her embrace.

"Damn it, Rachel, you better keep your promise."

Claire's words echoed in her ears as she slid hesitantly into the back seat and looked at Brice.

"Don't worry about Claire. She's in good hands. I know you don't want to do this, but it's the only way we can get into their systems and disrupt their global operations. Whoever is behind this has the power and ability to affect the international financial markets, which leaves major players in the market vulnerable."

As the wheels of the jet touched down on the Manila runway, Rachel continued to grab the armrests until the plane came to a complete stop. She was soaked in sweat from trying to fight the flashbacks. Would she never leave Alaska behind? She followed Brice into the airport as they turned right, away from the mass of people. The noise of the crowds was almost deafening—everywhere she turned there were throngs of people in motion.

"Two things you must always remember here in Manila, Rachel—there is always someone watching, and anyone can be bought." Brice said it as if he had spoken a written law of the land. He motioned for Rachel to follow him. The blast of hot humid air almost knocked her over when they went through the exit door. They immediately got into the waiting black Range Rover with heavily tinted windows and drove to the Manila Hotel near the old city wall. The small shanty-like structures that lined the dark narrow streets were jammed together haphazardly beside and on top of each other, seemingly with no uniform construction design, but each critical to the support and existence of the others.

Two men of slight build, in formal white traditional uniforms and salacots, greeted them at the entrance of the hotel, assisting Rachel as she got out of the vehicle. The scent of wood and flowers permeated the air as they walked through the hotel lobby with its high ceilings, carved wooden figures, and paintings of Filipino workers and villages. She was quickly escorted to her room by Brice.

"We have a little while until we leave, so try to get as comfortable as you can. I know this is a grueling schedule. Just a word of caution— don't drink anything that isn't bottled, including when you brush your teeth." Brice left her room.

She undressed and got into the shower, her muscles aching and her head pounding. She let the lukewarm water run over her shoulders and back, easing the tension. She changed into fresh clothes and lay down on the bed, drifting off into a light sleep. She woke suddenly, startled by the loud knock at the door. One of the agents, the one with perfect teeth and dark brown hair, greeted her and told her they would leave in thirty minutes as he handed her a mango, a banana, and two rolls.

"The rolls are called pandesal, a small sweet yeast roll. You'll like them."

She ate the delicious rolls and part of the fruit as she waited for the men to return.

❖

"Downtown Manila is very deceiving," said Brice. "The traditional jeepney and tricycle are not permitted downtown, and because of it, they have at least some regulated traffic control."

Rachel was surprised there was traffic in the middle of the night. The driver drove to the back of the Asian Mall and around the corner to a small cream and green colored older building. They got out of the Rover and climbed the uneven concrete stairs to the second floor, then walked down the open hallway to a room on the south side of the building. Two agents positioned themselves to stand guard outside the door.

"All right, Rachel, let's begin." Brice gave her the access codes for the satellite link and set the equipment down beside the electrical outlets.

She crouched in the dimly lit corner of the dilapidated concrete building. Her fingers flew across the lit keyboard as she entered the codes, sweat running down her face, dripping into her eyes. She wiped her eyes with the back of her hand and continued, her blouse soaked from the Manila heat and stifling humidity. "Start timing us as soon as I give you the signal...*Now.*"

"Started," Brice called out.

The data flashed onto the screen as she began to download the information, but the data suddenly started to corrupt. "They're fast. They're on to us already. Brice, we have to go." She yanked the cords from the booster and began shutting down the system, but it was too late—she knew whoever was at the other end had already tracked the origin of the signal. "We have to move now." She grabbed the flash drive and forced it into her pants pocket, disconnecting her computer and shoving it and the booster into the black bag. "Now," she said again, hearing the anxiety in her own voice.

She followed close behind Brice, her heart racing, feeling the sweat drip down the sides of her face, the overwhelming stench of mildew and mold invading the heavy air as she struggled to breathe. She put one hand on Brice's shoulder to balance herself as they went down the narrow steps almost two at a time. Once they reached the bottom step and moved out into the shadows of the night, she felt herself being guided into the black Range Rover.

The tires squealed on the pavement when the driver hit the main road, increasing his speed as the two black Cadillac Escalades approaching from the side and behind them raced across the parking lot to cut the distance between them.

"Go, go, go," Brice ordered.

The driver made three quick turns, trying to lose the SUVs, but they made each turn, narrowing the distance with each move, the high beams of their headlights flashing through the tinted back window onto Brice's shoulders.

Rachel struggled to put her seat harness on, missing the buckle twice, coming up off the seat, slamming into Brice but finally getting the harness connected. She looked over at Brice, his face ghostly, illuminated by the headlights of the vehicle close behind them and the light from his cell phone.

"This is Commander Chambers, we are on our way, get ready." He stuffed the cell phone back into the dark leather holder at his side.

The driver entered a tunnel. The sound of the car's engine echoed and bounced off the concrete walls, the lights flashing by so quickly they looked like strobe lights on a dance floor. Rachel's stomach began to churn. She closed her eyes and put her head down, but it only increased her nausea. She opened her eyes just as the SUV came up out of the tunnel, leaving the wet pavement, hitting back down hard onto the road, the driver never decreasing his speed.

The MI6 agent in the passenger seat called out to the driver, "Sixteen kilometers to go."

The lights, shining in through the rear window, suddenly changed.

Brice looked back. "They're falling behind. Something's wrong—they either don't want to risk it, or they have different orders. These people don't give up that easily."

"Pier seventeen," the agent in the front seat told the driver.

The driver slowed, maneuvering through the maze of barricades, making his way to number seventeen, where a light-colored cabin cruiser was waiting, outboard motor running, boarding lights on. They got out of the Rover, gathered their equipment, and hurriedly boarded the boat, the agent from the front passenger seat sitting Rachel down and telling her to hang on. She grabbed one of the inside rails along the starboard side of the boat but was suddenly thrown up against the railing, the tepid seawater spraying into her face as the skipper pushed the engine to full throttle, clearing the docks.

Thirty minutes later there was a bright beam of overpowering white light above and off to the left, as if scanning the ocean, moving toward them until it became fixed on their position. Shots rang out. Bullets hit the cabin windshield toward the bow of the boat, shattering pieces of Plexiglas over the forward deck. The skipper ducked and maneuvered the boat into a zigzag course as the two agents quickly knelt on the deck and fired their weapons up at the helicopter.

Brice rushed over and bent down to her, shouting into her ear, "No wonder they stopped following us—they knew where we were going. Bloody hell, this is a screwup."

As the MI6 agents continued to return gunfire, the light from the helicopter suddenly veered and went out completely. The skipper straightened out the course of the boat and continued for an hour more, and then cut the engine and began to slowly troll, flashing the running lights. A large beam of light, forward and on the starboard side of the boat, blinked in several bursts. The skipper turned the boat slightly, making his way toward the light, which was attached to a very large British naval cruiser.

Chapter Four

A female officer assisted Rachel on board the ship and escorted her to a compartment, gave her dry clothing, and placed a female guard outside the hatch. She shook so hard she could barely wash her face and hands or change out of her wet clothes. When she was ready, the guard escorted her to the captain's cabin where Brice, the captain, and two executive officers were waiting.

"Would you like some tea or coffee, or perhaps something stronger, Ms. Portola?" the captain asked.

"Just herbal tea or hot chocolate if you have it, please."

He looked at the steward, who acknowledged and left.

"Well, we have had quite a night. No harm done, I hope," Brice said.

"No, Commander. All reports are that no injuries occurred," said the captain.

"Rather good, that. We would like to go to a secure conference room, Captain. We need to debrief, and I need a direct link to MI6."

"Understood. The guard will show you the way. I'll have your drinks sent to you." The captain smiled and opened the hatch for Rachel.

She could taste the rich chocolate and cream as she sipped the delicious hot drink, listening to Brice talk on the com link as he reported the failure of the mission.

When he finished, he looked over at her. "Our air transportation will be ready in the early afternoon. I want you to get some rest. We'll meet back here at zero eight hundred."

She slowly got up from the chair. She had been awake for almost twenty-seven hours, and she felt exhausted. Her limbs were weak and her body ached from the physical exertion, stress, and the emotions of the night. The female officer escorted her back to her compartment and assured her someone would be watching over her if she needed anything. Rachel thanked her and said good night, shutting the hatch and immediately collapsing onto the berth.

She could feel the warmth of Claire's body against her, smell the faint scent of lemon and honeysuckle in Claire's hair as it brushed against her face, feel the softness of her fingertips as Claire touched her, and the wet of her mouth as they kissed, hungering for more. Suddenly she was standing on the outside railing of the mezzanine at the Henson building in Cleveland, looking down at Justin as he dragged Claire across the cold, hard tiled floor. "No, Claire!" She screamed as loud as she could, but the words caught in her mouth, coming out in slow motion, seeping out one syllable at a time, like trying to speak with a mouth full of cotton, choking her as she fell into nothingness. "Claire." She tried to get the word out but woke herself up.

She could feel the motion of the ship as she turned on the light. She got out of the berth and went to the sink, the mirror reflecting the night shadows, accenting the stress and anxiety in her face. She reached for a glass and poured the water, watching as it filled, trying to distance herself from the memories. She drank the water but thirsted for relief.

She went back to bed and tried to sleep, feeling the pressure of the handle of her grandfather's knife as it left her hand and sank deep into Justin's neck. In her mind's eye, she watched Claire push herself away from him as he reached up to his neck, and then fell backward against the wall, the bullet Jacob fired going deep into his chest.

She swallowed hard and sat back up in the bed, hearing the engines and feeling the rocking motion of the ship. Once again there would be little relief from her past.

Three more hours of restless sleep and she and Brice were back in the conference room.

"What happens now, Brice?"

"We're formulating an alternative plan. SeaBridge has relocated without a trace. It will take time to find them, but we aren't giving up—we have to shut them down."

She booted up her computer and loaded the flash drive, then searched for the information she needed. "I think I know a way. There." She pointed to a coding sequence.

Brice moved to her computer.

"My trigger embeds into the system my program's been illegally loaded to. As soon as SeaBridge's systems are up and running again, we can find them. You only need to monitor for that particular signature. I can't help you with locating their physical base, but if you monitor all international market activities, you will eventually find where they are secretly directing their funds."

Brice looked intently at the screen, "Astounding, Rachel, honestly, I've never seen anything like it."

"Well, you are going to see it used in corporate businesses now because I just sold the program to a corporation in the United States. I'll give you the information you need when we get back to London, and then I want to go home."

"We may need you in a few more weeks. Are you willing to come back to help us?"

She wanted to say no but found herself saying yes.

Eshee lifted the glass of lambanog to her mouth, drinking without stopping until the glass was drained, and then threw it across the room, shattering it against the wall.

"MI6 has been watching us for months—I don't care. I want whoever entered my system." She glared at the two men seated on the couch across from her. They would do her bidding. She had saved them from a certain death when they were caught trying to steal shipments of government medical supplies from a coastal port on Mindanao. "Find whoever tried to do this, and then do nothing until you talk with me. I want whoever it is."

"We already know who it is. We just need a little more information about her." Ondrada, the smaller of the two men, stood up and smiled coldly. "She's the same person who designed the program."

Eshee raised her right eyebrow, surprised it was a woman. "*She* is going to fix what she did and pay for it one way or the other. Use our sources in the United States to find her." She stood up, looking back at him as she started to leave the room. "When you find her, Ondrada, I want her untouched and unharmed—she's mine."

He lifted his hands slightly and shrugged.

Rachel pulled her seat belt as tight as she could and gripped the armrest. Her palms were sweaty and her heartbeat was in her throat as the plane started its descent into Las Vegas. She tried desperately to hold off the flashback of the plane crash and the smell of rubber, dust, and fuel. She tried to calm herself, fighting as hard as she could. When she felt the sudden jolt of the plane finally touching down, perspiration was dripping down her face, and her knuckles were white from gripping the armrests. She waited until she was ready to stand, quietly watching as the last of the first-class passengers emptied the section of the plane. As she descended the escalators to baggage claim, she saw Claire and Tilly waving madly, all smiles. She smiled and waved back.

Claire grabbed her and hugged her, kissing her face, not letting her go. "I'm so glad you're finally back."

They talked nonstop to Tilly's house. When she started to get out of the limo, there he was, standing straight, muscles bulging, a huge smile on his face. He reached in and took her hand, guiding her carefully out of the limo.

"Ms. Portola, welcome to Las Vegas," Jacob Locklear said.

Rachel smiled and hugged him. "Jacob, it's so wonderful to see you. How are you?"

"Good, Ms. Portola, I'm good." He wrapped his massive arms around her.

She stood looking at the people surrounding her, overwhelmed with love for all of them. She felt like she was home.

"I know you're tired, but we're going out later tonight. You can sleep for about two or three hours," Claire said.

Jacob carried her luggage up to her bedroom and set it down. She hugged him again and thanked him, feeling safe under his watchful eye. He left quietly and went outside to do his job.

She looked at Claire and then around their corner bedroom. There were two sets of windows and heavy dark curtains to block the sun, a large private bathroom on the left of the king-size bed, and a spacious walk-in closet just beside it. She could see Claire's clothes on one side of the closet, while the other side had four evening dresses, three of Rachel's favorite outfits, and some of her everyday clothes.

Claire closed and locked the bedroom door, then walked to her, taking her into her arms.

Rachel held her as close as she could, feeling Claire's body tremble.

"I've been so worried and lonely for you, Rachel. I feel like you've been gone for years."

She felt Claire's warm soft lips brush against hers, and then she opened her mouth and kissed her, probing gently, feeling the thrill of kissing her once again, holding her, feeling her exquisite body as she pressed against her, wanting her. She put her hand up to Claire's face and deeply kissed her again, feeling the wet of her mouth and the soft, warm, sweet sensation of her lips. She slid her hands over her body. "I've missed you so much, Claire. I can't even tell you how good it feels to be with you again."

They stood quietly embracing, rejoicing in each other's arms—until the knock on the door.

"Hey, you two can't stay in there the entire time," called Tilly.

Claire cussed under her breath and reluctantly went to the door and opened it. Tilly came in and sat on the bed as they lay on the bed beside her.

"When was the last time you had a good sleep, Rachel? You look awfully tired," said Tilly.

"It's been a while, long enough that I don't remember." Rachel put her hand to her mouth and yawned as Claire took her other hand and held it.

"Do you feel like eating anything?" asked Tilly.

"Maybe something light." She yawned again.

They got up and went downstairs to the kitchen.

While they ate and visited, she tried to drink as much water as she could. "What time is it?"

"It's seven p.m.," said Tilly, looking down at her diamond watch.

She stayed awake as long as she could but only lasted forty-five minutes. "I think I'll go to bed for a while and sleep."

She got up and slowly walked to the stairs, feeling like she was trying to swim against a strong current of water. Claire walked beside her to their bedroom, closed the door and heavy curtains, then gave her new silk pajamas and sat on the bed, watching her as she undressed to take a shower.

"You look exhausted."

"I'm pretty tired."

She showered and then got into bed, grabbing Claire's hand as she started to leave the room. "Be with me for a little while. I need to feel you next to me. I've missed you so much."

Claire kissed her and got in bed, scooting as close as she could next to her, slipping her arms around her.

Rachel smiled and yawned as she lay her head on Claire's shoulder, her body completely relaxed. "That's so nice."

CHAPTER FIVE

"Rachel, Rach, wake up." Claire shook her. "I brought you some food." She set the tray down on the dresser, watching Rachel as she slowly opened her eyes. She touched her face, as if to capture her beauty with her fingertips. It wasn't any particular part of Rachel's face that was stand-alone beautiful, not her high cheekbones, or her classic nose, or her full lips. Her eyelashes weren't particularly long, and her eyebrows were normally shaped, but it was the combination of all her features. Each individual asset seemed to accentuate and enhance the others, her eyes most of all. She moved Rachel's long dark hair behind one ear, desperate to see all of that face. Rachel's bright hazel eyes sparkled when she looked up at her. *She's a masterpiece. How could I have let her out of my sight for one second?* "How was your nap?"

Rachel smiled back as she yawned and stretched. "Good, I feel so much better."

Claire laughed. "You should—it's been thirteen hours." She saw the confused look on Rachel's face and laughed again.

"What? Has it really been that long? I'm so sorry."

Claire jumped up on to the bed and lay beside her. "It's fine. Tilly and I felt sorry for you last night and let you sleep. I laughed at you in the night because every time I put my arm around you, you would moan and say how good it felt and how much you missed me, and then you'd go right back to sleep. Let's go golfing."

"It's Thanksgiving week."

"Hey, we're in Vegas, baby. It's seventy-two degrees outside and sunny."

"I don't have my clubs, and it's too hard to find any good left-handed rental sets."

"No worries. Tilly and I made a trip to Cleveland to get some things, and I brought your clubs. I thought we could have an extended stay."

"You are the woman." Rachel half looked around the room. "Who's home?"

Claire tossed her head back and laughed. "I want you so badly. No one is here right now. Tilly left for an early rehearsal, Margaret, the housekeeper, went shopping for groceries, and Jacob is outside."

"Did you lock our bedroom door?"

"Yes, I locked the door." She brought Rachel's hand up to her blouse, her breasts aching to be touched. They kissed and began to hungerly undress each other. "I'm so glad you kept your promise. I told Tilly we would be at her show by seven forty-five tonight. I went shopping and bought you some things."

"That's nice." Rachel pulled her down and moved on top of her.

Claire's body throbbed, every part of her wanting to be touched. She wrapped her arms around Rachel's neck and pulled her as close as she could, pressing her center up into her.

They stayed in bed the rest of the morning and afternoon, making love, talking, enjoying the food, and then took a nap. Claire woke when Rachel pressed her body up against her. She slipped her hand over her waist, kissing her bare shoulders. "I have something for you."

Rachel laughed. "Mm, I have something for you too."

"I mean besides that." She reached into the nightstand and pulled out two beautiful black velvet jewelry cases, one twice the size of the other with ribbon tied around them.

Rachel kissed her and sat up and opened the cases. The larger case contained a three-carat diamond necklace surrounded by opals encased in gold. The smaller case contained two-carat matching earrings. Rachel stammered. She looked at Claire and then back at the jewelry. "I don't know what to say—they're magnificent. I've never seen anything like it."

"That's because I had them especially made for you. Thank you, Rachel, with all my heart. Thank you for your love, for all the sacrifices you made to save my life, but mostly thank you for making the choice to be with me."

She saw a solemn look come over Rachel's face.

"It was the best decision I ever made in my life." She moved Claire on to her back and got on top of her, kissing her, and then kissed her face and neck, all the time saying, "Thank you."

Claire laughed. "I think she likes it."

They showered together and began to get ready.

Claire looked at her, watching for any clues as to what had happened in Manila. "Can you talk about it?" She sensed Rachel did not want to talk, and she knew Rachel was hesitant to say anything that might alarm her.

"Not really."

"How much longer will we be under security?"

"I'm not sure, but for a while longer, at least until MI6 gets everything resolved with SeaBridge, and I don't know how long that's going to take. Does Tilly mind us being here?"

Claire smiled. "Are you kidding? She's so excited to have us here."

"I hope she continues to feel that way."

They walked down the stairway and out to the waiting limo.

"His name is Carl and he's Tilly's driver, but he will take us wherever we want to go," Claire whispered.

Frank Hawkins greeted the women when they got outside.

Rachel hugged him. "You look great, Frank."

"You look amazing, Ms. Portola. I bet you're glad to be back."

She touched his arm and smiled. "I'm so glad. Did you ask her to marry you yet?"

"Not yet, Ms. Portola, I'm still dragging my feet."

"Better not wait too long—she sounds like a pretty good catch."

He smiled and opened the door to the black limousine for them.

Claire laughed. "You sound just like Tilly's mom."

Rachel looked at her. "I do not."

Claire patted her hand. "Oh yes, you do."

When Carl turned onto Decatur Boulevard, Claire glanced out the rear window and saw Frank following them, keeping about two car lengths behind. Her dress shifted when she turned back around, and she saw Rachel looking at her thighs. She parted them ever so slightly.

Rachel smiled and laid her hand on her thigh. "I can't stand it. You couldn't be more beautiful if there were two of you."

Claire laughed, wondering how she was going to keep her hands off Rachel long enough to see Tilly's show.

When they pulled into valet parking, she watched as Rachel's aqua blue to black flowing evening dress shifted slightly up to her knees as she gracefully slipped out of the back seat, stepping lightly, leading with her right leg and reaching for the doorman's offered hand. The doorman smiled broadly as he took her hand and welcomed her, looking down at her long beautiful legs, accentuated by the black sequined heels. Her diamond and opal necklace and matching earrings glistened as they caught the lights from the entryway into the Royal Caprice Casino.

Another doorman helped Claire out of the opposite side of the limo. She watched as two men walked out of the casino doors and, ogling Rachel, ran right into the couple in front of them.

"Wow, do you see that?" Claire overheard one of the men saying, as he continued to stare at Rachel.

Claire wore a midnight blue and green sequined off-the-shoulder dress, and the diamond and emerald necklace Rachel had given her, accented with diamond earrings. Rachel turned and waited for her. As soon as Frank was behind them, they walked to the doors of the casino.

The two oglers continued to stare at them as they entered. Claire overheard one say, "I can see why they need a bodyguard. If that's the kind of women they have here at this hotel, I'm never leaving."

The other man elbowed his buddy. Claire knew they didn't realize she heard every word they said. She and Rachel smiled as they passed by.

They followed their escort into the theater and down to the front row center reserved VIP seating.

Once they were seated, Rachel leaned over to Claire. "I can't take my eyes off you. I don't think I have ever seen you look more stunning."

Claire reached over and briefly took her hand. "Thank you. I have no words to describe how absolutely beautiful you look in that dress." She lowered her voice. "I can't wait to take it off you later."

The theater lights started to dim. The orchestra began to play, and the curtain opened. The audience rose and began clapping as Tilly entered the stage and acknowledged the audience. Her beautiful full-length silver and red sequined gown dazzled as the lights followed her to center stage. Her microphone was so thin you could barely see it on her cheek and around her ear. She thanked the audience, welcomed them to the performance, then looked down toward Rachel and Claire, and blew a kiss in their direction. Each song she sang brought enthusiastic applause, winning over the audience with her powerful, flawless voice.

When she left the stage for the final time, Claire grabbed Rachel's arm. "Come on, she wants us to meet her backstage."

They stopped at security to get their passes. The backstage area was packed, everyone wanting to meet and greet Tilly. Claire waved to her from across the room, getting her attention. Tilly motioned she would be there in a few minutes.

Claire got champagne for herself and a ginger ale for Rachel as Rachel looked around at the crowd.

"This room is packed with money," said Claire.

"How do you know?"

"Well, look at the watches, shoes, evening dresses, and all the diamonds. I bet by now they have estimated that you and I are worth about ten to fifteen million—a gross underestimation. Next year they'll guess better." She took a sip of her sparkling wine. "By the way, I had Ash shipped here for you. He's at an exclusive stable about thirty minutes from Tilly's house, at the base of Mount Charleston." She took another sip. "Yes, sir, money."

"Who are you and what did you do with Claire?"

She smiled.

Tilly came up behind Rachel and hugged her, leaning into her ear. "You're awake."

Rachel turned around and returned the hug. "Tilly, your show was amazing, and that last song was so beautiful. I knew you could sing, but I never knew how well until now—that was unbelievable."

Tilly laughed. "Thank you."

Claire noticed a tall, well-built man dressed in a tuxedo, watching Rachel. He looked familiar and came up to them when he saw her notice him. Tilly took his hand.

"Rachel, I'd like you to meet a mutual friend of ours. You have spoken with him many times."

Rachel smiled as she looked up at him. "Jack Ralston. It's so wonderful to finally meet you in person."

When Claire looked more closely at him, she realized he was every bit as fine as Tilly had described him and even more handsome than his picture. His thick dark brown hair hung just above his brow and accented his long-eyelashed blue eyes and chiseled face, the face of a man experienced in life's trials.

He smiled at Rachel and shook her hand. "Rachel, you are more beautiful than any picture could convey."

They looked at each other for a moment, and then began to talk.

Claire watched them. *Go ahead and talk with her, but I'm taking her home, and I'm going to take her clothes off and make love to her.* She and Tilly left them and walked a few feet away.

She looked at Rachel and then Jack. "Poor Jack doesn't stand a chance, Tilly."

"Well, he can't help himself, but I'm afraid he's going to end up with friendship only. You two have each other's hearts. I think that's the way it's always been, now that I look back over the years." She put her hand on Claire's shoulder. "I have never seen a couple more in love with each other than you and Rachel. You can feel it when you're in the room with you two. I have always felt it, but now that you're together, you can almost reach out and touch it."

Claire continued to watch Rachel. "Thanks—you don't know how badly I needed to hear that. Look at her, isn't she gorgeous? My life with her is so amazing that sometimes I think I'm in a dream. When are Sarah and Ricky due in?"

"Tomorrow at three o'clock."

"Are they staying at your house?"

"Yes. You don't think it will overwhelm Rachel, do you?"

"If it does, we'll help her deal with it."

Rachel slipped off her high heels and put them carefully into the closet.

"Stop right there," Claire said.

Rachel turned toward her, a look of concern on her face.

Claire walked to her and kissed her, whispering, "I want to take it off." She reached behind Rachel and moved her long dark hair, slowly unzipped her evening dress, slid it off, then kissed her shoulders. "You feel so wonderful."

She turned around and Rachel returned the favor.

Claire pulled Rachel around to her and kissed her deeply, breathing in the sweet scent of her skin and hair, then softly spoke her name.

They carefully hung up their evening clothes and covered them, got into the bed, and lay beside each other.

"It hurts to look at you sometimes because I want you so badly. I feel overwhelmed to think I can touch you," said Rachel.

Claire moved to her and kissed her, sliding her mouth down her neck, reaching her hand up inside her silk slip and caressing. "You can definitely touch me all you want."

They undressed each other and lay naked, looking at each other.

"Rachel, I swear, you're more beautiful than when you left." She leaned over and began to kiss and caress.

Rachel pulled her to her. "I never thought I could ever feel more love for you than I did by that lake in Alaska, but my heart is so full, it's overflowing now. I love you so much. I love how relaxed you are and the light in your eyes."

"I see it in you also."

They loved each other into sleep.

CHAPTER SIX

The bright sunlight forced its way through the small opening in the heavy curtains, landing squarely in Rachel's eyes. She lifted her hand to block the light as Claire turned over toward her.

"Good morning, how'd you sleep?" Claire asked.

"Good morning, good enough to remember where I am and who I'm with." Rachel kissed Claire's shoulder, running her hand along the tight skin against her rib cage, feeling the curve of her hip, then brought her hand up and cupped a full breast, feeling the nipple rise. She wrapped her arms around her, their bodies molding into each other, sending rivets of exquisite want and desire shooting through her, first in her arms, then her breasts, and then down into her core. "You feel so good." She kissed Claire, lingering, exploring, enjoying each taste, each sensation—no need to hurry. "I'm famished."

Claire returned her kiss and teased with her tongue, then moved down her neck, then back up to her cheek. She interlocked their hands and slid out of bed, gently pulling Rachel. "Well, come on, let's get up and get you fed, and then we're going to the stable. The stable manager said I could ride three other horses there anytime I wanted."

They sat at the dining room table eating perfectly prepared Belgian waffles with slabs of melted butter and warmed homemade apricot syrup that filled the squares and spilled over the sides, running onto the plate.

Claire told her what she had been doing since she got to Las Vegas. "Besides making a quick trip to Cleveland and getting our things, mostly I've been waiting for you and trying not to worry. Sarah, Ricky, and Tommy will be here this afternoon and are staying until Sunday. We're having a group here tomorrow for Thanksgiving dinner. Tilly's manager will be here with his family, and Tilly has invited a couple of other people. It should be fun. Derrick called a couple of times. He wants to know if we want to come up to his place in Seattle and do some tours of the lights and take in a couple of shows."

"That sounds like fun. Let's talk about it when we get back to Cleveland."

Claire took her hand and held it. They finished their breakfast, thanked Margaret, and went back upstairs to change into their riding clothes.

Rachel put Ash on a lunge rein and worked him for about a half hour before she saddled him. The buckskin gelding jumped and bucked and tossed his head, his coat glistening in the sun. She walked up to him and soothed him in her tribal language, touching his ears and neck, and then stroked his withers and back. The horse rubbed his head up against her shoulder, and then stood quietly, lowering his head. She saddled him, then put on her Australian outback hat, which she found stashed in Ash's locker box.

Claire put her riding helmet on and started to saddle a bay mare with a Western saddle.

"I wish you would wear a helmet instead of that hat."

"It's heavy enough—don't worry. I'll be fine."

They rode the trails for two hours before stopping for a break near a group of mesquite trees by a shallow creek at the base of Mount Charleston. Rachel pulled two apples and a blanket out of her saddlebag. She gave one of the apples to Claire, and then spread the small blanket on the ground, looking around as they sat down to rest.

"This little area feels so much like home, where I grew up. Thank you for doing this for me. It means more than I can say."

Claire lay down with her knees up. "It was fun to do it. I'm so glad you're enjoying it. Can you tell me about what happened in Manila?"

"I can, but then I'd have to kill you." She laughed but knew Claire understood the anxiety behind it.

"The mission didn't go as we had hoped, but I was able to help MI6 retrieve information. There was some gunfire, and I got to ride on a British naval cruiser."

Claire sat up. "Rachel, damn it. Are you serious?"

"Well, they weren't exactly shooting at me—they were trying to hit the cabin cruiser we were in. The MI6 agents with automatic weapons solved that problem when they hit the helicopter that was shooting at us." She quickly changed the subject. "I got you an English tea set. It should arrive in a few weeks, back at the house. It's very nice—you'll like it."

"Are you all done with this stuff?"

Rachel brushed some dirt from her pants leg, purposely not looking at her. "No, there's more I may have to do."

"How soon?"

"Probably within the next several weeks."

"Damn it, I don't want you to be involved in this anymore."

"I know you don't, and I'm so sorry it's stressing you, but I have a talent and I can help, and I feel like I should do it."

"Damn your morals. I swear you're going to give me a heart attack."

Jacob watched the white man with curly blond hair through his binoculars. He knew neither Claire nor Rachel saw the sun's reflection off the man's belt buckle as he watched them from up above on the mountainside. Jacob suspected the man was scouting and that he had identified one of Rachel's vulnerabilities. And she was sitting right next to her.

When they arrived back at Tilly's, Jacob walked the perimeter one final time before he went off duty, discussing with Frank over a scrambled mobile connection what he had seen at the stables earlier. They were both concerned and knew they had to warn Jack.

"We may have a problem," Jacob said. "He's about six feet tall, around two hundred pounds, curly blond hair, and he was definitely watching her. I think he's scouting. I haven't seen him before."

"Tighten up," Jack said. "Good work, Jacob. I want to add another security detail. I'll speak with Rachel. I have a lot of questions to ask her, and I need to talk with Commander Chambers from MI6. What's Rachel's and Claire's schedule for the next couple of days?"

"Home tonight and tomorrow, unless they decide to go play somewhere. Don't know yet about Friday. The Reynolds family leave Sunday," said Jacob.

"Be prepared for all-out security on this one, and that includes the Reynolds family and Ms. Evans. Heads-up, guys. Do your homework."

❖

In late afternoon on Thanksgiving Day, Rachel went for a walk and visited with Jacob. She noted two new security personnel—Jacob told her they'd been added because there were more people in the house. That evening, she had a long catch-up call with Jack.

On Friday morning, after two of Jack's employees took Tommy out for a day of arcade and rodeo, Jack came to Tilly's house. Rachel gathered everyone into the living room and introduced Jack to Ricky and Sarah. Then Rachel broke the bad news.

"Jack's here this morning because we have a bit of a problem." She looked down at the burgundy carpet and then back up into Claire's face, seeing the color drain to a ghostly pale. Her eyes darted to the others, seeing almost the same reaction.

"Damn, Rachel, the last time we had a *bit of a problem*, people died," said Tilly.

She felt her cheeks flush as she stammered, frantically trying to find words of comfort, but suddenly Jack was standing beside her.

"I know what you're all thinking, and I know you're upset, but you hired me to do a job, and now we have to do it."

He motioned for Rachel to take a seat.

"I've studied SeaBridge. My guess is, after discussing this with Rachel and talking with Commander Chambers from MI6, they are looking for Rachel's vulnerable spots, learning about her, and then they're going to strike to get whatever they want. Commander Chambers told me SeaBridge has lost millions of dollars because Rachel's trigger corrupted the program they bought illegally, and more than that, their financial data continues to be exposed. They want Rachel to correct the problem, and they want their money. Somehow, they've identified her—most likely she was followed from London."

Rachel saw the expression on Claire's face change to apprehension. She took her hand.

"Now, the big question is how do we keep all of you safe? This will be all over in a matter of days. Here's what we propose—we divide our group. It makes it harder for SeaBridge to keep a watch if you are divided up. Ricky, you, Sarah, and Tommy will head back to your cabin in North Carolina, as before, under security. Two of our team will escort you via car. Ricky, arrangements have already been made at your work—don't ask how, just know you're getting an extra week off. Tilly, you'll be staying here."

Tilly threw up her hands. "Oh, goody, a holiday in jail."

"Rachel and Claire will not be separated since they are the most vulnerable but will be going to a safe house already arranged."

"Wait a minute, why can't they just stay here with me? I don't want to be alone, away from everyone. Shit, that's no fun. At least if they're here, Claire and I can get drunk together."

"Yes, I agree," Claire said. "We should stay here with Tilly."

Rachel leaned in. "You promised me you would do everything Jack told you, remember? You swore you would."

She could see Jack's jaw muscles flex as he rubbed his forehead.

"Tilly, you need to understand if they stay here it puts you at greater risk," said Jack.

"I don't care." She threw her hands up in the air again. "I don't want them off somewhere where I don't know what's happening to them, and besides, I want a chance to bitch-slap anyone who shows up here."

Everyone started laughing.

"Tilly, are you sure?" Rachel asked.

"Yes, absolutely."

Jack stood with his arms across his chest, looking at the group. Rachel could see he was mulling the risks. He rubbed his forehead again and then ran his hand through his hair. "Okay, they can stay."

Tilly breathed out a sigh of relief.

"MI6 has a plan. I can't tell you about it because it's classified, but I can tell you that while we are dealing with things here, MI6 will be taking a different direction," said Rachel.

While they all continued to discuss the needs of each of the group, Jack got a phone call and motioned for Rachel to follow him into the kitchen.

"It's starting. As of this moment, you are under constant surveillance. Go ahead and do what you want, but someone will be near you at all times. I'll be in touch. Call me anytime or if you need to talk. Keep me informed."

CHAPTER SEVEN

Jack drove into the security facility called the shed, closed the automatic door, and walked to the soundproof back room. Frank had the man who'd been scouting Rachel at the stable strapped to a chair, his mouth gagged and taped. The man was sweating, his face red, and he had a deep bruise on the left cheek where Frank had punched him.

"Is he cooperating?"

Frank kept his eyes on the man. "No, he's Mister Tough Guy."

Jack carefully went through the contents of the man's wallet, nodded to Frank, and then leaned down to the side of the man's face. "You're in Vegas, buddy. We do things a little differently here—besides guns and cannoli, we like to give choices. I'm going to give you some choices—choose what you want, makes no difference to me. We need some information about your boss. You can give it to us or not, but if I was you, I'd give it up."

Jack reached into the gray metal box on the table and pulled out a stack of hundred-dollar bills, then put it on the table in front of the man. He reached back into the box and brought out a small clear bottle of liquid and a syringe, placed it beside the money, and then slowly put on the leather gloves and the four rings that were set on the table by the metal box. The man's eyes grew wide as he looked up at Jack and then Frank.

Jack reached over and patted the man's chin with his gloved hand. "Now, these are your choices—in no particular order, you understand. If you choose to take the money, you get on the next plane out of here and never come back to Vegas again, and just for clarification, if I ever see you again, and you're involved in any way with anything I'm dealing with, we'll choose where you'll be buried. Option number two is a little concoction we like to call *Tell Daddy Everything*. And number three is—"

"Oh, three is his favorite." Frank leaned in and looked at the man. "Boxing…and he's good at it."

"What's it going to be, tough guy?" Jack gritted his teeth and watched the man's leg shake.

Frank leaned in. "He doesn't seem to be ready to make a choice, boss."

"Hmm." Jack pushed his leather gloves on tighter. "Maybe we can help him."

The man's eyes grew wider.

Jack drew back his right fist. The man started shaking his head and making noise through the gag.

"Speak up. I don't have all day."

Sweat began to drip off the man's eyebrows and down his cheeks. He looked down at the money and then up to Jack, back down at the money, and then up at him again.

Jack looked at Frank and nodded. Frank ripped the tape off and pulled the gag out of his mouth.

Jack put his foot up on one of the padded armchairs and motioned for the man to start talking.

"I'm here to—"

Jack put up his hand. "Pardon me for interrupting, but we know why you're here. You're scouting for vulnerabilities on Ms. Portola. I want to hear a better story."

He lifted his hand, motioning for the man to continue speaking.

"Eshee Yumiko, she sent me here. She wants to know her—"

Jack put up his hand again. "Oh, she wants to *know* her. Is that like in the biblical sense?"

Frank leaned in. "I don't think so, boss, I think he means Yumiko wants her."

"Oh, I see, she *wants* her. Have you seen her? I want her too. She is about the hottest woman I've ever seen."

Frank leaned in again. "No, boss, wants her, like to take her."

"Oh, she wants to *take* her. I'd like to take her. Man, she's hot."

"No, boss." He shook his head, smirking.

Jack looked down at the man. "Oh, now I understand." He drew out the sentence like he finally realized what Frank meant. He moved his foot and put it on the chair between the man's legs, leaning in. "Yumiko wants to kill her. Is that what she wants to do, tough guy?"

The man looked up at Jack and swallowed hard.

Jack leaned in closer and glared at him. "What's the plan, and don't leave out any details."

"She's going to take her girlfriend or one of the others and force her to fix the program. That's all I know. All I was supposed to do was report back on the best choice of target. I swear that's all."

Jack raised his finger, motioning for him to continue. "And then?"

No response from the man.

"And *then*?"

"And then the other two who were going to help me are at the El Rancho motel, room 214. We're supposed to take the target and hold her there."

Jack looked at him and punched his right fist into his left palm.

"And then we were supposed to kill her…but we decided we were just going to leave her there, take the money, and go. That's it."

"How much money?"

"Five thousand each."

Jack put his hands on the man's shoulders. "See, now don't you feel better about having this conversation? Wasn't that a great choice?" Jack looked at Frank.

Frank leaned in. "Smart, that's pretty good talkin', boss."

"Untie one hand and get him something to drink."

Frank reached into the refrigerator, pulled out a bottle of water, acted like he broke the seal on it, unscrewed the cap, set it down on the table in front of the man, and then untied his left hand. The man quickly picked up the bottle with his shaking hand and drank the cold liquid.

Jack left but came back fifteen minutes later. The man's eyes were barely open and drool was running down the corner of his mouth.

Frank checked his pupils. "He's good."

"Okay, bring him out of it. I want to know if he knows if Yumiko's coming, where exactly, and how. Find out the names of the other two idiots, and get all of the identification. I want to nail this guy and his buddies hard. Put the hammer down on them, Frank."

Frank nodded as Jack left. Jack was concerned, and he was angry. He'd never been personally involved in a case before. He went through the man's identification papers and the contents of his wallet again, finding an international number written on a piece of paper. He reviewed his notes, and then called Brice Chambers on a scrambled line and gave him all the information he had gathered about Eshee Yumiko.

More security staff arrived as the building began to bustle with activity. Jack called in his second-in-command, Steve Hathaway, and handed over all his cases but Rachel's. "I'm joining Frank in the chat room with our subject."

"How's it going in there?"

"I'll know in a little while."

He was going to get this one right, and no one he was responsible for was going to get hurt, especially Rachel. He called her and told her to come to the shed immediately.

As soon as Rachel and Jacob arrived, they conferenced with Brice Chambers. She and Brice reviewed their options and formulated a plan, but Jack objected.

"It's too much of a risk for Rachel. I don't like it."

"I assure you," Brice said, "MI6 resources are adequate to cover the operation and keep Rachel—and the rest of the team—perfectly safe."

"I'm with Brice on this, Jack," Rachel said.

Jack did all he could to talk her out of her decision to be human bait in a plan he didn't like, but she wouldn't budge, and in the end he had no choice but to accept it. He ran his hand through his hair, remembering what it felt like when he looked into her rich hazel eyes for the first time, but he also remembered she was someone else's. They worked out the final details and ended the call.

"Are you sure you're up to this? This is very dangerous. I don't like it—it's too great of a risk." His palms were sweating. He knew she was brave, but she was also headstrong and reckless at times.

"Yes. I'm sure."

He shook his head slowly, looking into her eyes, trying to convey his apprehension. "I wish you would reconsider." For one brief moment he caught a glimpse of hesitancy in her expression. "There are other ways to get the results Brice wants."

"No. We're doing this."

He sighed heavily and then reviewed with her once again what he thought was important for her to know and remember. Frank came in with a medical box, set it down on Jack's desk, and opened it, taking out an injector. Rachel looked up at him and put her right forearm on the desk.

"Can't inject that arm, Ms. Portola, too much scarring. I need to inject the microchip into your hip."

She stood up and pulled the waistband of her slacks down below her hip.

Frank rubbed her hip with an alcohol swab. "You're going to feel an ache, and then it's going to sting for a few seconds. Hold perfectly still until I'm done."

She rested her hand on the table, trying not to anticipate, but cringed. "Ouch!"

Jack touched her shoulder. "We can track you anywhere in the world to within about eight hundred meters, which is about a half mile, but you need to remember we have to be within ten miles of you to get your exact location. Brice's best guess is that Seabridge's new location is still somewhere in the Philippines, but there are thousands of islands. If they take you there, it's going to take time to find you. You have to stall for time. Remember, they need you alive to fix the program—that is your hole-card and edge."

"Jack, they need communications and sophisticated equipment. They were back up and running quickly, and because of that, Brice and I both feel they are still in the Philippines and somewhere not far from Manila."

❖

She got back from meeting with Jack and Frank just before Tommy got home. As they all sat in the living room, Tilly tried to convince them to go gambling.

"You can't come to Vegas and not go gambling. We're going to the Caprice tonight. We could go to Sam's Town or one of the other places for better odds, but the Caprice will appreciate that I brought all you high rollers to their hotel." She smiled. "Don't worry about Tommy—if he gets bored, he'll be fine in the game room. Margaret will make sure he's in bed at a decent hour."

They got ready and went to the Caprice. Rachel and Claire watched Ricky, Tilly, and Sarah as they played the slot machines, and then she and Claire walked around the casino. They sat at one of the restaurant tables near the blackjack tables, ordered something to drink, and people-watched as their security team watched them.

"Are you all right?" Claire asked. "You look so down."

Rachel reached down and gently rubbed her left hip, feeling the sting of the microchip. She wanted to tell Claire everything, throw it out onto the table and tell her the plan she was now a part of, a plan that put her life in jeopardy in order to get what MI6 desperately needed, but she knew Claire. She knew she would do all she could to stop it—

so Rachel held back, pushing it down inside, choking on it. "I'm just worried about everything. I hate that you're involved, and now once again, Sarah and her family, and Tilly. I've screwed this up so badly." A voice screamed inside her head, *Just tell her you're scared, afraid to leave her because you may never see her again. Tell her you got yourself in too deep and don't know how to get out.*

Claire reached over and touched her arm as Rachel tried to hide her trembling hands.

"Well, it's not so bad for us. Sarah and Ricky get an extra week of vacation and get to go to their favorite place, all expenses paid, and Tilly gets to have us here with her and an adventure on her week off, and we get to be together." Claire smiled at her. "That's not so bad."

"It's dangerous no matter how you paint it, and I've put you all in it, again." She looked around the casino, avoiding Claire's eyes as she tried to get herself under control, her hands shaking more. Flashbacks, stress, and anxiety began to flood her mind as the voices in her head got louder. She stood up. "I don't feel like being here. I'm going to ask Frank to take me back to Tilly's."

Claire reached up and took her hand. "Don't shut me out of this, whatever you're feeling."

She sat back down, feeling her body strain, her muscles tense. *Tell her.*

"Claire, I've screwed up. Damn it, I've screwed up your life, Tilly's, Sarah's, mine. God, I couldn't have destroyed so many lives if I planned it." She quickly stood up again. She couldn't breathe, and her heart pounded in her chest. "I have to get out of here." She immediately started to leave.

"Rachel, wait." Claire went after her, getting Frank's attention and pointing to Rachel, running up to him as they both followed close behind her.

"We have to get her out of here right now," Claire told him.

Frank talked into his microphone to the other two security guards, telling them to cover the others while he went with Claire after Rachel.

She watched Rachel walk quickly ahead of them to the entrance of the casino and push open the glass doors, practically falling out into the night, and then leaning up against the building, trying to take deep breaths, her body shaking. She and Frank came up behind her, called for their limo, and held Rachel up while they waited. Frank opened the car door and helped Rachel in, and then Claire slid in next to her as Frank closed the door. Carl pulled forward and waited until Frank got his car and positioned himself behind their vehicle, and then he drove out of the valet parking area.

"Where would you ladies like to go?" Carl asked.

"Take us to the Bellagio," Claire said, already calling Frank. "We want a suite at the Bellagio. I don't want to have to go to the front desk to check in. I just want to go directly to a suite."

Frank said he would take care of it and call her back.

"Drive around, Carl, and we'll eventually go to the Bellagio."

Rachel stared straight ahead, reaching over with her trembling hand and grabbing Claire's hand.

Claire put her other hand on top of Rachel's. "It's going to be all right."

CHAPTER EIGHT

Thirty minutes later they were in a suite at the Bellagio.

"I need you close by, Frank. We'll be here until the morning."

"Don't worry, Ms. Davenport. We'll be right outside your door."

She guided Rachel to the living room sofa and sat her down, got her a glass of ice water, and gave her a Xanax. Rachel took the pill, put it into her mouth, and drank the water. She didn't ask what the pill was.

Claire sat beside her and waited twenty minutes for the pill to work. Rachel stared straight ahead, and then stood up and started pacing, wringing her hands.

"Talk to me, Rachel."

"I don't know what to say."

"What the hell is going on?"

"I don't know." She began to slow her steps and stopped wringing her hands.

"Come sit down beside me." Claire patted the cushion.

Rachel sat down at the far edge of the sofa, took her shoes off, and put her knees up, finally making eye contact with her.

"I want you to tell me what's going on. Why were you with Jack so long?"

Rachel looked horrified. "I can't tell you."

"Yes, you can tell me, whatever it is."

She shook her head. "I can't. Don't ask me to do that. I...I'm under a legal restriction. I have put you and everyone else at risk because of my own selfish desire to help Brice." She began to wring her hands again.

Claire got up and went to the other end of the sofa near her. She could see Rachel's thigh trembling through her slacks. "In all the years I've known you, not once have I ever seen you be selfish when it comes to others—a little overly concerned sometimes, but never selfish, but I'm afraid this time you've stepped over the line. I have never seen you this upset. What have you gotten yourself into?"

Rachel looked at her and reached out, pulling her to her, wrapping her arms around her. "Claire, you are everything to me. I would tell you if I could, but I can't."

Claire held her and stroked the back of her hair. "Baby, it's okay. Whatever this is, it's going to be okay."

Rachel took her arms from around her and held her hand. "I need time with you. I need your strength, your patience, and your love."

"I'm here, I'm not going anywhere."

They sat close together in silence. Claire watched as the muscles in Rachel's face began to relax, and the trembling in her hands slowed. Her pupils were slightly dilated. The pill was working.

Rachel sighed a few times, rubbing her thumb over Claire's hand. "That was a Xanax, wasn't it?" She half grinned. "It's good stuff."

Claire brushed the hair away from Rachel's face. "Yes, and I want you to take another one in about three hours. You're under so much stress. I'm really worried about you."

"I don't want to think about anything but you."

"Okay, I like it. I need to call Tilly and tell her where we are. She'll be worried about us if she ever gets up from the slot machines and notices we aren't there anymore."

Rachel laughed and rubbed her face.

Claire picked up her phone and called Tilly, reaching over and holding Rachel's hand again. "Tilly wants to know if you want to go back over there for a while."

"Do you?"

Claire made a face and shook her head as she answered Tilly. "We're going to stay here, Till. We'll be back at your house in a day or so. Don't worry about us. Frank has security with us." She put the cell phone on the coffee table and looked at Rachel. "Well, they have anything you want here. What's your pleasure?"

"I want a beautiful woman with green eyes and long hair, who loves me like a rock."

"Oh, darlin', that can be arranged, this is Las Vegas." She stood and went over to search the music system. "A timeless classic is what we need." She touched the screen. "At Last" sung by Etta James started playing as she walked back, pulled Rachel up, put her arms around her, and started to sway with her as she kissed her.

When the song was over, she led Rachel to the bedroom. The curtains were open, and the lights from the Strip reflected back into the room, casting red, blue, and green shadows.

She turned to her. "If you expect conversation, it will be another thousand dollars." She unbuttoned Rachel's blouse as she began to kiss her neck. "I love to touch you."

"Does that count as conversation?" Rachel smiled demurely.

She laughed as she moved her down onto the bed, whispering in her ear, "Baby, you don't have to be nervous or do anything, just let me do it. I have lots of experience with this sort of thing."

She continued to take Rachel's blouse and bra off her and then unbuttoned and unzipped her slacks, kissing her again, feeling the warmth and softness of her skin as she moved down her neck and shoulders, kissing and caressing. She felt her calm as she slowly moved her hands down her body, feeling her muscles relax. She moaned with pleasure from the feel and excitement of touching her.

Rachel pulled her closer.

She reluctantly left her and got off the bed, taking her own blouse and bra off as Rachel watched, and then went to lie on top of her.

"Hey, sailor," Rachel said, pointing, "aren't you forgetting the bottom half? Did you have a busy night?"

Claire started laughing. "Now, that's conversation and will cost you."

"That's not conversation. That's a question."

"Technically, that's two questions." She slowly unbuttoned and unzipped her own pants and pulled them off, enjoying the sweet expression on Rachel's face as she watched her undress.

"Do you like what you see?"

"Mm, very much. You're worth every penny." Rachel smiled, putting her right arm behind her head, her eyes fixed on her.

She leaned over the bed and took the rest of Rachel's clothes off, touching her as much as she could while she did it. "I like what I see also." She got up on the bed and put the pillows against the headboard. "Sit up against the pillows."

Rachel complied.

Claire got on top of her, straddling her. "I'm going to give you a freebie flashback." She moved up closer to Rachel's hips, sitting on her, rubbing up against her and moaning as she felt the heat from her body.

"Do you remember when you straddled me the day of the plane crash to help Sarah set my broken hand?"

"Yes," Rachel moaned.

She moved up on Rachel and leaned in, pressing into her, their breasts touching as she moved against her, whispering in her ear, "I wanted you as much as you wanted me that day. When you came up against me, I wanted to rip your blouse off and touch you."

She began to caress her again, feeling her own heartbeat increase as she pressed her breasts into her. She slid down and took one of her hard erect nipples into her mouth, then moved to the other, desire and need pulsing, throbbing. "I love to love you."

Rachel pulled her up to her and kissed her, moving her mouth down her neck and shoulders.

Claire felt the desire increase with each breath, each touch. She threw the pillows onto the floor and pulled Rachel down, spreading her legs, pressing into her, feeling her hot wet welcoming center. She thrust against her, looking into her eyes, seeing the hungering want. She gathered her into her arms and rubbed her breasts against her again, feeling each nerve, each fiber reaching out as she grasped for her touch and feel. She slid downward, licking, kissing. She opened her thighs wider and spread her wet glistening folds, hearing Rachel gasp and cry out as she began to feast.

She woke in Rachel's arms, the sun shining into the bedroom. She called Jacob and asked him to arrange two more nights at the hotel. She got out of bed, filled the Jacuzzi, and went to the bar and poured a rocks glass of whiskey for herself and ginger ale for Rachel, taking them to the Jacuzzi and setting the glasses down.

They both got in the Jacuzzi and lay there, relaxing.

Claire put her leg over Rachel's thigh and scooted toward her, laying her head back on the padding of the Jacuzzi, reaching up for the whiskey and sipping.

Rachel ran her hand over Claire's arm. "Thank you for helping me through that. You're right—somehow it will work out. I don't want to talk about it anymore, okay?"

"Okay." She moved up and straddled her. "Ooh, turn the Jacuzzi down a tad, will you, baby?"

"A little too much for you, sailor?"

Claire nodded. "Just a bit." She reached up and made soft circles around Rachel's nipples. "I just realized we don't have anything to wear except what we had on last night, and I don't want to go back to Tilly's just yet."

"I guess we'll go shopping. It's on me, since you did stay over for free."

Claire looked at Rachel, moving her hands gently over her shoulders and arms, and then her face. "I love us. I love the way we are with each other. I love our tenderness and kindness to each other, and I love how we love each other."

Rachel slid her hands up her waist and back. "I know. I feel the same way."

CHAPTER NINE

Claire held her cell phone in one hand and held on to the rail with the other as she came down the staircase. "Rachel, the stable vet is on the phone and wants to talk to you."

Rachel took the call then handed the phone back to her. "Ash is lame. The vet said he checked his hoof and that it looks like laminitis. I need to go to the stable right away."

"Do you want me to go with you?"

"No, Jacob is going with me. I'll be back in a little while."

She watched the traffic and looked over at Jacob, his massive muscular body almost wedged behind the steering wheel.

"Jacob, you have never told me about your family."

"My parents live in Fairbanks, not far from my mother's family. My dad was in the military, so we traveled around a lot. He met Mother when he was stationed in Fairbanks, and they came back when he left the military."

"Do you have any brothers or sisters?"

"I have a twin brother who lives near me in Juneau."

"Are you close?"

"Pretty close. He just got married last year and they are expecting their first baby, a boy, in about three months."

He pulled into the stable driveway, across from the veterinarian's truck, then backed the car and parked so it was facing the driveway. He headed out to secure the perimeter while she went into the stables to talk with the vet and check on Ash.

The stable area was darker than usual, and it took a moment for her eyes to adjust. She got halfway to Ash's stall when she heard an odd sound and felt something sharp go into her right thigh. She looked down and saw a long, red dart sticking in her thigh, just above her knee. It stung and ached, but she half laughed, thinking it looked odd hanging out of her leg while she tried to walk. She took one more step but began to stagger, and then her vision blurred. She tried to look back at the entryway to call for Jacob but collapsed onto the wood floor, the smell of straw and dust filling her senses. She saw two men reach down for her and tried to call out for Jacob, but she felt like she was spinning, and then she slept.

❖

Jacob was on his way to the back of the stables when he noticed a black Escalade parked at the rear entryway. When he got closer, he saw a man standing by the vehicle looking directly at him, his gun tucked in the crook of his arm.

He pulled his gun out of the holster and aimed, but before he could fire, the man fired his weapon, hitting him in the chest. He went down to the ground on his back, his weapon falling out of his hand. He rolled and picked it up, firing once, then again, hitting the man in the right side and then in his chest. The man collapsed onto the ground.

He tried to get up, but a blast of heat and burning shot through his neck, and then something ripped through his left side, between the straps of his Kevlar vest. Deep radiating pain engulfed him, sending searing bolts of lightning through his neck and lungs, the pain pulsating into his spine. He gripped his gun and pointed it forward at another man standing near the stall entranceway, but it dropped out of his hand. He watched helplessly as two men put Rachel into the SUV. He tried to inch his hand to his weapon but couldn't reach it. He tried to roll to get closer, but he had no feeling in his lower body. He read the license plate as the vehicle sped past him, the rear tires spraying gravel. He managed to get his cell phone with his left hand and pushed the emergency code. "Three men, black Escalade, license Charlie Victor Charlie seven one seven five. They have—" The cell phone fell out of his hand.

He coughed, the taste of blood sickening as it came up into his mouth. He struggled to breathe. "I'm down." The sound seeped out his mouth and was absorbed in the space between his body and the earth that cradled him now. The pain flooded his mind. More blood. He gasped for air, choking, the sand and pebbles glistening in the sun, his handgun just inches away. He had to get up to go after them...they had her. One final choking gasp and his struggle was over.

❖

Jack ordered the team coordinator to call 911 as he jumped into his SUV and pressed the emergency broadcast to the team. "Jacob's down, target has been taken—repeat, target taken." He gave the license number and description of the vehicle and told everyone to track for the airport, private jet area. He ordered to secure Claire and Tilly and for everyone else to look for the SUV.

He watched the tracking system and then looked down the airport runway, seeing the plane's wheels leave the tarmac just as he got to the hangar. He drove to the tower, burst into the room, and asked for the supervisor on duty, showing his identification.

"The private jet that just now took off, where's it going?"

The supervisor looked down at the printout. "Final destination is Manila."

He drove to the stables. Police and emergency vehicles cluttered the driveway. He recognized the two detectives standing over Jacob's body.

"One of yours?" Detective Owens asked.

Jack nodded and gave them the information they needed. He knelt down and touched Jacob's body, laying his hand on his broad shoulder. "Thank you, you good, good man."

He moved Jacob's shirt collar to look inside his shirt. His protective vest was frayed and torn from the blast of the bullet. The shot to his neck had been destructive, but the side shot was the one that killed him.

He glanced over at the unidentified man lying on the ground, then got into his car, drove across town to the shed, and waited for Frank and the other members of the team to arrive.

They gathered stone-faced, somber and grieving.

"Jacob was murdered in cold blood. They shot him without any warning, and he never had a chance. They are going to Manila. We are running on borrowed time and have to be in the air within the next hour. I want a four-man team with me, and full tactical gear. We get her back. Her life depends on us getting there quickly and doing our job effectively and skillfully. In and out, no limits on body count on this one. This team has first option to go."

Frank, Katherine Henderson, and José Garcia wanted to go. Jack chose David Hampton as his final team member. "Prepare for a four-day mission. Frank, you are second-in-command. I will personally brief you after wheels up. Look sharp, people—we have a life depending on us."

He went into his office and closed the door, immediately going into the bathroom. He looked at his shaking hands with Jacob's blood on them. He washed and splashed water on his face, forcing himself to look into the mirror at his pale and defeated reflection. Jacob was dead, and now there was a high possibility Rachel was at a much greater risk then he had originally thought. As he walked to his desk, he cursed himself for not pressing harder to stop her from going through with her and Brice's plan. He picked up the office phone and called Brice, then had to do something he didn't want to do—he drove to Tilly's.

His secondary team reported Claire and Tilly were secure in the house. They were upstairs in Claire and Rachel's room. He asked Margaret to get the two women, pacing while he waited. They came down together, Tilly looking excited to see him but Claire just watching him.

"Sit down," he said, trying to sound as calm as possible.

They sat down on the sofa together, looking up at him. He avoided eye contact with Claire because he knew how she would respond—Rachel had warned him.

Claire jumped up. "No."

Jack put his hand up. "Rachel was taken at the stables."

Claire shook her head violently and brought her hand up in a fist. "No, you were supposed to protect her. We paid you to protect her." She moved toward him.

Tilly jumped up and grabbed her.

"Claire," Jack said, "time is critical. I have to go, and I only have a few minutes to tell you what I need to tell you."

Tilly led Claire to the sofa.

Jack continued. "They took her at the stables. Jacob was killed trying to stop them. They are taking her to Manila. We will be on a plane headed there in a little while. I'm working with Commander Chambers at MI6. Claire, we will do all we can to get her back."

Claire looked up, glaring at him. "You were supposed to do all you could to protect her, and look what happened." She stood up. "Get the hell out of this house, you bastard. You bring her back. I don't care how many of you get killed. Get out. Get out."

She shook, barely able to stand.

Jack looked at Tilly. "I will let you know the second I have any news."

He left the house, barely able to open the door and walk to his car.

❖

Tilly sat with Claire on the sofa but didn't know what to do or how to comfort her. "Claire, where's your phone?"

She didn't answer.

Tilly shook her. "Where's your phone?"

Claire looked up at her. "What?

"Where's your phone?"

"It's in my room."

Tilly ran up the stairs into Claire and Rachel's room, got Claire's phone, and called Derrick's number, telling him what happened.

He told her what to do and then said, "I'll be there right away."

"No, it's okay, there's nothing you can do. One of us will call you as soon as we know anything."

"Are you sure? It's not a problem to fly there. I can be there on the next flight out."

"I know Claire appreciates the offer, but I think it's best to hold off until we know more."

She ended the call and got into Claire's purse, ran back down the steps, got some water, and handed her two Xanax.

Claire pushed her hand away. "No." She stood up. "I'm going to Manila. I have to get her."

Tilly put the water and the pills down on the glass table and shoved her back down onto the sofa. "The hell you are, Claire."

She stood up again and shoved Tilly hard. "I'm going, and you aren't stopping me." She started toward the door.

Tilly grabbed her. "I said you aren't going, and if I have to tie you down or lock you in a room, then that's the way it's going to be." She turned Claire around and forced her back down onto the sofa. "You are hysterical—calm down."

Claire tried to stand up again, but Tilly pushed her down once more, picking up the two pills and holding them out in front of her face. "Take these."

Claire reached her shaking hand up and hit Tilly's hand, knocking the pills onto the floor, and then jumped up, trying to get past her. Tilly grabbed her and shoved her back down onto the sofa.

"Don't you dare move, Claire. I'm not kidding." She picked the pills up off the floor and shoved them at her again. "I don't care if they've been on the floor. You're taking them."

Claire took the pills from her, put them in her mouth, and drank the water as Tilly stood over her, making sure she swallowed them. She tried to stand up again, but Tilly shoved her back down.

"Damn you, Tilly, let me up."

"No. You just sit there and behave yourself."

Claire looked up at her. "They took her, Tilly. They took her." She put her hands up to her face.

Tilly put her hand on her shoulder. "They took her for a reason. They want her to correct her program. Jack has some time to find her."

"That bastard will screw this up." She grabbed Tilly's arm. "They took her. They took her."

Tilly sat down and held her.

CHAPTER TEN

R achel began to wake, feeling the bounce and motion of the plane, and realized her hands and feet were bound as she looked around the cabin. She tried to bite the rope and tape off her wrists, but two men suddenly appeared in front of her. One held her down while the other injected a syringe into her arm. It began to get dark, and a rush of wind filled her ears as she went back into a twilight sleep.

She woke again but had no idea how long she had been out. She needed to urinate and had a throbbing headache. "Bathroom," she moaned. The two men sat her up, untied her legs, and then they moved her to the lavatory, shoved her in, and shut the door. She looked in the mirror after she took care of her needs, staring at the dark circles under her eyes, trying to steady herself as she held on to the sink. When she opened the door with her taped hands, the two men grabbed her, pushed her back onto the couch, and tied her legs.

"I need water," she said, looking at the smaller man with short-cropped black hair.

He reached over and shoved a bottle of water at her.

She took it, but then shoved it back at him. "I can't open it."

The man opened the cap and placed the water bottle roughly into one of her hands.

She began to drink. "Where are we going?"

The men did not speak to her or answer her question.

"Who are you?"

The smaller man slapped the side of her face with the back of his hand. "Shut up."

The corner of Rachel's upper lip began to bleed.

The taller white man with dark brown hair looked at the smaller man. "Knock it off. You know she wants her unharmed."

The white man approached her again, reached for her arm, and injected the needle.

She felt movement and smelled gasoline but drifted back into darkness. Suddenly the movement stopped, and she felt herself being lifted, and then sunlight and extreme humidity engulfed her. Birds chirped, their noise echoing in her ears along with the sound of traffic all around her, as the overwhelming stench of sewage and garbage filled her nostrils. She felt weak and hungry. Her feet were untied, and she was pushed forward. She tried to walk but stumbled onto a smooth hard surface as rough hands guided her. She tried to see, but her eyelids were heavy. Then suddenly the sunlight was gone, and she felt a warm breeze against her skin.

"Bring her in here," a distorted voice echoed.

She tried desperately to focus her eyes, but everything was distorted. She felt the needle go into her arm, and she collapsed onto some type of bedding. She felt her feet being tied, the room spun around, and then it was dark and quiet again.

When she gained consciousness, she could hear faded voices and someone yelling off to her right.

"You gave her too much, and we've lost valuable time, you idiot." It was a female voice. "Get her hydrated and bring her out of it, now. You touch her again, and I'll shoot you myself."

In Rachel's mind she saw Jack. *Remember, when it happens and you're taken, stall for time, as much time as you can. The longer they have you—the better chance we have of getting to you.*

Keeping her eyes closed, she heard perhaps two sets of footsteps coming closer to her. A male voice spoke a foreign language. She recognized it from her trip to Manila—Tagalog. Someone lifted her to a sitting position, forced open her eyelids, and shone a light into her eyes. She instinctively tried to put her hands up to shield them.

"She's starting to come out of it," a male voice said.

She felt the shock of water being thrown into her face and struggled for air, putting her taped hands up to her face, wiping her eyes the best she could. Again, Jack's voice came to her. *Stall for time.*

She let her body collapse back onto the mattress.

"Damn it. Get her up," the female voice ordered.

They sat her up again and threw more water into her face. She drew in a deep breath, the shock of the water bringing her out of her stupor. She tried to wipe her hair out of her face and open her eyes to focus. Pain shot through her head as she slowly focused on the man in front of her.

"Where am I?" Her throat was dry, and her voice cracked. Her lips were sore and swollen.

"You're in the Philippines," a female voice answered with an accent of some type, possibly Asian. She wasn't sure.

She raised her tied hands and tried to move her head to the right where she heard the woman's voice. Her eyes slowly began to focus, and she could see a dark-haired woman sitting in a metal chair about six feet away. The woman got up and moved the chair closer to her, the chair legs making a scraping sound as she dragged it across the tiled floor. She sat down and crossed her legs, leaning in toward Rachel.

"Specifically, Quezon City, Philippines, our new location."

The woman handed her a bottle of water, but she wouldn't take it.

"I don't blame you. I wouldn't take it either."

The woman uncapped the bottle and took a large drink from it, then handed it back.

She quickly took the bottle and drank the water, her throat and lips burning as she drank. "Thank you."

"You are welcome, Rachel. I am Eshee Yumiko, and you are here to fix your program. I want the problem corrected—it's that simple—and as soon as it's fixed, I'll let you go."

"No, you won't," she shot back, wiping her lips. "As soon as I fix it, you're going to kill me."

"Rachel, I'm not a monster."

"No, you're a psychopath. I'm supposed to believe you're going to let me go—someone who kidnapped me, drugged me like an animal, and took me halfway around the world?"

Yumiko quickly stood up, and the chair fell over, making a loud noise as it hit the floor. "You are going to fix the program, Rachel." She stood back a few feet and signaled to the small black-haired man. He came forward and lifted Rachel up. She was at least three inches taller than he was.

"My, you are tall," Yumiko said, looking at her.

Rachel estimated the woman's height to be about five foot two. She looked like she could be blown over by a gust of wind and appeared to be either Filipino or mixed Asian, with long dark brown hair and light brown skin.

The same white man who was on the plane moved to the other side of Rachel and grabbed her arm. Yumiko motioned for them to untie her feet, and then they led her through the door to a larger room. The room smelled of mold and fresh paint and was not on the ground floor. It was dark outside, but light from other buildings was shining into the three dirty windows on the far wall to her left. The room was dimly lit, and she could see the mainframe computers lined up on the wall directly in front of her. A white plastic six-foot long table and a metal chair were placed in the middle of the room. On the table, directly in front of the chair, was a laptop computer with cables running to one of the mainframes.

"See, everything is ready for you. Let's begin, shall we?" Yumiko told her.

The men led Rachel to the chair and shoved her down onto it, untied her hands, and stepped back. She kept her hands in her lap. There was silence in the room as all eyes watched her. This was going to be a waiting game, and she knew the more she made them wait, the better Jack's chances were of finding her—but she also knew there would be a price to play the game.

Twenty minutes later, she had not moved her hands to the keyboard. Yumiko nodded toward the back of the room. The men stepped forward and led her back to the smaller room, took her shoes off, stripped off her blouse and pants, and tied her hands in front of her. The white man threw a heavy cord over the beam in the ceiling and tied her hands to it. He kicked the back of her knees, and she went down to the floor, and then he pulled until her hands were as high as they could be pulled, with her knees still on the floor. The small man forced a gag into her mouth and duct taped over her lips, then tied the cord off, and the two men stepped back.

Yumiko reappeared wearing black leather gloves and holding a heavy dark brown leather strap. She walked to her and shoved a color photo in front of her face. It was a picture of Claire the night of Tilly's show. She looked beautiful. Yumiko threw it on the floor and then shoved another picture of Claire at her. In this picture, Claire's face was bloodied, her eye swollen, and her lip bleeding.

Rachel was shocked. She cried out but then stared at it. It was another picture of Claire taken that same night, which had been photoshopped.

"I got you. I can get her," Yumiko said in her ear, handing the picture to the small man.

He taped it to the wall directly in front of Rachel, at eye level. Yumiko stepped slightly away from her and began to beat her back with the leather strap. Rachel cried out, but only her muffled sounds could be heard. She writhed from the sting and ripping of her flesh, feeling her warm blood run down her back as she hung her head and let the rope take her weight.

Yumiko stepped forward and looked down at her. "I want my program fixed and fully operational, Rachel, and then I'll let you go."

Rachel cried out and shook her head.

The small man stepped forward, smiling. He pulled the cord and raised her to a standing position, her feet barely touching the floor, and then tied off the cord.

Yumiko stepped behind her again and viciously beat her back once more. She cried out. The small man ripped the duct tape from her face and pulled the gag out of her mouth.

Yumiko leaned forward, grabbed hold of the back of her hair, and whispered into her ear, "I want my program fixed, and then I'll let you go."

Rachel lifted her head and stood straight. "No, never. I will never fix it."

The small man ripped more duct tape from the silver roll and taped her mouth. Yumiko stepped back and began to beat her again, hitting her with more force, beating her on the back of her thighs. Rachel shook her head back and forth and cried out, straining, trying to move away from the pain.

Yumiko stopped. Rachel watched as she walked to the table, picked up a clear container of liquid, opened it, and walked to her. She felt the liquid being poured all over her back and thighs—penetrating into her bleeding torn flesh, burning and ripping through her. She twisted and writhed, screaming, trying to get loose and away from the burning, excruciating pain. Yumiko stepped in front of her, capped the bottle, tossed it to the small man, and motioned toward the door.

The men untied her and dragged her to the laptop, forced her into the chair, and then untied her hands. Her wrists were bleeding, her body shaking from the pain and stress. She looked at the computer screen, tried to breathe deeply, and then placed her hands in her lap, forcing herself to focus on the small round red tag on the bottom right corner of the computer screen—its dimensions, color, shape, texture...Twenty more minutes went by.

Yumiko came up behind her, grabbed her by the back of her hair, and pulled her head back. "I want my program fixed, and then I will let you go," she said through gritted teeth.

Rachel moaned from the pain but didn't move.

The men dragged her to the back room again. The small man sat her in the metal chair, turned the chair toward the picture of Claire, tied her hands behind her and her feet to the front chair legs, and then stepped back as he ripped the duct tape off her mouth.

Yumiko stepped in front of her and punched her in the mouth, splitting open her lower lip. Blood splattered out onto Rachel's thighs as Yumiko stepped back and looked at the small man. He came up to Rachel and punched her on the left side of her jaw with such force it lifted the chair up off the floor. The pain from her jawbone breaking sent shooting white-hot images up into her head, and then she passed out.

She woke suddenly when water was thrown into her face. Immediately the small man punched her in the right side of her face. She felt the force vibrate into her head, images of light and pain shooting through her. She went limp and groaned, whimpering.

Yumiko leaned in to her again, grabbing a handful of her hair. "Fix it, Rachel."

Jack's voice came into her mind once more. *You fight back with any weapons you have: words, a gesture, a look, aggression, or submission—you fight to stay alive.*

She raised her bloody, swollen face and looked up into Yumiko's eyes. "Fix it yourself, you crazy bitch!"

The small man stepped in front of her and punched her in the nose. She heard it break as the pain shot into her head, and she felt the blood gush out, running over her mouth and chin, dripping down onto her thighs. She watched Yumiko walk to the table and pick up a metal bar the white man had brought into the room. The small man roughly wiped the blood from her mouth and face with a soft round cloth, and then duct-taped her mouth again.

Yumiko walked to her. "It's a shame really—you were rather attractive."

Rachel painfully shook her head back and forth and began to cry out, pleading.

Yumiko slammed the metal bar down onto her right shoulder, knocking it out of joint. She writhed and screamed out at the tearing pain, barely able to breathe, gagging on the blood running down the back of her throat from her bloody nose.

"Now, Rachel, I'm not going to ask you anymore because I know you want to help me, and soon I will give you morphine and the pain will not be as bad, but first you need to tell me you are sorry for calling me those ugly things."

Barely able to focus, crying and defiant, Rachel slowly shook her head.

Yumiko stepped back and swung the metal bar down onto her right knee, shattering her kneecap and flipping her chair backward. She screamed in agony, seizing from the pain, unable to focus on the brink of unconsciousness, the pain shooting up through her body as she cried out and screamed as loud as she could, gagging and trying to get loose from the chair. Someone grabbed the chair and set her upright.

Yumiko ripped the bloody duct tape off her mouth, throwing it onto the floor as Rachel vomited all over herself. All three of her captors left the room, leaving her alone, entombed in her own personal hell.

As she began to lose consciousness, she felt herself fall into the gaping jaws of despair, alone, without hope, consumed by pain, facing the end of her life with nothing more than a broken body and a broken heart. Her life was nothing, a worthless encasement of vomit and blood. She felt herself slip deeper into nothingness, isolated from human contact—no love, no warmth, no hope, only pain and dark, foreboding blackness. "Claire."

❖

Claire suddenly heard Rachel call out to her. She got up from the bed and staggered to the living room. Tilly and Sarah looked at her, worry and concern on their faces.

"What is it?" Tilly asked.

"Where's Rachel?"

Tilly looked confused. "Claire, what is it?"

"Where is she, Tilly? She just called to me."

"There's no one here but us." Tilly walked to her and then guided her down onto the sofa.

Claire's body trembled. She could barely breathe as she reached up for Tilly's hand. "Rachel called to me. She's in pain, Tilly—she's in pain, I know it." She clutched Tilly's arm. Sarah wrapped her arms around her.

"Rachel, I'm here," Claire cried out.

CHAPTER ELEVEN

Rachel felt the shock of the cold water as it was thrown into her face. She cried out when she moved her head. Yumiko went behind her.

"Tell me, Rachel," she said softly, stroking her hair. "Tell me what I want to hear."

Rachel coughed and gagged from the pain and beatings. She didn't want to say the words. She didn't want to surrender. She didn't want to let go, but she couldn't hold on any longer. She was defeated—she had nothing left, and she knew she had done it to herself. Her pride had led her to it. *Who did she think she was? She was nothing.* Barely able to speak, she choked out the words, "I'm sorry I said those things."

Yumiko poured water over her head, letting it run gently down her face, mixing with the blood, then she poured it on her shoulder, and then her knee.

"That feels good, doesn't it?"

Then someone injected Rachel's hip. Morphine, she realized. She felt the momentary welcome relief of the drug as it surged into her body but then quickly left.

"More," she begged.

Yumiko grabbed her by her hair, jerking her head back, and then reached down and moved her broken kneecap. She screamed out in agony as the pain shot up through her body, choking again as blood ran down the back of her throat.

"Fix my program."

She moved Rachel's kneecap again.

The pain exploded into her mind, surging, grabbing hold of her, dragging her down into that dark horrifying pit, wrapping its gnarled twisted claws around her throat. She was going to die here in this place, alone. She no longer cared what she did. Why should she resist? All she could think about was getting relief from the pain, and she would do whatever she had to do to get it—she let go.

"Morphine, and I will fix it."

The men untied her and carried her to the computer, dropping her down onto the chair. She cried out in consuming pain. The white man injected the needle into her hip. She felt the rush of the morphine go into her body—soothing, comforting, desperate relief. She slowly reached her shaking hands up to the keyboard and began to enter the code to correct the program, her fingers awkwardly touching, incorrectly hitting keys, correcting, and then struggling to hit the correct keys again, trying to hold her right hand in position as her shoulder pulsated and pain shot through it. She finished the first phase in twenty-five minutes.

"It's halfway, please, more. I can't concentrate because of the pain," she looked Yumiko in the eye and pleaded, as she tried to hold her fingers over the keyboard.

Yumiko nodded to the white man, and he injected her with more of the morphine. The rush engulfed her, the stabbing, aching, bone-crushing pain floated, drifted away as the drug pulsed through her body. She lowered her head and breathed deeply, coughing as blood dripped back down into her throat.

"Rachel," yelled Yumiko, "focus, finish the coding."

She opened her eyes, raised her head, and looked at the monitor. She tried to remember the sequence, forcing herself to focus, dragging out the process as long as she could, but thirty minutes later she placed her hands in her lap.

"It's done," she said, shattered and broken.

"Run the program," Yumiko ordered.

She rebooted the program.

The program redirected, automatically corrected, and rerouted actions to the best possible solutions.

"Morphine," Rachel begged, pain ripping through her body.

"Perfect job, Ms. Portola," Yumiko said. "Kill her."

They roughly carried Rachel into the back room and threw her on the bed. Rachel knew the end had finally come. In one brief fleeting moment she thought of Claire, and then of Brice and Jack, and how she had failed them all. *I'm sorry. I'm so sorry.*

Then shots rang out and she heard Yumiko call for her men.

❖

Jack came through the door, shouting and firing his weapon, followed by the rest of his team. The two men with Eshee Yumiko were instantly killed. Yumiko backed up against the wall and threw her hands up, begging, "Don't shoot. Don't shoot."

"Where is she?" Jack yelled, desperately demanding an answer.

Yumiko pointed to the back room. Jack and Frank ran to the room while Katherine and David pointed their weapons at Yumiko, daring her to move, José positioning himself at the door.

Jack saw Rachel lying on the wet, bloody mattress. When he saw her face, he groaned. "Son of a bitch."

He and Frank put her blouse around her and lifted her off the mattress. She cried out in pain. Jack placed her over his shoulder and then quickly moved to the outer room. He looked at Yumiko. "Bring her," he ordered Katherine and David.

Rachel moaned, barely able to speak. "Computer. Take me to the computer."

Jack sat her down on the chair as gently as he could. "Rachel, we have to go now—forget the damn mainframe."

Jack watched as she lifted her shaking hands to the keyboard, straining, fighting to focus. She typed a sequence on the keyboard and touched *enter*. The computer screen images began to corrupt.

He picked her up again. She groaned in pain as they moved quickly down the stairwell, Katherine dragging Yumiko down the steps. They reached the outer exit door, where two MI6 agents were waiting in the SUVs. The bodies of three brown-skinned men, dressed in camouflage fatigues, lay by the door.

Jack and Frank put Rachel into one of the SUVs and got in beside her, while Katherine and David shoved Yumiko into the other vehicle and got in as José joined them from the passenger side.

They drove fifteen minutes to the rendezvous point where the helicopter was waiting as promised. Jack and Frank carried Rachel to the helicopter, and Katherine and David followed with Yumiko. But as they lifted Yumiko in, she grabbed Katherine's weapon, maneuvering her fingers onto the trigger and firing, hitting David in the upper arm. Katherine punched her in the jaw, knocking her out of the helicopter. Yumiko attempted to flee, but one of the MI6 agents opened the SUV door and fired his weapon, hitting her in the right shoulder, the impact knocking her to the ground. Jack watched the agent run over and check her. The agent looked up and crossed his hand over his neck, motioning that Yumiko was dead, and then gave a thumbs-up.

Frank and Jack wrapped Rachel in a blanket as the helicopter lifted off. She screamed out in pain from the movement. As the helicopter banked, Jack looked out and saw two MI6 agents lifting Yumiko's body. To his shock, she moved her arms and struggled to get free. He knew then they had hit her with dummy shots. She was too valuable for them to kill and that they would use her as a bargaining tool. He turned, disgusted, and bent down, taking Rachel's hand. "Hang on, Rachel."

Katherine dressed the wound in David's arm as Frank worked on Rachel.

Jack lifted the light over Rachel with one hand and held her hand with the other. Frank inspected her body, grimacing when he saw the damage to her face, right shoulder, knee, and back. He gently moved her head, but she cried out in pain. He reached into the emergency bag, taking out what he needed.

"Ms. Portola, I'm going to give you something for the pain. You are going to drift off. We won't leave you," he assured her.

He took a curette and plunged it into her thigh. Jack watched as she began to drift off and her body started to relax. He knew she felt the welcome relief from the pain and mental anguish as the morphine pulsed throughout her body—he knew too well. She remained still but cried out when Frank wrapped her shoulder and knee. He activated cold packs and placed them on her face, shoulder, and knee, and then strapped her into the harness.

The helicopter landed on the HMS *Hampshire*, and Rachel and David were taken to the ship's medical facility for further treatment. She and the team were then transported to a military helicopter. As Frank monitored her condition and IVs, Jack contacted Tilly and told her what had happened. Both Tilly and Sarah insisted Rachel be flown to Las Vegas for treatment.

❖

Derrick sulked after disconnecting the call from Sarah. He'd offered to fly in to help, but she'd shut him down.

He threw the lamp against the bedroom wall and rubbed his lips so hard it left a bruise on the corner of his lower lip. How could he be with Claire if everyone kept interfering? He went to the far wall and stood in front of the framed poster-sized photo he'd taken of her in Alaska, the last time they'd been together. He touched his lips and then hers. "I'll be with you soon, don't worry."

❖

Tilly and Sarah went into Claire's bedroom, each sitting beside her on the bed.

"Jack's team has her, Claire. They are on their way back," Tilly said, taking her hand.

Claire hugged her but saw the concerned look on both of their faces.

"What's wrong?"

Tilly looked at Sarah and then Claire. "She has some injuries, serious ones."

"Tell me."

Tilly hesitated.

Sarah put her hand on Tilly's shoulder. "She will have to have emergency surgery for some broken bones. They won't know until they get her into the hospital and can see how badly she's injured, but it's her right knee, right shoulder, and face."

Claire felt the flutter of her heart as it skipped a beat. She grabbed Tilly's hand. "What happened? Tell me, tell me now."

Tilly looked at her. "The bastards tortured her."

In that instant Claire felt her life collapse and crumble like pieces of dried clay on a potter's wheel. Nothing meant anything without Rachel being a part of it. She put her face in her hands.

Sarah knelt beside her. "She's going to get the best care possible."

"It's my fault."

Sarah took her hands. "Why would you say that?"

"I knew something was wrong. I knew she was upset, and all I thought about was myself."

At that moment Claire hated herself. She hated her selfishness and her insecurities. She hated how she put herself first and didn't give to Rachel like Rachel had given to her. She vowed she would change. She would be different. She would be a better companion and partner to Rachel. She would be stronger for her.

❖

They stood at the side entrance ramp to the hospital, waiting for the paramedic rescue squad to transport Rachel from McCarran airport. Claire saw Jack walking beside her gurney as they brought her through the side entrance and up the ramp to where they were waiting. Claire gasped and grabbed Tilly's arm. What parts of Rachel's face that could be seen were so badly swollen and bruised she was unrecognizable. Claire put her hand on the top of Rachel's head and stroked her hair, bending down and calling to her, but Rachel was still heavily sedated and didn't respond to her voice.

Jack stepped off to the side as they walked beside the gurney as far as they could until the hospital staff took her to the surgery suites where the team of surgeons was waiting. When the automatic doors closed behind Rachel and the medical staff, Claire turned and looked at him. He was leaning against the wall and looked exhausted. She started to walk toward him.

Tilly grabbed her hand. "Be nice, Claire."

Claire shoved her hand away. "The hell with nice."

She walked up to him, but as they looked at each other, she suddenly realized the agony and pain he was in. She hugged him, and he put his arms around her.

"I'm so sorry, Claire. I'm so sorry. I'll give you a full written report in a few days. I believe the danger is over, but if you would like, we will have security outside her room until we are absolutely sure she is out of danger."

"Yes, I want that."

He turned and walked down the hallway, not looking back at her or the others.

Hospital staff came into the surgical waiting area periodically and gave her updates, but it did little to decrease her anxiety. The surgeon finally appeared after almost thirteen hours of surgery and took her into a private room to discuss Rachel's condition. She insisted Tilly and Sarah be with her.

"She will be kept on heavy medication because of the trauma and pain. She had to have a partial right knee replacement, major repair of the right rotator cuff and the ligaments in her shoulder, and pin placement in the left side of her jawbone. I repaired the bone in her nose and cheek, and the plastic surgeon reconstructed the damage to her face and did what he could to her back. Her jaw is wired shut, and she won't be able to chew or open her mouth for at least six weeks. She will have a long, long road to recovery."

Claire looked intently at him, hanging on every word he said. "When can I see her?"

"As soon as she comes out of recovery and they get her settled into ICU. Ms. Davenport, I don't know yet how well she will recover from all of this. She's in pretty bad shape, and she will be in a lot of pain. We will just have to take this one day at a time." He touched her elbow. "The best thing you can do is be positive and help her find her own pace in this."

Claire thanked him, and he left.

They went back to the waiting area.

"I have to fly back to Cleveland tomorrow," Sarah said.

Claire hugged her. "I know you have to get back. Sorry you're not getting the extra vacation at the cabin."

"I promise, I'll be back as soon as I can."

Claire's cell phone rang. Derrick.

"I'm so very sorry, Claire. I would like to come be with you if you'd like."

"Thank you so much," Claire replied, "but Sarah and Tilly are here with me and I'm good for now."

"Well, let me know if you need anything, anything at all."

She was finally able to go into Rachel's room in ICU three hours later and stood by her bed, holding her hand as she lay motionless, the sound of the machines intensifying the quiet in the room. Except for her eyes and forehead, her face was completely wrapped in bandages.

She lifted the sheet and blanket to look at Rachel's body, trying to see the damage, but put the covers back. "Rachel, what did they do to you?"

Rachel lifted her left hand slightly, her fingers jerking, as her monitor began to beep. A nurse came in to check her.

"Do you think she's in a lot of pain?"

The nurse checked her IVs and the monitor. "I think she's comfortable. All of her vital signs are strong and not elevated. She's being given pain medication through her IV, and she seems to be tolerating everything well." The nurse left the room.

Claire sat quietly beside her bed, holding her hand, watching her.

CHAPTER TWELVE

She stayed at the hospital around the clock, visiting Rachel as often as the ICU staff would allow. Sarah flew home, but Tilly stayed as long as she could in between rehearsals and performances.

As the hours and days passed, Rachel began to moan and cry out when she started to reach awareness. Claire was by her side, holding her hand when she finally opened her eyes. She groaned when she moved her head to look at her.

Claire smiled and stroked the side of her head. "Rachel, you're safe and back with me."

Tears ran down the corners of Rachel's eyes. Claire wiped them away with a tissue.

"Blink once for yes, twice for no. Are you in a lot of pain?"

She blinked once.

"I'll get the nurse to give you some more medication."

Tilly and Claire were by Rachel's bedside when she next woke. She tried to speak. Claire saw the panic and confusion in her face and tried to comfort her, leaning in over her, touching her left shoulder, trying to calm her.

"Rachel, your mouth is wired shut to help heal your broken jaw." She offered her water with a straw. Rachel sipped slowly. "The doctors say you are healing nicely."

A look of panic once again crossed Rachel's face.

She stroked Rachel's hair. "I know you have a lot of questions."

Rachel slowly nodded and forced her speech through her teeth.

"Damage?" she said, barely understandable.

Claire looked at Tilly, not knowing how much to tell her, but Tilly nodded. Rachel deserved the truth.

"It's extensive, but you're healing."

Rachel tried to move. Claire watched as her eyes widened and Rachel gripped her hand, looking at her.

"Face?"

She stroked Rachel's head again. "Broken nose, broken right cheekbone, broken jaw on your left side."

"Scars?"

She put her hand on the side of Rachel's face and gently held it. "You will have some scarring on your nose because of reconstruction and a small scar over your cheekbone and on the left side of your jaw, but the surgeon has assured us the scars will fade rapidly and be barely visible in a year."

"Nose?"

"It's as beautiful as ever, Rachel, except you still have some swelling," said Tilly. "It will eventually go down."

Rachel looked exhausted. "Pain."

"I'll get the nurse," Claire said.

Claire sat on the couch in the lounge down the hall from Rachel's room with her hands pressed tightly together, her knees shaking as she tried not to listen to Rachel's pitiful screams when the medical team removed the special skin barrier from her back and thighs, and then reapplied the medication and new bandages. She paced, relieved when Rachel's screams began to subside. They must have given her more pain medication.

It took every ounce of energy Claire had to watch Rachel struggle to deal with her injuries and the pain. She felt totally useless. There was nothing she could do but be beside her and try to comfort her.

She was sitting in a chair next to her bed, working on a design for a new piece of pottery, when Rachel woke and looked at her.

She took her hand. "You all right?"

"Jacob?"

She leaned in and looked at her, shaking her head slowly, forcing back her tears.

Rachel grabbed the bar on the bed and began to shake it, moaning, "No."

The nurses came in and sedated her.

❖

Rachel was slipping into a deep depression. Three days later after learning of Jacob's death, she refused to eat. Claire begged, and Tilly pleaded, but she would not eat.

The next day, Claire came into the room and insisted she eat.

"Pain," Rachel said, looking at her.

She told her she had to wait for more meds.

Rachel grabbed the side rail, shaking it. "Pain."

"You eat something, and I'll see what I can do."

Rachel scowled through her teeth. "Screw you."

Claire looked at her, half smiling. "You already did, and I enjoyed it immensely. If that's an offer, it's a little crude, but I think we should wait until you recover a little more—no pain meds until you eat something."

She helped Rachel hold up the power drink to her lips. Rachel took a small amount and then refused to take any more.

"Rachel, you can act like a two-year-old all you want, but you won't get any more pain medication until you drink some of this. I will do what I have to do to get you well again."

Rachel took the straw and drank half the liquid.

"Good job, I'll tell the nurse."

❖

As the days passed, the injuries began to heal and the swelling subsided. The doctors said Rachel was ready for physical therapy. They put her in her wheelchair, and Claire walked beside her as the aide took her down to therapy. Sweat ran down Rachel's face when the therapist worked her knee, and as hard as the therapist tried, Rachel would not cooperate. After her session, they brought her back up to her room, and Claire gave her ice water and more power shake. Rachel had lost a significant amount of weight, and everyone was concerned.

"Pain."

"Rachel, you just had a shot two hours ago. They won't give you another one for two more hours."

Rachel grabbed Claire's hand and pleaded.

Two days later the team psychiatrist, Dr. Sharon DeYoung, paid Rachel a visit. Claire held Rachel's hand as the doctor talked with her.

"Rachel, your doctors are taking you off the pain shots and putting you on oral medication. You're in danger of becoming addicted to the pain medication, and we have to wean you off."

"No." She slammed her left fist into the bed. "Pain."

"Yes, Rachel, I know you're in pain, but you have to come off the drug, and your surgeon wants you in physical therapy every day for at least an hour working that knee. They won't start therapy on your shoulder for a while yet. They are sending you home in two days."

"No." She slowly shook her head.

Claire leaned down to her. "I've rented a one-level house not far from Tilly, and we will be staying there."

Rachel looked at her. "No."

"Tough, you're going there."

Rachel turned on her side and refused to look at them.

Dr. DeYoung and Claire stepped out of the room. The doctor put her hand on Claire's shoulder.

"She'll be all right. She has a lot to deal with, and she needs time, and lots of love, understanding, and patience." She handed Claire her business card. "If you need anything, don't hesitate to call me. I can come see her at the house if it's necessary. I can see it's been very difficult for you."

Claire took a deep breath. "It has, but I just want her to get well."

"You know, Rachel has to come to terms with the changes in her life—and so do you. This has affected both of you."

"What can I do that will help her the most?"

"Be patient and accept her the way she is right now, and enjoy each day with her, the good and the not so good." Dr. DeYoung patted her hand. "I assure you, there are better days ahead."

Claire nodded.

"Rachel has withdrawn for a time, but that doesn't mean you should. It's very important for caregivers to take good care of themselves."

❖

Claire repositioned Rachel's wheelchair facing the outdoor pool area, and later wheeled her through the house, showing her the rooms.

The house had been decorated for Christmas, in hopes it would help Rachel's mood, but she continued to slip further into depression.

"It's a furnished rental, so it's not that great, but the three bedrooms are nice, and all the beds look comfortable."

Claire pushed her into the master bedroom where she had arranged to have a treadmill, exercise bicycle, and a few other needed pieces of equipment.

"This is your room."

"Pain," Rachel said softly.

"No pain medication for another hour."

"Merry Christmas."

Claire did not respond.

She agonized as she watched Rachel's days begin to pass in unnoticed succession, each one fading into another: morning stretching and exercises, afternoon workouts, swimming, physical therapy, an endless parade of people in and out of the house—and always there was pain.

Rachel was consumed in night terrors, her cries and screams filling the house in the early morning darkness. Claire would go to her room to try to comfort her, but with little success, and in desperation, she called Dr. DeYoung, telling her the situation and asking what more she could do. She suggested one more thing.

And so, in the long dark nights, when she heard Rachel's night terrors reach into her soul and overshadow her, she went into her room and got in bed with her and held her. She cradled her in her arms, told her it would be all right, that they were just dreams and she was safe. She told her the good and positive things that had happened that day, or week, or in days past. Rachel went back to sleep, and then once she was in a deep sleep, Claire reluctantly left her bed.

Slowly, Rachel's night terrors began to subside.

❖

Anna, Rachel's aide, wheeled her out to sun by the pool and wrapped her in a light blanket. Claire came out and sat down beside her.

"It's snowing and twelve degrees in Cleveland. I don't know that I ever want to go back there." Claire closed her eyes and held her face up to the sun.

"Jacob."

Claire took Rachel's hand and held it. "It's not your fault. He died doing his job, trying to protect you. His last thoughts were of you."

Rachel wanted to tell her she knew it was her fault that Jacob was dead. She'd gone along with Brice's plan, she'd supported it, and because of it, Jacob was killed. She had failed Jacob, and it had cost him his life.

"Tell me."

Claire told her how he died.

Rachel's sadness engulfed her, surrounding her like she had fallen into a deep vat of thick turbulent liquid, and no matter how hard she struggled she couldn't get out.

"Sarah?"

"She's doing great, and so are Ricky and Tommy. They'll be down to see us in a couple of weeks."

"Ash?"

"He's fine. I hired a rider to take him out every couple of days. He wasn't lame. It was just a ploy to lure you to the stables. They found the vet in one of the empty stalls, shot in the head."

"Jack?"

Claire grew quiet. "I don't want to talk about Jack. I hold him responsible for what happened to you."

"Saved me."

"Yeah, well, if it wasn't for his screwup, you wouldn't have been taken in the first place."

"Trap. Plan."

"I don't understand what you mean, Rachel. He should have tried harder because he knew it was dangerous, and he knew Yumiko was plotting."

Rachel couldn't explain that it was her and Brice's plan to have her be captured, not Jack's.

"See him soon."

"Okay, that's your business, but don't expect me to be around when he comes over."

They sat quietly in the sun.

CHAPTER THIRTEEN

Yumiko looked up at the two-way mirror and then back at the MI6 agent but didn't speak.

The agent leaned forward. "Either do this or spend the rest of your life here, locked away, without contact. I rather think the choice is obvious."

She saw the sweat on his upper lip and watched his eyes dart down and to the right. He was lying.

"What guarantees do I have that MI6 will keep their word? You people are notorious for lying."

"You have us confused with the CIA. Wear the wire, set your stepfather up, or stay here the rest of your life—those are your only options."

"I want to be set up in the United States when it's over."

"That can be arranged."

"And not some horrible place that snows or rains all year long. California, or somewhere in the Southwest."

"Yes, we can do that."

"New name, new identity, and one hundred thousand pounds?"

"Yes, in exchange for all the information, if you wear the wire and cooperate fully."

MI6 might have wiped out her holdings in the European markets, but Eshee knew they still had no idea of the operations in the United States, and once she sold out her stepfather and got rid of his leadership, she would be at the head. He was right—*all things come to those who wait.*

"All right, I'll do it."

❖

"Okay, Rachel, open your mouth slowly." Dr. Murphy touched both sides of her jaw.

Rachel carefully opened her jaw and went through the exercises.

The orthodontist worked inside her mouth, and then his assistant cleaned the inside of her mouth and teeth.

When his assistant was finished, Dr. Murphy inspected Rachel's mouth and jaw again. "How's it feel?"

Rachel smiled. "Clean."

After six weeks, her jaw muscles felt weak, and she slurred her words, but the pain was not as bad as she had thought it would be.

Anna drove her back to the house and walked beside her as she walked through the living room, using her cane. Claire was out sunning by the pool and waved for her to come out to be with her.

Anna readjusted Rachel's right arm sling and walked with her out beside Claire, helping her sit down in the cushioned chair.

"I'll take it from here, Anna. You can leave for the day," said Claire. "Let me see you." Claire bent over her, leaning in, looking intently at her face. "Both sides of your jaw look exactly the same."

"Claire."

Claire held her face in her warm, soft hands. "It's so wonderful to hear you say my name again."

"Thank you."

Claire sat down and hugged her, kissing her hair. "Oh, Rachel."

That night Rachel screamed louder than she had ever screamed and called out Claire's name. Claire came into her room and got in bed with her.

"It's all right." Claire held her in her arms as Rachel trembled. "You're safe. Are these damn nightmares ever going to stop?" Claire kissed her head and face.

The next afternoon Rachel heard Claire do something she thought she would never do—she called Jack. When Jack came to visit that evening, Rachel watched as Claire let him into their home, walked him to the living room where she was sitting, and then excused herself, leaving Rachel alone with him.

She looked up and smiled. "Jack."

He sat on the couch across from her. "You look good—thin, but good."

"Jack, how are you?"

"I'm okay."

She heard sadness in his voice and saw it written on his face. Silence filled the space between them, and then she spoke. "Where's Jacob buried?"

"In Fairbanks, where his mom and dad live."

"I want to go to his grave."

"You can't for a while yet."

"I want you to take me when I can go."

"All right."

"Thank you for saving me, Jack. I hoped you would come, but I didn't know." She moved her mouth slowly. It would be a while before speech was automatic.

"Rachel, I'm so sorry this happened to you. I have gone over in my mind a thousand times how I could have done things differently to prevent it or get to you sooner, but honestly, I don't know how we could have done it. They set what we call a kill-trap. Jacob was dead the moment you two pulled into the driveway. They knew exactly where he was vulnerable."

She lowered her head. "I feel responsible for Jacob's death."

"You are not. Jacob was a professional, and he did his job. He knew the risks. We all did."

"I wish there would have been some other way to do what we had to do."

"Jacob knew our plan, so did Frank and the other team members guarding you and Claire, and they were all willing to do what they had to do. There was nothing we could have done differently to prevent Jacob's death. They wanted to murder Jacob, not wound him. Jacob died with honor, doing what he loved, protecting you, and if we hadn't put that tracking chip in you, we would have lost you too."

"I want you and Claire to work out what's between you."

"I don't know if that's possible. She doesn't know there was a plan to have you taken, and I cannot tell her."

"Still, promise me you'll try to fix things."

"Yes, I will."

They began to talk about the rescue and what happened. She grew quiet, hesitating to talk about what Yumiko had done to her, and her night terrors. She saw the concern in his face.

"I want to show you something." He stood up, unbuttoned his shirt, and turned around. With his muscular back toward her, he took off his shirt, and then his undershirt. Raised long thick scar tissue riddled about sixty percent of his upper back. He turned toward her, showing her his chest that bore similar scars. He put his clothing back on and sat down again.

"I was captured in Africa, beaten, and tortured for information. I'm a trained professional, and it was all I could do to deal with it. You did well. You survived, and you accomplished the mission. No mission ever goes perfectly. I have a message for you from Commander Chambers. He wants you to know that his team will be forever in your debt for what you did, and if you ever need anything, you are to call him. I don't think you realize the significance of what you did."

"I broke, Jack, in the end I fixed the program for her, and I would have done anything she wanted. If you hadn't gotten to me when you did, she would have been unstoppable."

"You can't think in terms of *if*. You helped stop her. No one but you could have done what you did. I know you gave our team the code in case something happened to you, but you were the one she wanted. Rachel, it was an incredibly unselfish and brave thing you did. Your mission was a success."

"But I broke, and I gave her everything she wanted."

"But now you're stronger than you've ever been, and you are so much more capable of survival in other situations. Rachel, if my team hadn't gotten me out when they did, I would have given up the information they wanted."

"Jack, I have vivid night terrors, and they are not going away."

"You may have them the rest of your life, but hopefully they won't remain as severe as they are now. I still have them once in a while myself."

"What can I do to stop them from being so threatening?"

"Face them, Rachel. Face the demons and defeat them."

"But how?"

"You have to find a way that works for you. Don't allow fear to overpower you—do whatever you can to help yourself. Fill your mind with positive, good things, so when the terror does come, your arsenal is full to fight back. When you're fully recovered, I'd like to talk to you about coming to work with me—not for me, but with me. I think it would be good for you, and you have some skills we desperately need."

They talked about his business and then he left.

❖

Rachel started more intense physical therapy on her shoulder. By the end of six weeks, she was at ninety-eight percent mobility, walking without a cane, and had gained seven pounds. She started tanning her body and building herself up. Her muscle tone increased, her movement was balanced and graceful, and her body became sleek with muscle. The pain decreased, and she began to feel strong and healthy again.

On a Friday night, she knocked on the open door of Claire's bedroom and was invited in. She propped up some of Claire's pillows and climbed carefully onto her bed, leaning back on the headboard.

Claire put the book she was reading down on the nightstand.

"It's wonderful to have you in here, Rachel. Everything all right?"

"Claire, I don't like the distance that's between us. We're not the same as we were before. I'm so sorry for my behavior."

Claire turned to her. "Rachel, there's no need to apologize. You went through hell. I'm sorry I wasn't more helpful."

Rachel touched her face. "You have been wonderful through all this. I couldn't have asked for a better companion through this." She grew quiet but then finally spoke again. "I need to talk to you about what happened." She watched Claire's reaction, trying to get a read on what she was feeling.

Claire looked down and wouldn't make eye contact. "I've dreaded this moment for a long time. I'm afraid to hear it, but I know you need to tell me." She looked up into Rachel's eyes. "Tell me."

Rachel didn't tell her that she was used as bait, she was too ashamed to tell her that, but she told her the details, from being darted in the stables to the torture and beatings. "I need to show you." She stood up and took her blouse and slacks off. She watched carefully as Claire looked at her. She showed her the scars on her shoulder and knee, then slowly turned and showed Claire her back—the raised, ugly, ribbed pink scars all over her back and thighs. And then she turned around and told her Yumiko had poured acid over her back and down her thighs.

Claire put her hands up to her face.

She dressed and got back into the bed, pulling Claire to her and holding her. "I can't let you touch me again. If I do, all I will ever think about is you enduring my scars. I can't bear the thought of you touching my scarred body. I love you. I don't want to hurt you, please understand."

Claire kissed her face and stroked her hair. "I can only see the beautiful person you are. Yes, your body is scarred, but it's because you thought more about others' lives than you did about your own. If it's your wish we not be lovers, then I have no choice but to accept it, but remember, just because your body is scarred, doesn't mean my feelings or your feelings will change. I know right now you're sensitive about it, but I'm hoping over time you'll change your mind."

They lay in the bed and held each other.

❖

A few weeks later they rode the equestrian trails at the base of Mount Charleston, enjoying the morning sun as the birds sang through the pines. Rachel made Ash pick up his pace, as Claire followed on a beautiful chestnut mare. Claire had on a new gray Stetson with a silver band that Rachel had bought her. She had told her laughing, "You can't ride Western style with a helmet in the west, Claire. If another rider sees you, they'll beat you up."

They stopped by a cluster of pine trees and got off their horses to take a break. Claire reached into her saddlebag and got out the snacks she had brought for them.

"Rachel, please make sure you eat all of that sandwich and fruit."

Rachel smiled. "Yes, I will."

They sat down on a rock formation.

Claire looked around as she drank her water. "It's so beautiful here." She looked back toward the Las Vegas skyline. "Not so much there, but here is gorgeous. Are you all packed?"

"Yes, I just need to call the equipment company and confirm a time for them to pick up the treadmill and bike. What time does our flight leave on Wednesday for Cleveland?"

"One o'clock." Claire started eating her sandwich.

Rachel took a big bite of her apple, put it in her hand, and walked over to Ash and gave it to him. She wiped her hand on her jeans and then came back to Claire. She gazed down at her and stood quiet for a long moment, worried how Claire would react to what she was about to tell her.

"I've decided to move to Las Vegas, and I want you to move here with me."

Claire stopped eating and looked up at her.

"Jack has asked me to come work with him, and I've decided to do it. Join me, please? There's nothing in Cleveland, Claire. Tilly would love it if you were here too, we won't be separated, we can build you a new studio, and the weather is great here." She stopped pleading her case and was quiet, watching her, trying to get a sense of her reaction.

Claire put her half-eaten sandwich back into the plastic bag, set it down on the rock, and was quiet for a long time. She picked up a pebble and tossed it, then watched as it went through the air, hit the ground, and rolled. She brushed her hands together and then looked up at her.

"I think that's a great idea. I'm sure we can agree on a house, and our attorneys can work up a joint purchase agreement. I have some things I need to tell you too, so come sit down beside me."

Rachel slowly sat down. "What is it?"

"Your hospital bills have been covered, in full. I got a call from Commander Chambers two days after they brought you back. Evidently, when you corrupted SeaBridge's system, you wiped out all their holdings and eliminated MI6's headache. They were so grateful, they picked up all the expenses of your surgeries, hospital stay, doctors, and rehabilitation. The costs were profound. You have some serious friends in high places."

Rachel was quiet. She wanted to tell her she already knew, and she wanted to tell her about what she and Brice had planned, and that Jack had been against it from the start, but she knew she couldn't because she had signed a confidentiality agreement and had sworn an oath, and her shame overwhelmed her.

"Rachel, there's more. While you were in the hospital, and then later recovering at the house but incapacitated, Michael called me regarding some decisions that had to be made about your finances—remember, you gave me power of attorney?"

"Yes."

"Well, I've been monitoring your funds closely, and as of last week your cash and assets are now worth over fifty-eight million dollars."

Rachel's mouth dropped open and she stared at Claire.

Claire reached over and took her hand. "It seems I have a talent for managing your money, who knew? I think, if you'll allow me, I'd like to continue to watch over your funds, while you go off and play with Jack and his friends. I'm going to scale down my pottery business and just work on special pieces. I can do it anywhere." Claire smiled and looked more intently at her. "What do you think?"

Rachel stood up and walked to Ash, grabbed his reins and the saddle horn, and swung up on him without using the stirrups. She looked down at Claire. "For the first time in years, I feel alive again, and I think I can't wait for the rest of our life to start."

CHAPTER FOURTEEN

They purchased a three-acre estate one-third of the way up Mount Charleston, in a secluded, partially wooded area of the mountain. It had a sweeping view of the beautiful rock formations, and from the living room's vaulted windows they could see for miles. Jack's team renovated the security system and installed state-of-the-art technology in every part of the estate, which had four bedrooms, six bathrooms, a heated pool, a Jacuzzi, and gardens in the back courtyard. They both loved the house and settled in quickly. They hired a full-time cook, a housekeeper, and a landscaping service to care for the grounds. Rachel began working with Jack and would often be gone long hours.

Claire had her studio built and began to focus on only special ordered pieces. She tried to keep her mind occupied, but her desire and sexual need for Rachel continued to build. Each time Rachel walked by, she felt like pouncing on her. Rachel dropped her car fob on the hallway floor, bent over to pick it up, and Claire felt like she was in heat. In desperation, she fantasized about ways to get Rachel to have sex with her. Pity sex might work—no, too needy. She could get her drunk—no, she didn't drink. Get her stoned—no, she didn't indulge. Slip some porn on the TV when they were in the living room—no, Rachel would just turn it off. Claire felt like she was in love with a saint.

They went riding frequently up onto the mountain and into surrounding areas, but today Rachel seemed not to enjoy the ride. She sat stiffly in the saddle and acted irritated and restless as they maneuvered the horses back and forth on the brush-covered trail.

They arrived back at the stables just as the sun was setting, and it was fully dark by the time they took care of the horses and started back to their estate.

"Rachel, you're so quiet. Are you all right?"

Rachel shrugged and looked out the passenger window.

They pulled into the gated entryway, and Claire parked her silver Maserati GranTurismo in the six-car garage next to Rachel's black Viper. They walked through the vestibule to the kitchen.

"Do you want a salad?" Claire asked.

"No thanks, I'm not hungry."

She watched from the French doors of her bedroom as Rachel went out to the pool with her camisole on over her bathing suit, dived in, and swam underwater the entire length of the pool. Claire paced and then turned on the sauna in her bathroom and stayed there for thirty minutes before she showered.

When she came out of the shower, she dressed in the sexiest outfit she had, one she knew Rachel liked, went to the media room, and poured herself a glass of red wine. Rachel came in twenty minutes later dressed in her pajamas, stared at her for a few seconds, and then picked out a movie and turned it on, but a few minutes later she grabbed the remote and started channel surfing.

"Would you like some ginger ale?" *Perhaps a Xanax to help you relax and not be so uptight?*

"No, I don't think so." Rachel sighed and continued to surf.

Claire sipped her wine, watching her. *Is she finally ready? Thank God for sex drive.*

Rachel turned the TV off and looked at her. "Claire, can we talk?"

"Of course. What would you like to talk about?"

Rachel tossed the remote aside. "I know I said I didn't feel I could have sex because of my scars, but I...I..." She stood and began pacing.

Claire could see the strain in her face. She wanted to help her get through it. "Rachel, I know how difficult this is for you, but I think you're putting way too much pressure on yourself. We are human beings with human emotions and needs, and no couple has a greater need to be together than we do. The love between us that we enjoy so much is also entangled in our sexual needs. I told you—I don't care about your scars, and I mean it. I'm not just saying it. I know you want me, and I want you so badly I'm dreaming about you. If we don't get this resolved pretty soon, I'm going to turn into a drunk." She took another drink of her wine.

Rachel moved toward her. "Screw this." She took the glass of wine out of her hand.

"Don't you dare drink that, Rachel."

"I'm not going to *drink* it."

She set the glass of wine down on the coffee table, grabbed Claire's hand, and quickly led her to her bedroom. When they got to her room, Claire wrapped her arms around her and kissed her. They had their hands on each other in a matter of seconds, and then fell onto the bed kissing, touching, and caressing.

Claire moved on top of Rachel, feeling the warmth of her body, aching, throbbing. "It's been forever. I've missed your touch so much."

"I'm starving for you." Rachel kissed her, groaning, sliding her arm around her back and then intertwining her fingers into the back of her hair, bringing her against her.

Claire looked into her eyes. "I know how we can work this out so you're comfortable. All you have to do is leave your pajama top on over your back. I promise I won't touch you anywhere you're uncomfortable."

"You're okay with me leaving my top on?"

"Yes, of course."

"Promise me if this doesn't work, you won't push it?"

Claire kissed her and whispered, breathless, "I promise. And it's going to work. Quit worrying."

They began to kiss more deeply as Claire unbuttoned Rachel's top and exposed her full, firm breasts and her toned stomach. She looked down, completely lusting for Rachel's body.

"Rachel, you do know your body is more beautiful than before. I didn't think it was possible, but it is."

She bent over her and cupped her hand on Rachel's breast, kissing her shoulder and neck. Rachel's hand rose slightly, as if to guard from any unwanted touch. She put her hand on Rachel's face and whispered to her, "Baby, you have to relax. I promise I won't touch you anywhere you're uncomfortable."

She lowered Rachel's hand gently and began to caress and touch her, moving slowly down her body. She could feel Rachel flex her stomach muscles as her hair fell onto her, and her lips touched her stomach.

Rachel raised her hands and put them on Claire's shoulders. "I can't." She sat up. "I want to so badly, but I'm afraid my scars will be a turnoff to you."

Claire sat up and looked at her. "Are you kidding me? You just don't see it, do you? You look like something out of a...Rachel, you're gorgeous and ripped. I want to see—please let me look at you and touch you."

She peeled Rachel's pajama bottoms off her and moved her hands down the front of her thighs, being careful not to touch behind her. "Let me take your top off. You can lie on your back. I promise I won't touch your back."

"I'll take it off." Rachel took off her silk top and threw it onto the floor, then quickly lay on her back again.

Claire looked at Rachel as she lay naked in front of her. Her muscles were tight, her curves smooth and defined, her skin tanned and toned. She couldn't take her eyes off her. She sat up in the bed looking at her.

"Holy crap, you're intimidating. I don't want to get naked in front of you."

Rachel started to take Claire's blouse off, but Claire reached up and stopped her.

"I'm not kidding, I don't think I can lie beside you."

Rachel pulled her down on top of her and kissed her. "Yes, I've wanted to be with you, please. If I can let you touch me, then you can let me touch you."

Rachel lifted her slightly and began to undress her, kissing, caressing.

Claire put her head back, "Rachel, I'm so sorry my body is not in its best shape."

"Claire, you are so beautiful. I don't think you have ever realized how beautiful you really are. You walk into the room, heads turn, and the whole room lights up. You are stunning. I have seen men and women trip over themselves and do double takes when they see you."

"No, it's you they see, not me."

"Not anymore, those days are gone for me."

"Oh, Rachel, no, you're still so beautiful."

Rachel kissed her shoulders, slipping her blouse off, unhooking her bra, letting it fall off her, and then unzipped her slacks, reached inside her panties, and peeled them off, throwing all of her clothes onto the floor. She guided Claire and brought her down on her, kissing, touching, caressing, gasping.

"I know you don't see your own beauty, Claire."

Claire began to moan as she moved her hands over Rachel's toned body.

"Promise me, Rachel, if we start this again, we won't stop until we both agree."

Rachel kissed her, breathing deeply. "Yes, yes, anything, I promise."

Claire kissed her, running her fingers through her hair, touching her. "I'm drooling all over you, Rachel. It's been so long I can't catch my breath. I've wanted you so badly."

Their bodies merged, desire and pleasure surging.

CHAPTER FIFTEEN

D errick called a few days later, anxious to speak with Claire.
"Now that Rachel is doing well, I want you two to come to Seattle and stay a few days. It will be good for both of you."

"Wait, I'll put you on speakerphone."

Derrick made a face and threw his hand up. He didn't want to be on speakerphone. He didn't want to talk with Rachel. He didn't want to pretend anymore. He needed to be with Claire. He looked over at her picture on the wall.

"Hey, Derrick."

Hearing Rachel's voice made him nauseous. He wanted to reach through the phone and grab her by the throat. He didn't think he could keep up the facade, but he decided he would do it for Claire's sake.

"Hey, Rachel. It's wonderful to hear you're doing well. When are you two coming to Seattle?"

"That sounds like fun, but with everything going on right now it will have to be in a few more months. How are you doing? Are you doing a lot of surgeries?"

Small talk, just blah, blah, blah. Get off the phone, you bitch. "My schedule is pretty hectic, but I'll always make time for you and Claire."

"We appreciate that, Derrick." Finally, Claire was talking again. "We'll be in touch, and we promise we'll come see you soon."

He threw the cell phone onto the floor when the call ended and kicked it across the room.

He called again two days later, but Claire didn't answer. He walked over to her picture on the wall. "I swear to you—I will save you from her soon." He picked up the rocks glass and took another sip of The Macallan single malt.

❖

Rachel lay awake, feeling the warmth of Claire's body, but in this moment when she felt closest to her, the fear and anxiety of the possibility of losing her was at its peak. The shame and guilt she felt because of Jacob's death and that she withheld why it happened caused an unbearable ache, like a wedge being driven between them. She knew she needed to tell her, but the fear of Claire's rejection was overwhelming. The risk was too great, and so she pushed it down, driving the wedge deeper.

Claire turned over and slipped her leg over her. "Good morning."

Rachel rubbed her thigh. "Are you feeling better now?"

"Mm, how could I not. How about you?"

"Oh yes, you have the touch."

Claire laughed. "Are you still concerned about how I feel about your scars? I've never enjoyed sex so much, ever. We may mess up some things, but *that* is one thing we get completely right."

"Thank you. Thank you for loving me with a love I don't deserve."

The smile left Claire's face and a deep frown appeared. "Rachel, that's so not true. How can you possibly feel that way after everything we've been through together?"

A quiet voice spoke inside Rachel's head. *This is an opportunity to tell her. Tell her what's in your heart.* But she lay silent in Claire's arms.

"Rachel, I've been thinking about your scars."

"I'm so sorry."

"No, no, I mean in a good way. Don't be ashamed of them. Every time I see them, I think how brave you are and what you did to help others. I love your scars—I don't love that you had to get them, but I love them because I know what you did."

Coward. Liar. She could feel her body tense at the thoughts.

Claire began to kiss her nose and cheek, and then moved to her shoulder. "Do the scars on your back hurt?"

"Sometimes my skin feels really tight and aches, and it's always sensitive. I use the special applicator to put the lotion on, and it helps."

"Will there ever be a time when you'll let me put the lotion on your back?"

"I just don't see that ever happening, but thank you for being so caring and understanding about it. I feel fine now about all the other scars, but the scars on my back are just too much for me to deal with, thinking about you having to see or touch them."

Claire kissed her. "You know, this is Saturday. We can stay in bed until Monday morning if we want, or longer. You can tell Jack you can't come into work because you're busy."

"I do need more time with you, Claire. Each morning when I leave for work, I can't wait to get back to you. I feel this thing always hanging over us, that it may be the last time. It drives me crazy. I have enjoyed every second with you, each and every time we've been together, but I have never been able to lie with you and think, we're together now and you'll be with me next month or next year. We've only been able to make love in moments. I would love nothing more than to know you'll be with me each morning when I wake. I love knowing you'll be next to me tomorrow and for a few more days. It is the sweetest feeling. I love it."

"I know. I feel it too. I hate that we starve each other and then feel like we have to cling to each other every second we're together. It's not right, and it's stressful. I'm sure it's from everything we've been through. It's all right, though, really. We'll eventually get this right."

Tell her. Rachel took her hand.

Claire kissed her arm. "There's no one else I'd rather be with than you. I feel totally complete and happy with you. You're beautiful, smarter than anyone I know, my best friend, the most tender, focused, considerate, fulfilling lover I have ever known or even imagined, and I feel completely safe and protected when I'm with you. Why the hell don't we make a permanent commitment to each other? I don't want to be desperate for you. I hate that—it's a horrible feeling."

Claire kissed her then, fully, deeply. "Rachel, I want to enjoy you as much as I can. I want to come up to you, take you in my arms and kiss you, or come in when you're taking a shower and strip off my clothes and get in with you. I want you to be in my bed and make love to you in the middle of the night or in the morning. I want to feel you beside me. I want to wake up next to you. This time is finally for us. Look what we went through all those years trying to fight our feelings for each other. We were so miserable, and it damn near killed both of us. I still don't know why we feel the way we do about each other. All I know is we do. I would be content to spend the rest of my life with you, and it makes me sick to my stomach to think we might not be together."

"Claire, are you proposing?"

Claire sat up in the bed and met her gaze, smiling. "Yes, I think I am. I know what you went through has changed you, and it's changed me also. I don't want to risk losing you ever again. I guess it's selfish on my part, but I don't want to risk that you might leave me. I don't want to have an affair with you. You and I both deserve more than that. If you drifted from me, I couldn't bear it."

"Claire, if we don't stop soon, I'm going to reach a point where I won't be able to separate from you. My life is so entwined in yours now, that I can't see where I end and you begin."

"Is that such a bad thing?"

"No, I love it, but where do we go from here?"

Claire cupped her face in her hands. "I know...I know you have always been concerned for my wellbeing. I look back over our years together, and I know you've always been so concerned about how I felt and how whatever you did would affect me. You are the person I want to be with for the rest of my life. Marry me, Rachel? Our hearts are already bound—let's bind ourselves together legally for the rest of our lives. I don't care about anyone but you. We've been through so much—now let's spend the rest of our lives together."

Rachel took her hands and held them. "Claire, I...I'm..."

"What is it? Why do you hold back from me? I know you love me, and I know you feel just as strongly about me as I do about you."

"I'm not who you think I am."

"That's not true. You are *exactly* who I think you are."

"I have to tell you something."

Claire continued to hold her hand. "It's about time. I know you've held back for a long time, since you were with Jack, just before you were taken. Did you sleep with Jack?"

Rachel touched her face. "Oh, Claire, no. There's no one in my life in that way but you, but I...I—"

"Rachel, you can tell me. No matter what it is, you can tell me."

"It's my fault Jacob was killed."

"It is *not*. You have to know that."

"It is. It's my fault because Brice and I planned for me to be taken in order to trap Yumiko and take down SeaBridge. It was all a plan, and I let you hold it against Jack, knowing he opposed it and wanted nothing to do with it. He tried to talk me out of it, and because of what I did, Jacob is dead."

"Rachel, you deliberately put your life in danger again?"

"I was naive enough to think we had the resources and skill, and we could do it without anyone being at risk but me, and look what happened. So many lives were affected by what we did, and more people could have been killed. I'm so sorry, Claire—please forgive me. I've broken my obligation to MI6 by telling you this, but I can't let this be between us any longer. I'm so sorry." She put her face in her hands.

Claire put her hands on her shoulders. "Listen to me. Do you honestly believe I don't understand you? I get you. I know your great desire and need to help wherever you can. How many times have you put your life at risk because others needed your help? Rachel, look at me."

She knew she couldn't hide. Every feeling, every emotion was exposed. If Claire rejected her, she knew she would never recover. At that moment, when she had nowhere to hide, she realized trust was what completed intimacy— not sex, but total trust. It was what would fuse them together. With every ounce of courage she had left, she took her hands from her face and looked up into Claire's eyes.

Claire continued, "How can I judge you about this, when you did exactly the same thing for *me*? I know you would have given your life for me. You did when you offered Justin your life for mine, and I know Jacob understood what he was doing, and he understood the risks you both were taking. He knew you. You can't go through what you and Jacob went through together and not understand, and I think that's why he had such great respect for you. You were willing to give your life. Do you think Jacob was willing to do any less than you? Jacob and I talked about you one day when we were in the car together. He admired you so much, and he loved you, and I know he felt it was an honor to watch over you.

"Baby, I know you're not perfect, and I know your weaknesses. I forgive you, and I want you to let this go and forgive yourself, but I also want you to promise me you will never, never do anything like that again. You're mine now. You can't make those decisions on your own anymore—above all, your life is mine."

The wedge was gone! Her heart burst open, and relief and joy and love poured out. She put her arms around Claire and kissed her, drawing her down on the bed.

"Yes, I promise, never again. I love you so much. Let's marry and give our lives to each other. My heart is yours, Claire. It's always been yours."

Claire wrapped her arms around her. "The damn MI6 or CIA or whoever no longer have you, and God help them if they even act like they're getting near you again."

CHAPTER SIXTEEN

Claire, please let's stop for the day. I can't look at one more ring. We've already been to the three top jewelry stores in Las Vegas."

"Let's go to one more place. Drive to Le Beau Carreau."

"I don't think that's a good idea. It's the best diamond house in practically the world. We're going to pay premium price."

"I don't care. They have the most exquisite pieces, and we should have gone there in the first place."

Rachel delivered the car to the valet, and they went into the store, walking over to the mirrored display counter of diamond wedding rings. Immediately an impeccably dressed sales representative—Eric—asked if he could be of assistance.

She pointed to Claire. "My friend is looking for a wedding ring."

"That's it," said Claire, glaring at her and then looking at Eric.

Eric's eyes grew wide as he looked at them.

"Eric, this is Rachel," Claire announced, moving her hand to Rachel's arm. "We have loved each other and struggled about it for years, and now we've finally decided to get married."

Rachel turned three shades of red and put her hand up to her mouth.

"Excuse us." She led Rachel by the arm to a private corner of the store. "I don't give a flying monkey's ass who knows or what they think about us, and it's about time you did the same. Now come on, Elphaba, let's go pick out *our* wedding rings."

Rachel looked at her and started laughing. "Well, okay, get on your broom and let's go."

Claire grabbed her arm and herded her back over to the counter. "Show us the best wedding rings you have, six to eight carats, and we don't want to know the price until we've picked out a ring."

Eric's eyes lit up as he reached down, unlocked the cabinet, and brought out the black velvet case of diamond wedding rings. Claire knew this sale meant a huge commission for him, and she knew he wasn't going to leave them unless they walked out of the store. She also knew he was going to make sure they didn't leave empty handed.

Rachel scrutinized the rings closely, stopping to study an eight-carat marquise cut, surrounded by a cushion of cut diamonds. "That's gorgeous."

"Do you really like it?" Claire watched her eyes as she inspected the ring. The expression on her face changed from curiosity to excitement.

"Yes, I do, very much."

Eric took it out and explained to them the carat size, clarity, color, and cut.

"Do you see any you like, Claire?"

"There it is." She pointed to a pear-cut eight-carat diamond, surrounded by smaller diamonds.

Rachel leaned in to get a closer look. "Well, it sure will shine in the moonlight when you're riding your broom."

Claire grabbed her arm.

Eric smiled and placed the ring Rachel had picked out back down on the black velvet cloth and picked up the pear-cut diamond for Claire.

"You two have exquisite taste," he said, explaining both of the rings' attributes, adding where each diamond had originated, the designers, and the rarity of the diamonds.

"Are you sure?"

Rachel looked into her. "Absolutely, are you?"

"Definitely." This was the moment. The moment she knew Rachel was hers, and they were actually going to get married. It penetrated her heart, spread out into the sinew of her bones, and flowed into her soul. She held back. She wanted to wrap her arms around her, hold her in one of those dramatic poses from old photos, dip her and plant a kiss on her, a kiss that said, *It's official, you're mine.*

She slid her hand down Rachel's arm and grasped her hand, looking back at Eric. "How much for each?"

Eric told them the prices. "And congratulations, both of you are gorgeous and glowing."

"Nothing helps a woman glow more than diamonds." Claire led Rachel back over to a private corner. "What do you think?"

"I think I love them both, and I couldn't be happier, but if you want to keep looking, we will. Just not today. I'm shopped out."

"I love them also," Claire said. "Since my ring is a little more expensive, let's split the cost down the middle?"

"No. I love my ring and I don't care if yours is more expensive. I want to pay for it. It's important to me," Rachel insisted.

"Okay, I understand. I feel the same about yours. Are you sure you like it, and you aren't just trying to be frugal and nice?"

Rachel laughed. "I love it. I really do. It's perfect for me. I'd kiss you, but we're in public."

"Oh, don't start." She smiled, thinking of how she wanted to kiss Rachel. "I'll give you a little break since it's been such a hard day for you, and you had to bring your broom out of the closet."

They walked back to the counter arm in arm and finalized the purchase of the rings, as well as a pair of simple gold and diamond wedding bands.

Rachel sat beside her on the soft leather sofa in their living room, the sun filling the room.

Claire reached for her hand. "Are you ready to do this?"

"Yes, stop fidgeting."

"They'll be here any second. Are you sure you want to do this?"

"That's the fourth time you've asked me."

"So you don't want to do this?"

Rachel put her arm around her. "That's enough, Claire. I mean it—now you're making me nervous. Do you want to tell Derrick our news?"

"No, we can tell him some other time. Tilly and Sarah should be the first to know. I'm glad we're going to get married in October. It will give us some time to get things in order. Are you nervous?"

"Yes, now I'm nervous. Are you?" Rachel started laughing.

"Very." Claire looked at her and shoved her arm. "You aren't having second thoughts about this, are you?"

She saw the stress and concern on Claire's face and tried to put her at ease. "No, not at all. As a matter of fact, I'd rather do this as soon as possible instead of waiting until October. Why are you so nervous?"

"I'm not nervous about us getting married—well, maybe a little— but mostly I'm just nervous about their reaction." Claire smiled slightly.

"Remember, flying monkey's ass."

Claire laughed. "It may take until October to get the legal issues of our individual finances worked out. I want to be as smart as we can about this, and I'm happy we're both going to sign prenups. I think it's an excellent idea for you and for me."

"Claire, I want you to get your paperwork done for your durable power of attorney. I can't tell you what a comfort it was to me, knowing you were watching over me and making decisions for me when I couldn't."

"I'll do it this week." Claire sighed loudly.

"Claire, stop. It's going to be fine. Everyone who knows us knows how much we love each other. This won't be a surprise to any of them."

The doorbell chimed, and Claire jumped up. "Oh, shit, they're here. What are we going to do?"

"First of all, you're going to sit down before you fall down." Rachel took her by the shoulders and lowered her back down onto the sofa.

Claire swallowed hard and looked up at her with pure panic in her eyes. "I don't want to tell them."

"Okay, then we won't. Just relax." Rachel couldn't help but smile as she turned to go to the door.

When she opened it, Tilly burst into the house. "What's going on?" she yelled from the doorway.

Rachel hugged her and then Sarah and ran interference for Claire. "Would you two like something to drink?"

"Oh yes, whiskey, and plenty of it," Tilly announced.

"I'll have some merlot," said Sarah.

She poured their drinks as they hugged Claire and then followed CeCe, the housekeeper, to their rooms to freshen up.

"I'll show you around as soon as you get back," she told them.

Sarah looked around the rooms as she came into the living room. "What a house. You two outdid yourselves for sure. This is hands-down gorgeous."

They all sat and admired the view from the huge glass entryway and the vaulted windows.

"That view is breathtaking," Sarah said, taking the drink from Rachel's hand.

"This really is unbelievable. Well done, you," Tilly told them, raising her drink.

Rachel fixed Claire a drink and got herself a ginger ale, raising her glass. "To change."

"To change," said the others.

Claire looked at her like a deer caught in the headlights.

Still not ready. Rachel looked back to Sarah and Tilly. "How was your flight? Were you able to fly straight through?"

"Yeah, yeah, we had a good flight. I want to see the house," said Tilly.

Rachel laughed. "Come on, we'll give you the thousand-dollar tour."

They began to move through the eight thousand square foot house as she and Claire told them about it.

"I don't believe it, Rachel," Tilly said when they got to the game room.

"We can't take any credit for it, Tilly. It was already complete when we bought the house."

"That billiard table is gorgeous. Do you play, Rachel, because I know Claire doesn't?"

"Actually, Tilly, I do play. Rachel taught me."

"Good, I can't wait to beat you," Tilly said.

"You might have some competition, Tilly—she's pretty good," said Rachel.

After a complete and thorough tour of the house and grounds, they went back into the living room and sat down, Sarah and Tilly in the overstuffed chairs, she and Claire on the sofa.

Tilly and Sarah sat looking at them, sipping their drinks.

Sarah finally spoke first. "So, what's going on? I'm sure we didn't fly all the way out here just for you two to show us the house."

Claire shifted her weight and cleared her throat. Rachel sat quietly and waited, then reached over and took her hand, trying to ease her stress, knowing it would be up to Claire to tell her childhood friends.

A concerned look slowly appeared across Sarah's face. "Is everything all right, Claire?"

Claire held Rachel's hand tightly, trembling. Rachel reached over and put her other hand on top of Claire's.

Claire cleared her throat again. "Rachel and I are getting married, and we wanted you two to be the first to know."

Tilly jumped up. "Fork it over, baby, five hundred big ones, Sarah." She held out her hand, leaning toward her.

Sarah slapped the palm of her hand. "Oh, shut up, Tilly, you'll get your money."

Tilly wriggled her way in between them. "I knew it, I just knew it. When is it going to happen?"

Sarah was smiling, but deep concern was written on her face.

"Sarah?" Claire got up and went over to her, putting her arms around her.

"She's from Ohio, what does she know," said Tilly, taking a sip of her whiskey.

Claire looked over at Rachel. "Please pour us more drinks, Rachel. We're going to need more alcohol."

"Yeah, Rachel, we need more booze, sorry about your luck." Tilly raised her glass to Rachel.

Rachel laughed as she took her glass.

Tilly looked at Sarah. "Sarah, I'm not in the mood for any heavy conversation about sexual behavior between consenting adults, and please, spare me your dissertation on the lasting effects of a bad relationship. I haven't gotten over the last tongue-lashing you gave me."

"Oh, go to hell, Tilly," said Sarah. She drank the last of her merlot and held out her glass to Claire. "Whiskey, please."

"Are you sure you want to switch?" Claire asked.

"Yep."

Tilly looked at Rachel. "It's a bad sign if she goes for the whiskey this early. All right, Sarah, out with it. Bring it all out in the open, and let's hash it out. Get it out on the table, and let's sort through it."

"You think you're so damn liberal, Tilly, but you aren't," said Sarah. "You don't know the first thing about being liberal. You aren't liberal—you're just someone who doesn't give a damn about the rest of the human race, so why do you care what they do?"

"Now, Sarah, that's mean-spirited," Tilly said.

Rachel handed Sarah the rocks glass of whiskey.

"You want to know why I'm so upset about Rachel and Claire's relationship?"

"Yes, Sarah, that's the general idea." Tilly smiled.

"You can be so damn smug sometimes, Tilly." Sarah took a drink of her whiskey, then drew in a deep breath and sighed. "All these years I've watched you and Rachel, Claire. I've watched you fight your feelings and your desire for each other. How many nights on the phone or how many nights have you been to my house crying, sobbing, on the verge of a nervous breakdown because you couldn't take one more day of being without Rachel, or one more day of the suffering loving her brought. Why? What was the point? Why did you both fight it so hard?"

Everyone was silent.

"Why, Claire? Why did you fight it so hard?" Sarah demanded an answer.

Claire didn't answer her. No one spoke.

"I'll tell you why," Sarah said. "You fought it because you knew what you would be up against if you gave in to it. People are cruel—society is cruel—life is cruel. You both have money, and that puts you in a special place in society, but believe me, that bubble won't go completely around you. I'm upset because I don't want you hurt. I don't want your lives to be ripped apart. We have spent our lives together, and now I'm going to have to watch you be subjected to cruel comments and become the brunt of someone's joke."

Sarah finished her drink and held out the empty glass for more. Rachel poured more whiskey into her glass, and after hearing what she had to say, felt like pouring some for herself.

Claire knelt down beside Sarah's chair and took her hand. "Sarah, I know you love me, and I know you love Rachel, and I know you're scared for both of us, but you don't have to be afraid for us anymore. We are stronger together than we ever were apart. There is nothing Rachel and I can't face together—look what we've already been through. Yes, we're going to have to go through some rotten, stinking, shitty situations, but that's just the way it's going to be. Bad times and good times are part of life. Look at the life together we would miss if we didn't take this opportunity. Our love will help us get through whatever we have to go through.

"Life is for living, loving, and sharing, Sarah. There is no one on this earth I want to be with more than Rachel. In my entire life there has never been anyone I have ever wanted more than her. It's always been Rachel—you know that—so put away your fears, put away your worries for us, and rejoice with us. You are part of our family, so celebrate our love with us, bask in its light and warmth, and let it help carry all of us into the future."

Rachel knelt down on the other side of Sarah, setting Sarah's glass of whiskey down and taking her other hand.

Sarah squeezed their hands. "You two have the most amazing love I have ever seen in my life."

"Now, let's celebrate," Tilly blurted out, holding up her glass.

CHAPTER SEVENTEEN

Jack held his glass of champagne up to Rachel's glass. "Rachel, you joining the business was the best thing that ever happened to it. Thank you for all of your help. To a successful expansion, more than we ever dreamed."

Rachel raised her glass of ginger ale. "Success, Jack, more than we ever imagined."

He smiled as he brought the glass up to his lips and drank. "Now that we have that out of the way, there's a client in Houston who wants to talk about renovating their security system, and I need to talk to you about that new app you designed."

She turned to Claire. "You okay going home without me? I should be back by around nine tonight."

Claire took her arm. "Walk with me out to the car."

Claire put her hand on the Maserati driver's door handle. The scanner swept her fingerprints, and the car door popped open. She started to get in but turned to Rachel. "I swear to you, if I ever, and I mean ever, find out you have gone with Jack on a dangerous assignment, you will wish you had never been born."

Rachel moved closer to her, looking into her eyes. "I promise you there will never be any more of that going on unless I tell you first."

Claire started laughing. "You want to kiss me so badly right now, don't you? Go ahead, do it—I dare you."

Rachel's face turned red and she laughed.

"Well, someday you will in public." Claire reached up and touched her face. "But I still mean it, nothing dangerous."

"It's dangerous enough just being with you."

Claire smiled and got into the car, and Rachel closed the door.

❖

Claire was in bed reading when Rachel got home. Rachel took a long hot shower, wrapped a towel around herself, and jumped onto the bed.

Claire kissed her. "I don't want to wait until October to get married. I want to do it now. There's no reason to wait—it's only four weeks anyway."

"I don't want to wait either. Let's get married as soon as possible by a judge or someone. I don't care who it is, just as long as it's legal."

Claire kissed her again as she slipped the towel off her.

Rachel's cell phone rang, but she didn't answer it. It stopped and then rang again. She groaned and reached for it on the nightstand, seeing Jack's name on the display before answering. Claire continued to kiss her neck as she listened.

"Rachel, it's Jack. Your alarm system just went off. We're on the way and will be there in a little while. It will take the police a while to get there."

She handed the phone to Claire, turned off the bedroom lamp, told her to get down on the floor, and reached into her nightstand, pulling out the 9 mm Glock. She checked the mag and then took the safety off. She crawled around to the far side of the bed, away from the window where Claire was waiting.

"God, Rachel, I'm so scared. What is it?"

"I think someone's on the property. Don't worry—I locked all the doors when I came home. Jack and the guys are on their way and will be here in a little while. The police are also on their way. We have to get some clothes on."

Claire crawled to her dresser, pulled out two running outfits, and handed one to her.

"I'm not wearing *that*. It cuts me in the crotch."

"Rachel, put it on or go naked. We haven't moved our clothes into one bedroom yet."

"Fine, but I'm going to look ridiculous in this, and I hate this fabric. Can't I have the other one?"

Claire pulled her outfit away from her. "Absolutely not, this is my favorite one."

"Oh, sure, you get to look good, and I look like Miss Hand-Me-Down of America on a bad hair day."

"Rachel, what is wrong with you?"

She reluctantly put on the clothes and then chambered the gun. "I'm not sitting here waiting to be attacked. You stay here. I'm going to go check it out."

"Oh no, not in a million years are you leaving me here alone while you go play GI Jane. I'm coming with you, so lead on, Sarge."

They crawled to the bedroom window.

"Now what do we do?" Claire challenged. "You stick your head up there, and you could get shot."

"We have to see if anyone is out there."

Rachel crawled to the nightstand, opened the drawer, and pulled out a round five-inch mirror, then brought it back to the window. She scooted to the side of the window and slowly held the mirror up, trying to see the reflection.

"Hey, that's pretty smart. Where did you learn that?"

"Jack."

"Of course, Jack."

"Oh, stop. Be grateful we're friends with smart people. I don't see anything or anyone out there, not one solitary person."

They heard the front door open. Rachel pointed the gun toward the hallway.

Claire grabbed her sleeve. "Oh God. I thought you said you locked the doors."

"I did. There's a key at the shed. Let go of my sleeve. I can't aim with you pulling on me."

Jack called out from the foyer.

Claire let out an audible sigh of relief.

They stood up and went to him.

Rachel saw the stress in his face when he hugged both of them. "What happened, Jack?"

"Didn't your alarm system go off?"

"No, I reset it when I came in from the garage when I got home, and I didn't hear anything."

Jack told the technician to go through the system while he sat down at the kitchen table with them, and the rest of the team inspected the grounds and buildings.

"Your security system alerted at 9:32 p.m.—according to the record, you arrived home at 9:20 p.m."

"I know, I reset the system when I came into the house."

Jack shook his head. "No, someone screwed with the system. It would not have alerted with a simple command like that."

"The system was working fine when Olivia and CeCe went home. CeCe left about four p.m. and Olivia left at around seven p.m.," said Claire.

Jack sat quietly, but then suddenly put his finger to his right ear. "Go," he said. "Okay, we'll be right out. The guys want to show us something."

"I'll be right back. I need to change." Rachel touched Claire's shoulder as she started to leave the room.

Claire smiled. "She'll just be a minute."

They all met at the front entrance and walked to the main gate, where three of Jack's men were waiting for them.

Jack pointed to the fresh scrape marks on the security transmitter box. "Here," he said. The group walked to the pine trees and the landscaping facing Claire's bedroom window.

"Freshly matted down area where someone helped themselves to a bird's-eye view of your bedroom. How often do you close your curtains in the bedroom, Claire?" asked Jack.

Claire looked sheepishly at him. "Never."

Jack bent down and looked closely at the prints in the soft mulch. "It looks like from the shoe prints whoever it is wears a size eleven or twelve. Okay, that's enough for me. You two are getting full-time guards."

"Damn it, is this never going to end?" Claire turned back toward the house and walked away without saying anything more.

Rachel and Jack talked for a few more minutes.

"Whoever it was tampered with the system or at least tried to. They didn't know what they were doing, but they got lucky. It won't happen again. Scott fixed the system, so it's back up and running. There will be a security guard at the gate and one around the house at all times from now on for a while until we find out what's going on. Rachel, you can't risk not having them, not with your history."

"I know, Jack. I completely agree. Don't worry about Claire. It will be all right."

"Look, Rachel, I know you both are under a lot of stress right now, and you don't need this, so let me tell you what I think. Judging from the length and depth of the shoe prints, I'd say it's likely a male. He didn't move around very much, which means he's methodical and focused, and he was watching that bedroom for a while. I assure you, whatever went on in there tonight, he saw it. This person is probably between thirty and fifty, white, intelligent, and he's probably going to be back. There's a lot of nutjobs out there, and you and Claire seem to bring them out of the woodwork." Jack laughed. "Why don't you two go away for a while. It would be good for you. Take a cruise or something."

"I think I have a better idea," Rachel said. "I'll be in to wrap some things up, but then I won't be coming in for a week or so."

The guards were posted, the security system rechecked, and then Jack and the team left. Rachel went back inside the house and went to the bedroom, got on the bed beside Claire, and put her arm around her.

"Don't say it," Claire said.

"Say what?"

"Don't say how it's going to be fine and everything is going to work out, and we'll just go on with our lives. I can't take this anymore."

"Claire, it is going to be fine, and they're going to catch this creep, but meanwhile, you and I are going on a trip, an extended trip. I already cleared it with Jack, so wrap up any projects you have going on, and I'll let you know what you need to pack. I see you closed the bedroom curtains."

"Yes, I figure what we do in our bedroom is our own business and no one else's. I'll be damned if I'm going to allow someone else to see us."

"I don't like it so dark in here. I feel closed in."

Claire got up and switched on the bathroom light but left the door slightly ajar, allowing only a shadowy light to fall into the bedroom. When she walked back, the light caught her and held her. Rachel watched as she walked toward the bed, the way she moved, her graceful features, her beauty.

"Rachel, I can't take this anymore, I really can't."

"You'll feel better once we get out of here."

❖

Derrick made sure Claire did not suspect she had been followed, staying enough car-lengths directly behind her to blend into the traffic. Last night he had taken the red-eye from Seattle, checked into the Bellagio, and slept a few hours. He needed her, more than he had ever needed anyone in his life. He couldn't wait any longer. He had to find out what she was doing, why she sounded so distant and cold when they talked. When he rented a car that afternoon, he purposely chose the silver Mitsubishi Lancer, a car that would not draw attention in traffic and not look out of place near her home.

He had watched with his binoculars from a safe distance when she went through the security gate. He parked the car well off the road about a quarter of a mile past her house, then walked back to the cluster of trees near the property. He went to the edge of the tree line to remain hidden, but close enough to see her with the binoculars. He knew that the cook and housekeeper had already left for the night, and that Claire was alone. He had bought her engagement ring last week, a ten-carat diamond. He would propose soon. He was ready and couldn't wait to put the ring on her finger.

When he saw Rachel pull into the garage, park the Viper, and walk into the house from the garage entryway, he made his move. He waited long enough for her to reset the security system, and then he put on the gloves, disarmed the system, slipped through the gate, and positioned himself in the pine trees and large shrubs, close to Claire's bedroom. The curtains were open, and he had a clear view of the room. He began to breathe heavily, feeling his erection when he watched Claire undress.

He saw Rachel move through the bedroom. A little while later he watched as she pulled Claire on top of her, forcing her to love her. He felt nauseated and almost threw up as he choked the bile back down his throat.

He returned to his hotel suite, stomach churning, hands shaking, and poured himself a scotch. All he could see was Claire lying naked on top of *her*, touching *her*. He downed the drink and poured another one, trying to get the image out of his mind.

He reached into his pocket and pulled out the jewelry case, opened it, and looked at the ring. Tomorrow he would call her, and tomorrow night he would take her for a ride up into the mountains overlooking Las Vegas, and he would tell her he loved her and ask her to marry him. *I love you so much. I am at the point in my life where I can't picture my life without you beside me. I'll do anything for you. Will you marry me, Claire?* He closed the lid and put the case back into his pocket. The sooner he got her away from Rachel, the sooner he would be able to save her.

He called her at eleven the next morning. He lied, but he had to. It was the only way to get her away from *her*. He told her he would be coming to Las Vegas for a conference and asked if she and Rachel would like to go out to dinner, but she refused, saying they were going out of town. He knew Rachel was standing next to her, making her lie. He tried to find out where, but she told him she didn't know where they were going—another lie. He knew Rachel had her claws in her, and it was going to be difficult to get her away from *her*, but he had do it somehow, and soon.

Chapter Eighteen

Olivia greeted Rachel when she came home in the early evening. "How was your day?"

"Good, Ms. Rachel."

"Where's Claire?"

"She's in her bedroom, showering."

Rachel sat at the kitchen bar, reading her mail. Michael called.

"Rachel, will this new program you're working on for the government affect how we do business here in the United States?"

"No, it will only affect how the government monitors itself."

"Will it go on the open market?"

"No, the government bought the program exclusively and it won't be sold to any other entity, that's why they're going to pay so much for it, but part of the deal is that I can modify it and use it myself for our business, but not anywhere else."

"When will the paperwork come through to my office?"

"Probably not until the end of this month, but you should be getting their statement of intent within the next three days. Michael, this is very confidential—Claire doesn't even know about it yet. I'm not taking cash. I'm taking a land deal instead."

"Did they offer you cash?"

"Yes, but I want the land. I have enough money to last a lifetime. The land is more important to me, and I made them an offer they couldn't refuse and pushed with some help from friends in high places. Meanwhile, I'm glad you called. Claire and I are going out of town for an extended vacation, off the grid. You can get a message through the tribal council like before if you need me, or if it is an extreme emergency, Jack can helicopter in, but otherwise, I'll call you in about two weeks."

They discussed a few more financial matters and then ended the call.

Rachel's next calls were to her tribal leader on the reservation and to her cousin Joseph to discuss getting the help she would need from her extended family.

The last call was to the stables to have horses and all of their tack transported to their destination.

Claire came up behind her and kissed the back of her hair and then moved in front of her and kissed her face and lips.

Rachel put her arms around her. "You all right?"

"I've missed you so much."

"I've missed you too. I'll explain what you need for our trip later, but for now, I want you to relax, rest, and be with me. Would you like to go for a swim?"

Claire kissed her cheek. "No, baby, I just took a shower, but I'll come out and watch you."

Rachel spoke to Olivia about dinner plans and asked her to make a fire in the fireplace, and then gave her the rest of the week off. "You can put our security guards on hold until we get back."

After her swim, Rachel set out the food in the living room. Claire helped bring pillows and blankets and placed them in front of the fireplace.

Claire sat quietly as they ate, leaning against the pillows, looking around the room. "We really do have a beautiful home, don't you think?"

"Yes, we do, but it's only beautiful because you're here in it."

Rachel reached up and touched Claire's face, then unbuttoned three buttons and slowly moved her blouse partially open, bending down and kissing her above her breasts, catching the familiar scent of her skin, feeling the warmth of her body on her lips. She felt Claire's muscles tense. She tried to stop her own hands from trembling.

"I feel so much a part of you when I touch you, and when we make love."

Claire put her hand to the back of Rachel's head and gently held it there. "I feel it also—your touch is indescribable. Where are we going? Can't we just be together without anyone around? I want to spend this time with just you. I need you so much."

"We're going to be so alone you're going to get sick of me."

Claire reached up and cupped her face with her warm hand.

"Never. I will never get sick of being with you. You should know that by now."

Rachel's alarm was set for seven the next morning, but she woke at six thirty and turned it off, hoping Claire would sleep as long as she needed. Stress had demanded its toll and claimed its bounty—she saw it in Claire's face. Even in sleep, her face looked tense and pale.

She carefully got out of bed, and for one brief moment longed to lie beside Claire and make love. She walked to her own bedroom, showered, and dressed. As she walked past Claire's open door, Claire called out to her.

"Are you leaving for work so early?"

Rachel made coffee for her and cinnamon herbal tea for herself and took them to the bedroom, setting the cups down on the nightstand. She climbed into the bed as Claire reached out for her, moving beside her.

"You dressed already?" Claire asked, pulling her down to her.

"Do you think I'm sexually okay?" Rachel asked, without preamble.

Claire looked at her, giving her a half smile. "What on earth do you mean?"

"I mean, do you think I'm overly sexual? I'm not a pervert to want you all the time, am I? This morning when I got up, I wanted so much to get back in bed and make love to you."

Claire laughed. "Absolutely not, I think about making love to you all the time." She began to unbutton Rachel's blouse.

"Really, or are you just saying that to make me feel better?"

"You really are concerned about this, aren't you?"

"Yes, I am."

"We both have a voracious sexual appetite, and there is nothing wrong with wanting to fulfill it. We both love sex, and we both love having sex with each other. I have never in my life been so completely sexually fulfilled as I am with you. I don't want you to ever be embarrassed or worried no matter how many times you want it."

"Promise me if I ever want sex with you and you don't, you'll let me know. I would never want you to feel uncomfortable."

"Only if you promise you'll tell me if you feel the same way. I told you, Rachel, you can touch me anytime you want, and I meant it. It thrills me to think you want me. I'm yours. I know you're a much more private person than I am, and I know you need a little more personal space than I do—that's part of getting to know each other's intimate boundaries and limits. I love that you brought this up because it's a good thing to talk about. Now, as far as you wanting to make love this morning, I can help you with that."

❖

When Rachel got home that evening, she went into the bedroom and lay down beside Claire. Claire put her book down on the nightstand and they began to talk, but Derrick called, interrupting them.

Rachel went into the kitchen to fix them something to eat.

When Claire hung up from talking with him, she told Rachel, "He asked me again if we wanted to come to Seattle for a couple of days. I think he was really disappointed when I put him off again."

"We'll eventually go. It's a long trip. And speaking of trips, let's pack for this one. You'll only need three complete changes of clothing, and a pair of pajamas."

"What about my makeup, and my hair and beauty supplies?"

Rachel reached for the plastic bag she had brought into the room. "Here's a small bottle of shampoo, a small bottle of liquid body soap, and a bottle of hand sanitizer. That's all you'll need." She had already packed Claire's hat and boots and food for her in the car. Everything else was going to be waiting for them when they got to the reservation.

"That's it?"

She heard the disappointment in Claire's voice and laughed. "It will be fine, I promise. We have a four-hour drive in the morning, and we need to get a good sleep tonight."

The next morning, they drove to the south end of the reservation. Rachel could see Claire's excitement when she saw Ash and the chestnut mare saddled and ready. Her cousin was sitting quietly under a canvas lean-to. She walked over to him and hugged him.

"Claire, this is my cousin Joseph."

Claire shook his hand.

Rachel handed him the keys to her Viper and whispered instructions. He nodded and helped them unload the car.

"Claire, carefully pack your gear in your saddlebags. The canteens of water are already over the saddle horns." She reached into the trunk and gave Claire her boots, hat, and food.

"Aw, you brought them for me. How sweet."

"You're going to need them because we aren't just riding for the

day. We're going up into the Arizona, and we aren't coming back for
about a week."

"Great." Claire stuffed the items into her saddlebags, half into
each side.

"No, one side has to be reserved for the grain for your horse," said
Rachel.

Joseph put the bags of grain into the saddlebags, added some items
to Rachel's bag, double-checked the gear, and then brought the sleeping
bags, tying them to the back of each saddle. They said good-bye, and
then he got into her car and slowly drove out the way she had come in.

She strapped her grandfather's knife to her back and checked her
saddlebags.

"There's cold water and sandwiches over there under the shelter.
Let's take a break, drink some water, and then mount up. We are now
on reservation land, by the way."

Rachel watched Claire as she surveyed the surrounding land,
looking at the foothills, the distant mesas and buttes, and the foliage.

"It's so beautiful here," said Claire.

They stretched out under the lean-to and ate. Ash shook his head
and stomped his front hoof.

Claire laughed. "Ash is bored and wants to go."

Rachel drank the last of her bottle of water. "Are you ready?"

Claire patted her leg and pushed herself up.

They mounted the horses and left, stopping for the night just before
dark near a running stream. They made a fire, watered and bedded the
horses, and sat on their sleeping bags side by side and ate their meal of
packaged beef Stroganoff.

Claire sat reading the ingredients. "This isn't half bad." She
looked over at the stream. "Can we fill our canteens with the water in
the stream?"

"Yes, but we're going to be extra safe and filter it first. I brought a
water filter in my saddlebag."

When they were done, they lay back, looking up at the night sky
filled with stars as the sounds of the night creatures and the distant
running stream serenaded them.

Claire took her hand. "This reminds me of the little lake in Alaska,
but so much more peaceful and comforting. Our love is so much
stronger now. I feel like we were babies back then—it feels like such a
long time ago."

Rachel closed her eyes and listened to the comforting sound of

Claire's voice as she moved closer to her and held her. "I want you to get into the environment and relax. This time is just for us."

The next day they rode for three hours and then took a break beside some large boulders and cactus. She searched carefully for snakes and scorpions before she let Claire put her sleeping bag on the ground. She walked over to Ash and spoke to him in her Native American language and then came back and sat down beside Claire.

"Rachel, what do you say to Ash when you talk to him?"

"I tell him what a good friend he is and thank him for his service to me. I tell him to be careful and sure-footed. Just then I thanked him and told him we had a long ride ahead and to be careful."

Claire took her hand. "You're such a wonder to me. Did you travel in this area when you were little?"

"Yes, many times—I rode and walked all through here."

"I see you change as we go deeper into this territory."

"What kind of change?"

"You become more serious, pensive. I think you become more... yourself."

Rachel smiled. "Soon we'll dance."

They mounted their horses, turned east, and rode until evening.

They lay on their sleeping bags after supper.

Claire watched the sky, the pale pink and orange sunset fading over the mountains. "My lower back and knees are killing me. I need ibuprofen or something. I hurt."

Rachel reached into her saddlebag and brought out a bottle of liquid.

"Is that whiskey?"

Rachel laughed. "No, it's a special concoction Joseph put in my saddlebag. Lift up your top and lie on your stomach."

She turned over onto her stomach and brought her shirt and arms up, laying her head down as Rachel straddled her thighs and began to rub the soothing, warm oily liquid onto her shoulders and lower back.

"That feels wonderful." She moaned several times, feeling Rachel's hands slide over her body, massaging and touching. She began to breathe deeply, feeling her arousal start to build. "Mm, that feels so good."

"Turn over on your back, and I'll do your knees."

She pulled her top down and turned slowly over onto her back, unbuttoned and unzipped her jeans, and lifted her hips as she felt Rachel slide her pants down to her ankles. The warm liquid instantly stopped the ache as Rachel rubbed slowly, massaging.

"How do you feel now?"

Claire moaned as she lifted her hips and pulled her pants up. She had an overwhelming desire to keep her legs open and pull Rachel to her, but she sat up. "That's wonderful. Do you think there will ever be a time when we won't think of each other sexually? Even before we actually made love, it seemed as though I wanted you so badly for so long."

"I hope we never lose our sexual desire for each other. I don't see anything ever stopping us until we're just too old to enjoy it, and even then, just lying with you and holding you and being next to you would be enjoyable." Rachel leaned over and kissed her.

Claire felt Rachel's warm lips part and opened her mouth wider, encouraging her to enter her mouth more deeply. She lifted her hand behind Rachel's head, wove her fingers into her long dark hair, and with her other hand brought Rachel's hand up to her breast.

The night sounds seemed to increase.

She softly kissed the side of Rachel's neck as she leaned into her, putting her head on her shoulder.

Rachel wrapped her arms around her.

"It's so beautiful here," Claire said, "being out under the stars and the night sounds. The stars seem to go on forever. I've never seen so many."

"There's a peace here like no other place on earth. I want you to experience it." Rachel got up and put more wood on the fire. "I want you to dance for me."

"I don't know how to do that kind of dancing."

Rachel stirred the fire with a stick, and then sat quietly, her arms folded. "Yes, you do. Close your eyes. What do you see?"

Claire closed her eyes. "You, making love to me in front of the fireplace in Cleveland." She laughed, "You, making love to me at Tilly's. You, making love to me at our house in Las Vegas."

"Listen to the sounds around you."

Claire listened closely. She could hear an owl calling for its mate, crickets, and the wind in her ears as it gently blew around her.

"What do you see?" She felt Rachel's whispered breath in her ear, sending rivulets of sweet chill down her body.

"I see your beautiful face. Tilly, Sarah, Ricky and Tommy, and Jack. I see my mom and dad."

Rachel lifted her by the hand. "Open your eyes. Listen and feel what's all around you and appreciate it."

Claire went to the fire and moved her hands over the warmth of the flames. She began to sense the rich environment around her as she tried to focus—the wind gently touching her skin as she breathed, the crackle of the fire, the scent of the smoke, the open expanse above her. She heard the rhythms of the night sounds of the creatures and felt the comfort of the earth beneath her. She felt herself move effortlessly and freely, as if every part of her body reached out and was greeted and welcomed…and then she came back to Rachel's eyes as she watched her, seeing the gentle smile on her lips as she greeted her.

No words were spoken as they lay together upon the earth, under the stars, in each other's arms.

CHAPTER NINETEEN

Very little was spoken in the morning, but Claire felt their love flow between them. It seemed the deeper they rode into the Arizona, the less she wanted to talk. The splendor of the blue-gray vistas was overwhelming. She felt the spiritual influence of her environment: the landscape, the foliage, the horses, and most of all Rachel. She was right—there was great peace in this land, and she began to feel it deep within her.

When the sun began its descent, they were riding northeast. Ahead and about a quarter mile up past Rachel, she saw what looked like a teepee. Off in the distance to their left she heard several wild horses. Ash whinnied and nickered, returning their call, and her mare also called to them. When they approached the teepee, there were tie downs for their horses, grain, and hay. They unsaddled and led the horses to drink at a small stream west of the teepee. They bedded the horses for the night as Rachel quietly spoke to Ash, stroking his neck and withers.

Rachel lifted the flap on the front of the teepee and motioned for her to go in. Inside there was a fire of hot coals, fresh cooked meat, beans, and simple fry bread. Water was hanging in a skin pouch. Rachel took the water pouch and sat down, putting the pouch beside her. She washed her hands with the hand sanitizer and then handed it to Claire, motioning for her to sit down beside her.

Claire was too overwhelmed to speak. She was in a Native American teepee, with items she felt were too sacred to even ask about. They ate in silence. The meat was flavorful and delicious, the beans filling and sweet to the taste, and the bread warm and light flavored. Rachel showed her how to open the container of water and drink, and then handed it to her.

When they were finished with their meal, Rachel reached for her hand. "Let's bathe now."

They gathered their items from their saddlebags, and she led her out and behind the teepee down to the small stream, a little distance from where they had watered their horses. Stones had been placed to collect the water into a small pool, which had been warmed by the sun.

Rachel took off her clothes, and Claire noticed this time she was not self-conscious of the rippled, gnarled scars on her back and thighs. She picked up a cream-colored bar of what Claire thought might be soap, went into the water, and sat down, motioning for her.

She took her clothes off and followed Rachel into the water. Rachel lay in the pool and let the water wash over her as Claire began to wash, feeling the welcome relief of the water. Rachel began to wash Claire's back, rubbing the scented bar over her. She moaned from the touch of Rachel's hands gliding over her stiff muscles. She lay down in the water, rinsing and watching her bathe with the bar of soap and then wash her hair.

When Rachel was finished, she turned to Claire. "Would you wash my back?"

Claire was speechless. She tried to get the words out. She wanted to tell Rachel how honored she was, how it meant so much to her that she had asked, how she knew Rachel was giving her a great gift of trust, but she was so full of emotion all she could choke out was, "Yes."

She took the bar of soap from Rachel's hand and gently rubbed it over her, feeling the undulation of the tissue, seeing every scar, trying to imagine what she must have endured—every agonizing rip of her flesh and searing of her skin. She cupped her hand in the water and raised it to Rachel's back, gently letting it run over her, as if to bind her wounds, to wash away her pain. If she could have been there in those agonizing moments of unimaginable pain and suffering, she would have gladly taken her place.

Rachel turned and took the bar of soap from her and laid it on the stones. She put her hands to Claire's face.

Claire saw the reflection of a billion stars and the moonlight dancing on her face. She looked into her eyes and saw their love, deep and pure and strong.

Rachel leaned in and kissed her. "Now there is no shame between us."

Claire put her arms around her and fell on her neck. She felt the water from Rachel's hand run over her shoulders. Rachel lifted her up with her and walked her to their clothing, handing her a small simple cloth to wipe her body.

When they were dry, they put on their nightclothes, picked up all of their items, and went back to the teepee.

Rachel told her they would not be sleeping in their sleeping bags. She noticed a large bearskin on the teepee floor near the fire with several blankets covering it. Rachel led her to the bearskin and motioned for her to lie down, and then she lay down next to her, covering them with the blanket, moving close to her.

"Give me your right hand."

Claire brought her hand up as Rachel interlocked their fingers.

"I have loved every moment of sharing my body with you, Claire, and the joy I feel as you share your body with me is indescribable. I will always honor you as long as I live upon the earth."

She brought Claire's hand up and kissed it, and then gently lowered it, removing her hand from hers.

Claire kissed her and whispered, "Rachel, I will always honor you as long as I live upon the earth."

They undressed each other and made love, giving themselves to each other.

Rachel rose early and dressed, stoked the fire, and went outside. She went about a quarter of a mile from the teepee and sat down and meditated, searching for strength to be the woman she wanted to be. She saw Joseph quietly approach, but he waited patiently until she was finished. As always when their conversations were private, they spoke in their tribal language as they walked back to the teepee. Joseph handed her their food.

"Today we hunt. In two days, we'll be ready for the family gathering."

They discussed what needed to be done and then she and Joseph quietly said good-bye.

She returned to the teepee and woke Claire. They sat outside and ate in quiet reflection.

"Life is so much simpler here," Claire said softly. "There are no schedules to keep, no man-made noise, no conflict, only the peace of our environment and the love we share." She reached for Rachel's hand.

"How did you sleep, Claire?"

"Very well."

Rachel taught her how to say their conversation in her native language. She repeated her question and Claire answered her in perfect dialect.

Rachel's heart swelled with pride. "We're going hunting today, but we're walking. While we're gone, Joseph will come and get our equipment and take the mare, but he will bring her back in a few days. Ash will be here, in case we need him." She walked to the back of the teepee and brought items wrapped in cloth, setting them down beside Claire. "You'll need these."

Inside the cloth were moccasins, a knife and sheath with a leather tie, and a small drawstring pouch about ten inches square with a leather strap to tie around her waist. She helped Claire with her moccasins and knife, and then Claire tied the pouch around her waist.

"You must be careful with the knife. It's razor sharp—always make sure your fingers are never near the blade."

"I love being with you like this, Rachel. Thank you for sharing this with me. I will treasure this time always. I feel like you're giving yourself to me. Sometimes when we make love, I feel you inside my soul. I feel like you're inside me now, like those moments."

Rachel stroked her face with the back of her hand and then came closer and put her arms around her, whispering words of love.

Claire smiled and shrugged her shoulders. "I have no idea what you just said, but I loved it."

Rachel laughed. "I told you I loved the light in your eyes and the peace in your soul."

They walked up into the mountains, hunting for whatever they could find.

"Do you remember how to set the trap like we did in Alaska?"

Claire nodded and placed the thin leather in a loop, placed small sticks around the loop, and tied the end to a tree branch. They walked farther up the mountain and stoned a quail. When they returned to the trap, a rabbit dangled from the end of the trap. They had enough for their meal and returned to camp. They sat outside near the teepee the rest of the day, Claire sharing as much detail of her childhood as she could remember, and Rachel sharing her memories of her grandfather and being in the land as a child.

"Rachel, tell me about the symbols on that leather scroll in the teepee."

Rachel went into the teepee and brought out the scroll. She sat down beside her and untied the leather straps and unrolled it in front of her.

Claire touched the rich tanned leather, admiring the colors and symbols. "It's a beautiful piece of art, Rachel."

"My grandfather was chief of our tribe. I am a direct descendant because my mother was his daughter. He helped me make the basic part of my teepee and the first part of this scroll. I've worked on it since I was about ten years old. The symbols represent my struggles and heritage. You are here." She pointed to the white female figure enclosed with colorful lines of various lengths and surrounded by a circle of purple on the scroll.

Claire touched the surface of the carved painted figure in the leather, feeling its delicate features with her fingertips. "When did you do that?"

"I did it the summer of our senior year in college."

Claire looked at her and then down at the scroll again. "You knew then?"

"I've always known. From the moment I met you, I knew."

Claire didn't say anything for a long time, continuing to stare at the scroll.

Rachel put her arm around her and pulled her close, feeling her warmth.

Claire still didn't speak.

She ran her hand over Claire's arm and kissed the side of her head. "Your heart is full?"

Claire nodded. "I know what we're doing."

"It's a time for doing, Beloved."

❖

Claire surveyed the vista, taking in the view of the sun as it began to set, the colors spreading out in a never-ending array of purple, pink, and varying shades of blue across the skyline. She realized as she watched it that in some way she was part of it through her connection with Rachel. She belonged here with her. She watched as the sun set on the horizon.

Rachel went to Ash, put his bridle on him, and then grabbed his mane and swung up on him. Claire never lost sight of her as she rode for a few minutes before sunset.

Claire continued to sit quietly, watching twilight appear, and then darkness. After they ate, they went to the creek and washed, then returned to the teepee. She lay down in Rachel's arms, engulfed in her love, and slept in a peace she had never known.

She rose early in the morning and was sitting outside watching the sunrise when Rachel came out of the teepee and guided her to a standing position. She turned her toward the sun, then she also faced the sun but raised her hands and said, "For the joy of our life, the quiet morning stillness, for the earth and all she offers. Help us to live worthy of her blessings." She then offered the prayer in her tribal language and motioned for Claire to repeat it, helping her with the words.

They ate their breakfast outside, watching the glory of the earth and the sun greet each other.

"We will dance tonight," Rachel said, as if declaring a great insight, a revelation of importance.

Claire looked at her, watching as the morning sunlight touched Rachel's face, revealing the woman inside, whose capacity to give of herself knew no bounds. This was an extraordinary human being, and she knew at that moment there was no finer person on the earth.

They spent the day gathering herbs and carried them back in Claire's pouch.

Derrick pushed the automatic door release and left the operating suite. After he talked to the family of his afternoon knee replacement, he stripped off his gown, cap, and mask and threw them into the bin. His legs ached, and he had a headache. He picked up his phone and started to call Claire. He wanted to leave another message, tell her he was sorry he'd missed her again, but he stopped himself and decided if she didn't call him back by tomorrow, he would fly to Las Vegas and surprise her.

Chapter Twenty

Claire, just so you have a sense of geography, we're no longer on the reservation. We left it when we turned east and then northeast."

"Where are we?"

"We're on my land."

"Your land? When did you get this land? How far does it go?"

"About ten square miles?"

"Rachel?"

Rachel took her hand, sat her down on the blanket, and then sat beside her. "Claire, I sold a new security program exclusively to our government. When we negotiated, I exchanged the program for the available acres near the reservation. My land connects to the reservation, which connects to a national park."

Claire looked at her and then at the surrounding area, shaking her head, not speaking. They gathered firewood for their bonfire, and then danced and celebrated.

In the morning Rachel gathered a few items, put them inside two of the blankets, rolled the blankets, and strapped the bundle to her back. She took Claire to a series of natural caves in a canyon about an hour's walk from the teepee, where they spent the day exploring the caves and surrounding area, finding hieroglyphs in some of the caves.

She put her hand up on the cave wall beside the markings. "These have been here for hundreds of years. It is a history of my ancient people. They traveled from across a water—here." She pointed to one of the hieroglyphs. "There is sadness in this story. I wish I could interpret it." She touched the cave wall beside the markings once more and then turned to Claire. "I'm so glad I can share this with you. My life feels so different with you, Claire. I loved Alex, but I never wanted to share these kinds of things with him. I feel like I don't want to ever stop sharing with you. I feel my heart is so open to you. I don't want to hold anything back. I think the word I'm searching for is…" She spoke a Native American word Claire had never heard before. "It means complete or whole, but more than that."

Claire stood next to her, putting her arm around her as they looked at the unknown lost history of an ancient people.

In the evening, Rachel built a fire inside one of the caves.

"We haven't been in a cave since Alaska," said Claire. "That cave saved our lives."

"I don't really remember much about the cave."

"I remember how warm it felt once we finally got the fire going." They made their beds for the night and slept.

In the morning after breakfast, Rachel asked her to sit down across from her.

"Claire, are you ready?"

Claire was quiet for a long time, pondering her question. "Yes, I'm ready. I want to make this commitment to you. We are a family, and although my love for your body burns hot inside me, my love for your soul burns stronger. I'm yours. There will not be anyone else for the rest of our lives. I want you with every part of me." She smiled and moved to Rachel. "I feel so happy in my heart about you and me. I feel love and safety, and peace. I know we will have to go through some hard things, but I want you beside me—I need you beside me."

Rachel wrapped her in her arms and kissed her face, stroking her hair.

"I feel peace because I have confidence in your love, Rachel. I feel your love for me, and it covers me like a blanket, and I wrap myself in it and feel warmth, security, and assurance." She lay quiet in Rachel's arms and then reached up and ran her fingers over her cheek and lips. "I want to tell you something…I heard you call to me when you were going through your suffering when you were taken." She looked into Rachel's eyes, watching, feeling their souls entwine more deeply.

"At my darkest moment, I did call out to you," Rachel confessed.

Claire reached up and embraced her. "I still don't understand the bond we have, but I know it's real."

Rachel kissed her and held her for a long time. "As much as I would love to stay here with you like this all day, we need to go soon."

They gathered their things and left, walking two hours north to a beautiful canyon with a rock formation filled with water.

"Rachel, look at this, it's beautiful."

"Yes, it is. We're going to stay here for the rest of the day and relax and then go back. We're about an hour and a half northeast from our teepee."

They ate the food they had brought and explored the canyon, and then started back.

When they arrived at their teepee, Claire was surprised to see a large fire about twenty-five yards east of the teepee.

They washed off in the stream.

"Claire, we're going to have some of my family come this evening, but don't be concerned or worried about anything."

She walked her to the teepee and opened the flap, motioning for her to go in. Claire was surprised to see flowers hanging on the poles, wooden bowls of food near the fire, their things neatly placed at the far edges of the teepee, and two beautiful beaded necklaces hanging on the main pole. They ate a simple meal of beans, squash, and fry bread, and when they were finished, Rachel stood up and reached for her hand, pulling her up to her. She took one of the necklaces and placed it over Claire's head and around her neck, then slipped the other necklace on.

Claire suddenly heard a soft drumbeat and chanting outside. Rachel took her by the hand and led her out of the teepee. Claire was shocked to see about thirty people gathered around the fire. Rachel led her to the group, and they stood watching as the people moved gracefully around the fire, chanting softly. Claire put her hands to her face when she realized they were welcoming her.

The group stopped dancing and faced them. Claire recognized Joseph, Rachel's cousin, as he walked up to her, dressed in his beautifully decorated Native American clothing. He held out a long flowing hand-beaded scarf, handed it to her, and then rejoined the group. Rachel helped her place it over her shoulders.

Each member of the group—men, women, and children—went up to Claire and greeted her, touching her hand or arm, and then went back to their place.

Rachel turned to her. "These are members of my mother's family. You are one of us now, a part of me and a part of this family. We will always be safe here on this land, supported and protected by those who are here this evening."

Rachel took her by the hand, and they sat down together, watching

Rachel's family dance and sing as the glorious sunset spread out over the horizon.

When the dancing and visiting ended, and darkness began to engulf them, they said good-bye to the group as they quietly left.

Rachel led her back to their teepee and closed the flap. They built up the small fire, and then Rachel brought Claire to her, kissing her deeply, lingering in her mouth, softly touching her face and hair. Rachel whispered, "In all my life I have never known such beauty and fulfillment. Claire, I know we aren't married yet in the eyes of the law, but in my eyes and heart, and on this land where the spirits of my ancestors live, I feel you inside me." She reached into the cloth bag hanging on one of the poles for their diamond rings. She slipped one on Claire's finger and then handed hers to Claire.

"I feel the same way, Rachel." She placed Rachel's ring on her finger.

"Come to me, Beloved," Rachel whispered. Rachel embraced her fully and they kissed, then began to undress each other slowly, as if it was a dance.

Claire felt her clothes slide off her body, each touch of Rachel's hands sending pulsating surges over her skin and into her core. She felt her heart pound and her body yearn as her fingertips glided across Rachel's body.

They lay down together. Claire leaned over her as Rachel reached up and drew her down onto her, fingers caressing aching breasts, moving across soft curves, probing hot wet folds of desire. They kissed deeply, lingering, each caress of their tongues, each touch of their lips building their need and want for each other.

Claire felt Rachel wrap her arms around her, engulfing her, and then she lifted her, guiding her. As they began to completely give themselves to each other, holding nothing back, Claire felt their souls entwine, and she felt the fullness of their love, and her want and desire merged with Rachel's.

Claire woke slowly in the early morning, hearing the birds chirping outside the teepee. She opened her eyes to see Rachel lying beside her, gazing at her. She reached to touch her.

"Rachel, never have I ever imagined a night of lovemaking that could be so glorious." Rachel held her, and Claire spoke as she lay in her arms. "You're mine now, and no one can ever take you away from me."

They loved each other into the evening. When they got up from their bed, Rachel opened the flap of the teepee, and they took a blanket and lay outside, watching the sunset as they held and caressed each other. They ate the food that had been prepared for them, and then they lay under the stars, overwhelmed by each other and the beauty and magnificence of the night.

CHAPTER TWENTY-ONE

In the morning, Claire woke to the nicker of horses. Rachel was already awake, lying beside her. Claire rolled over and put her leg over Rachel and touched her face. "How does it feel to wake each morning beside me, knowing it will be for the rest of our lives?"

Rachel smiled. "I have to remind myself it's real."

Claire leaned in and kissed her. "Oh, it's real, my love." She breathed deeply and curled up next to her. "Since the legal paperwork is in order, let's get married when we get back to Nevada, with our wedding bands instead of these rings." She touched her diamond. "I want these rings for our love—and the bands for the law."

Rachel smiled. "I like that." She raised up on her elbow. "Are you up to making some visits later today? I want to take you to some of my family. They want to spend time with you and get to know you."

Claire moved over onto her. "Much later, yes." She kissed her, eager to touch, to love, and to bring her to fulfillment.

That evening Rachel gave her soft cotton clothing, a top and tie pants. "Joseph brought these for us. We'll be more comfortable riding in these." She bridled Claire's horse and then Ash, putting a thick girthed pad over each of their backs.

"Those look so comfortable—what are they?"

"They're bareback pads." She taught her how to swing up onto her horse. "If you want, I can give you a lift up onto her."

"No, I think I can do it. I've seen you do it several times."

"The trick is to keep your momentum."

Claire tried once but couldn't do it, her horse shying sideways.

"Make her stand still, and get a big handful of her mane. Stand back a little more toward her head."

Claire tried again, this time easily mounting. She adjusted and looked down at Rachel, smiling. "See, nothing to it."

Rachel smiled, patted her thigh, and swung up onto Ash. "It will take about an hour and a half to get there."

They rode southwest for an hour, and then Ash tossed his head and whinnied.

"There's a herd of wild horses somewhere up and to the right of us. Make sure you have a secure seat."

Not one minute after Rachel said it, Ash reared up and bucked. She went flying off into the air and landed on her left side, moaning, but managed to keep hold of one side of his reins.

Claire called down to her and started to get off her horse.

Rachel quickly jumped up and faced Ash. "I'm good, Claire— back her away from Ash."

Claire quickly moved her horse. As soon as the mare was clear, Rachel moved to Ash's left side, cupped her right hand and forcefully slapped his neck, swung both his reins over the right side of his neck, and pulled his head hard toward her. Ash lost his balance and went down on his left side. She moved up toward his neck and put her knee on his shoulder and kept it there, speaking loudly and firmly to him.

Claire watched in amazement, even though she couldn't understand what Rachel was saying to him.

Ash quivered and lay there, his nostrils flaring, his eyes wide, breathing heavily. Rachel brushed herself off, keeping her knee on his shoulder, and continued to pull the reins with her left hand. She spoke more and then slowly lifted her knee and released the reins. Ash rolled to his knees, pushed himself up, and shook, then lowered his head and brushed against Rachel's shoulder, as if to apologize for his behavior. Rachel stroked his neck, gently touched his ears, and rubbed his head, softly speaking to him.

Claire leaned forward, watching and shaking her head slowly. "Rachel, I don't know what to say. That was audacious. I take it Ash was chastised."

Rachel laughed. "Just a little." She took Ash's reins and mane and swung up on him. "There's a stream just up ahead."

They watered the horses, and then Rachel led Ash to a small grouping of mesquite trees and tied him. Claire followed and did the same with her horse, and then they walked to the stream and Rachel washed herself off.

"Are you all right? You took a pretty hard fall."

"I just got the wind knocked out of me. I'll be all right."

"Take your top off—I want to make sure you're okay."

Rachel slipped her top off. There was a large bruise on her left upper arm by her shoulder.

"That looks bad, Rachel."

"I'll be okay. I'll soak it tonight." She put her top back on and touched Claire's worried face. "It's all right, Claire. Believe me, it's nothing." Rachel kissed her. "Thank you, baby, for the worry. Come on, let's get going, your future in-laws are waiting."

Claire's mouth dropped open. "Oh, Rachel, they will be my in-laws. What if they don't like me?"

Rachel smiled. "I don't give a flying monkey's ass if they don't like you."

Claire laughed.

Joseph and his wife Elaina warmly welcomed them into their modest home. The interior walls were covered in intricate stencil patterns, and contrasted colors were used to highlight architectural features. There was hand-carved wood furniture and bright tapestries that enlivened the rooms. Claire couldn't take her eyes off the decor, complimenting both Joseph and his wife.

Rachel held their year-old baby son, as their four-year-old daughter, Ela, sat beside Claire and held her hand. Claire enjoyed their visit and getting to know Rachel's cousin and his beautiful family. The family ate and shared stories, and then Joseph led the family in prayer and said good night to his children. Ela hugged Claire tightly and kissed her cheek. Once the children were in bed, Joseph and Elaina continued to visit with them. When it was time for sleep, they said good night and Joseph led them to a camping trailer in his yard—their guesthouse, he joked. Elaina gave Rachel a salve and a hot compress for her arm.

In the morning more family members arrived, visiting, laughing, and sharing stories of Rachel when she was a child. In the evening, as Rachel and Claire prepared to leave and were saying their final good-byes, Elaina brought out a bow and handmade leather quiver of arrows, handing them to Claire.

"This is from all of the people to you, Claire. It was made by Moon Shadow's cousin Ilesh, who couldn't be here with us but sends his love to you both. Moon Shadow will teach you how to use it, although don't expect much from her."

Joseph laughed.

"Everyone knows Moon Shadow can't shoot a bow for squat," Elaina said. She hugged Claire again. "We wish you both well. Please come back often to visit us."

Claire thanked her again. She mounted her horse and Elaina handed her the bow and quiver. Claire placed the bow over her shoulder and then the quiver of arrows. She turned her horse, and she and Rachel rode back toward their camp.

Claire was overwhelmed with a sense of Rachel's heritage, as well as her family's love, acceptance, and compassion for her and for Rachel. "Your family is so loving and kind and accepting. Are they like that with everyone?"

"They are with family members."

"There's no judgment or any kind of limitations on their love, is there?"

"No, because family is family—whether you are born in, adopted in, or married in, you are family. American Indians are just like everyone else—some people are very judgmental and have attitudes, but for the most part, especially within my own family, they are accepting."

"Rachel, was your family surprised when you told them about me?"

"No, I told Joseph about you when you and I were in college, and I have talked with my elder family members and others about you over the years."

When they arrived back at their camp, they fed and watered the horses and then settled in for the night, lying close together in their bed.

"Rachel, your family has great love and respect for you. I see it in how they treat you and how they talk with you."

"Yes, I suppose they do."

"Do they think any less of you because you're with me, not only white but especially because I'm a woman?"

Rachel put her arm around her. "Claire, I'm half white. You're a part of me, an extension of me, and they think of you like that. They know the love we have for each other. Those members of my family I have been closest to know the years of loneliness and yearning I've had for you. Like you said back in Cleveland, true love has no regard for race, religion, culture, social status, or gender. We didn't ask to have these feelings—it's just something that happens. When it comes to true love, my people have always understood that true love can only dwell in a true heart."

"Rachel, I've never known a truer heart than yours. I'm so blessed to have your love."

Claire moved closer to her and they loved each other through the night.

❖

Claire's arrow missed the bull's-eye again.

"Damn it, I'll never get it. I thought you weren't any good at shooting arrows. You haven't missed one time yet."

"I've hit the target, but not in the center. Patience, you'll get it. You have great eye-hand coordination, much better than mine. Try it again."

Claire took aim, slowly pulled the bowstring back with even pressure, adjusted her arm, and breathed the way Rachel taught her. She tried to focus and then let the arrow fly, hitting the bull's-eye exactly in the middle.

"Wow, Claire, you nailed it."

"Hey, I did it." She raised her arm in triumph.

They walked to the makeshift target and pulled the six arrows out, putting them back in the quiver. Suddenly an arrow came flying between them and landed in the target. Claire screamed and jumped back. Rachel turned quickly and smiled.

"Ilesh, you finally made it," she called out.

A tall, handsome Native American man with long dark brown hair stood where she and Rachel had been standing when they shot the arrows, and when he smiled, his hazel eyes twinkled, and his face lit up.

"Claire, it's okay, that's my cousin Ilesh. He made your bow and arrows and quiver. He is the best marksman in the tribe and would have never missed his aim."

Ilesh laid his bow and quiver of arrows down as they approached him. He embraced Rachel, picking her up and spinning her around. When he put her down, he turned to Claire, looking at her from head to toe, putting his hands on his hips.

"Well, now I see what all the fuss has been about. I can see why your heart was captured, Moon Shadow." Ilesh held out his hand to Claire. "Hello, I am Ilesh, the renegade of the family. I'm sorry I frightened you." Claire took his hand and smiled. "May I say, I am quite sure the sun does not rise without asking your permission."

She blushed. He put his arm around her and Rachel and walked them back to the teepee. His beautiful paint horse stood by Ash and Claire's mare without being tied, munching on hay.

"I'm afraid Itza-chu is going to eat all of the hay—he's a horrible pig."

He pulled his saddlebags off the horse and carried them to the teepee. He brought out two blankets and spread them on the ground, sat down, and patted beside him for them to sit down. Then he pulled out what Claire thought looked like a very expensive bottle of wine, uncorked it, and handed the bottle to her. She happily took a drink.

"Greetings from civilization." He reached into the bag again and pulled out gourmet coffee bags, creamer, herbal tea, and three cups. He reached in one last time and pulled out a collapsible cooking pot. "Ladies, I give you what you have been missing all these days."

Claire clapped her hands. "I know Rachel doesn't miss it, but I have been craving coffee."

"Now, while Moon Shadow heats the water, you, dear Claire, will spill your guts about what it is like to love my cousin. You do know you have fallen in love with the only female road warrior in the West. God, this woman—I could tell you stories that would make your toes curl."

Rachel shook her head, took the pot, and went into the teepee.

Claire noticed the lighter flesh around Ilesh's left ring finger. She knew he saw her notice it and he sighed deeply.

"Alas, my second wife did not appreciate my need for social interaction, especially at all hours of the night. I'm afraid I pushed the bounds of her love once too often, and she divorced me."

Claire grew sad to hear his news. He touched her face.

"Oh, dear Claire, do not fret—yours truly will recover, and someday I will find the true love I have always searched for."

That statement made her even more sad. "Ilesh, don't give up. She's out there somewhere, I know it."

Rachel rejoined them, and Ilesh turned to her and said, "Moon Shadow, my love, you have what we all search for, the true love of a good human being. My God, you have been blessed. I have decided to stay here with you two for the night so that we might philosophize upon life's important truths."

Claire instantly loved him.

They talked through supper, a bottle of wine, two cups of gourmet coffee, herbal tea, sunset, seven shooting stars, Ilesh's two ex-wives, and Claire's ex-husband. They lay on their backs watching the stars, Rachel and Claire close together, covered in a blanket.

"Claire, did you know Moon Shadow saved my life when we were twelve?"

"You must tell me about it, Ilesh." She wrapped her arms around Rachel and held her as he told the story.

"We were with my father and uncle hunting. We had been out most of the day and had not found any game. As we set up camp for the evening, I decided to go up into the canyon. Foolish as I was, I wanted to go by myself, but Moon Shadow insisted she go with me. We got into the canyon, climbed up into a crevasse, and suddenly there was a cougar on a ledge just to my right. It lunged toward me and ripped my right upper arm, pulling me closer so he could get a better hold on me. All at once it screamed out in pain and released my arm. I looked up and there was Moon Shadow, repeatedly stabbing it in its neck with her knife. He flipped sideways trying to get at her, but I threw my bow at his legs, trapping his front paws, and he lost his balance, slid down on the ledge, and fell to his death onto the canyon floor. Moon Shadow and I just stayed there looking at each other, not knowing what to do. When we finally came to our senses, she ripped a part of her blouse off and wrapped my arm up, and we went back to camp, carrying the ninety-five-pound cougar on a large limb, to the amazement of my father and uncle."

"Why does that story not surprise me?" asked Claire, reaching up and touching Rachel's face.

"I helped a little," Ilesh's said, laughing.

"You saved my life," Rachel said. "That cat would have had me for supper if you hadn't prevented him from turning on me."

"It sounds to me like you two saved each other," said Claire.

"Well, that's what family does," said Ilesh.

Claire yawned.

"You two go in to bed. I will sleep out here and guard your lives."

Ilesh wrapped himself in his blanket as Rachel and Claire got up, said good night, and went into the teepee.

❖

The next morning, Ilesh stood close behind Claire, coaching her archery skills. "Your anchor point is off. Put your chin closer to the bowstring and line your eye straight down the arrow. Breathe."

By the afternoon she was hitting the middle of the target almost all the time.

In the early evening, he saddled Itza-chu and prepared to leave. "Claire, I know you and Moon Shadow will have a blessed life because of the love you have for one another, but I also know you will have pain. When you need to escape or need someone to lean on, please come to visit me in Phoenix. I confess, I googled you and went to your website. I love your pottery and would love to display them in my gallery, which would be the better for it."

He hugged her and then Rachel, mounted Itza-chu, and rode off, waving again before he was out of sight.

"That's quite a compliment," Rachel said. "He's quite famous in his own right, world renowned for his leatherwork. He has nothing but the best in his gallery. If your pottery is displayed in his gallery, you can ask whatever price you want, and you will get it."

"Oh my gosh, he's The Tribesman." Claire gasped.

Rachel smiled. "Yes, but to me and you he is Ilesh."

As they sat out on their blanket, watching the sunset, Claire felt reborn, renewed with a passion for life and a desire to become the best she could be, and to make the best possible life she could for Rachel. She leaned on Rachel as the last of the golden sunset colored the horizon, spilling over the distant mountains. They lay on the blanket and made love. As they lay in each other's arms, Claire touched Rachel's face. "We are one. I feel it in the depths of my soul."

CHAPTER TWENTY-TWO

Derrick arrived in Las Vegas and rented a car. He drove directly to Claire's house, but no one was home, no guards at the gate or around the house, no movement in the house. He went past the house and parked, watching through his binoculars for five hours, stewing in his own juices of self-pity, lust, and denial. He blocked his number and called Claire seven times, but she didn't answer, just her voice mail, which he was sick of hearing. He finally went back to his hotel, drank more alcohol, and seethed. When he woke in the morning, he blocked his number again and called her another four times.

Joseph arrived midmorning with a pack mule loaded with their supplies.

"So, what's the plan, Rachel?" Claire asked.

"We start back by no later than eleven tomorrow morning, alternating our route just slightly to get back to our original starting point, and then home to Las Vegas. Are you ready to go back, Claire?"

"No, I don't ever want to leave this place, but I know we have to go back."

Joseph took their horses to the creek for water and then packed their food and grain for their horses in the saddlebags, showing Claire how to roll her sleeping bag and tie it to the back of her saddle. He said his final good-bye to them and left with the pack mule.

"He'll come back tomorrow with some of the family after we leave and pack everything up in the truck. When they're finished, no one will ever know we were here, and that's the way it should be," Rachel told her.

They spent the evening out on the blanket, once again watching the sunset and making love. They lay naked under the stars, caressing, talking, and planning for the future.

❖

At two thirty a.m., after Derrick showered twice and dressed, he drove away from the Strip. He threw the soiled clothes and the cheap tool kit into a dumpster on one of the side streets near the El Hacienda motel. He couldn't get the smell of gasoline out of his nose.

❖

In the morning, Rachel and Claire made love one last time and then dressed and prepared to leave. When they were ready, Claire drew her close, wrapped her arms around her, and held her.

"Rachel, my heart, my love, how can I ever thank you?"

Rachel put her arms around her. "My heart is so full it's overflowing. Thank you for your love and making this the most wonderful week I have ever known."

They reluctantly broke their embrace, mounted their horses, and left.

In the early afternoon, three hours into their ride, the helicopter came in low and circled. Rachel knew something was wrong. They both dismounted and waited as Jack got out and quickly walked to where they were, the helicopter engine slowly winding down.

He grabbed Rachel and held her, reaching one hand out to Claire. "I'm so very sorry to have to tell you that your house was set on fire sometime in the night, and by the time the fire trucks arrived, half of it was destroyed."

Claire grew pale. Rachel looked up and saw Joseph's truck on the horizon coming toward them. Jack told her he had called him en route to meet them. Jack took their horses and motioned for them to go to a nearby rock formation where they could lean against the rocks. He got their canteens off their saddles and gave them water.

Rachel looked up at him. "What happened?"

"It's under investigation. All they know right now is that it was deliberately set and started in Claire's bedroom."

She looked at Claire. "What would you like to do?"

"I want to go home and check it, and then we can decide."

She nodded, watching Joseph pull up with the horse trailer. Jack helped him unsaddle the horses and put the gear into the back of the truck, and then they loaded the horses into the trailer. She and Claire got what they needed from their luggage, hugged Joseph, and said good-bye. As soon as he drove off, they got into the helicopter and were back at the shed within two hours.

They started making calls, and then Jack drove them to meet their insurance agent at the front gate. The agent introduced himself, shaking hands with them.

"The cars are fine, other than needing a good cleaning. It was the back half of the house that took the major damage."

As they approached the house, Rachel thought it looked like it had been hit by a wrecking ball. Black soot was on two-thirds of the facing, half the roof was damaged, and one third of it was caved in. They walked through what was left of the front entrance way. Rachel held back her tears, but Claire started crying. The house was almost a total loss. By the time they walked through where they were permitted to go, they were heartsick—what wasn't destroyed had smoke damage.

Claire grabbed Rachel's arm. "Let's get out of here. I can't take it anymore." Her phone rang, but she refused to answer it—someone had called twenty-one times while they were out of range in Arizona, leaving only dead air in the voice mail. No way was she answering an unidentified caller.

Rachel walked into the back pantry and moved burnt wood from the shelving and pieces of charred fallen ceiling to get to the safe. She unlocked it and pulled out their wedding bands and their legal paperwork. Other than reeking of smoke, it was all intact. She gathered up the folder, checked to make sure all the documents they would need were there, took the rings, and relocked the safe.

They walked back to the main gate, where they discussed their concerns about the house with the agent. He handed them his business card and an envelope of forms, and told them he would get back to them as soon as he had more information. They shook hands once again and got in the car with Jack.

Jack told them a guard would be at the estate twenty-four hours a day. "I don't have to tell you two how concerned I am about this. Rachel, I don't want to say I told you so, but you know it was a mistake to remove security from the house when you left. We're going to have security with you there at the hotel."

Claire reached from the back seat and took Rachel's hand as she called CeCe and Olivia.

"Jack, we're going to be busy trying to sort through all of this, but I'll call you sometime tomorrow," said Rachel.

The assigned security took Rachel and Claire to the Bellagio VIP desk, and Claire arranged for a suite. They went up to their hotel room in silence, staring at the elevator door until it stopped on the seventeenth floor. One security guard took his position outside their door as they went into the suite, took a long hot shower, and collapsed onto the bed.

"What the hell happened?"

Rachel stared up at the ceiling. "I don't know."

She got under the covers and lifted them for her. As Claire crawled in next to her, her cell phone rang again.

"I'm not going to answer it. I don't want to talk to anyone right now."

She turned off her phone, set it on the nightstand, and rolled over close to Rachel.

Rachel put her arms around her and kissed her hair. "If it's all right with you, we're getting legally married tomorrow."

"Isn't there anyplace open tonight?" Claire half laughed. "It's a good thing we just had the honeymoon of a lifetime because this legal wedding is going to suck."

Rachel smiled and kissed her. "Let's just get through the next couple of days." She sighed heavily again, pushing the flood of thoughts about the house, insurance, damage, her work, and everything that had to be done out of her mind.

"I'm not getting married in the clothes I have. Let's go shopping and do it up right," said Claire.

❖

Jack and Tilly met them at the county courthouse as witnesses. After the ceremony, they all went to Lil' Nell's lounge, three blocks from the shed, where employees and close friends were waiting for them, and then everyone started drinking. Before Claire got too drunk, Rachel told her how beautiful she looked.

"Me? Rachel, you look like you just stepped off the fashion runway. I love that dress on you." She leaned in close to her. "I'm going to really enjoy taking it off you later." She raised her glass to her.

Everyone started clinking their glasses and looking at them.

"No, not hardly," Rachel protested, putting her hand up in the air.

Claire laughed when she looked at her. "You know I'm game."

Everyone started shouting *Do it!* and kept clinking their glasses.

"We're going to get kicked out of here," Rachel told them. She looked over at the bar. Louie, the owner, raised his glass of ginger ale to her and smiled. "The hell with it," she said and leaned in and kissed Claire.

Claire put her arms around her and returned her kiss. Everyone started cheering, yelling, and clapping.

Claire kissed her again. "Love you, baby."

"Love you back."

And then the drinking really got started.

Rachel helped Claire into their security guard's car at one a.m. Whoever wasn't passed out and was able to stand up cheered and threw birdseed at them as they drove away from the lounge. Claire was passed out by the time they got back to the Bellagio, so the security guard carried her to the suite, put her on the bed, and congratulated Rachel.

Rachel started laughing and thanked him, then led him out of the suite and bolted the door. She undressed Claire, covered her up, and then she undressed and took a hot shower. She stood in the shower for twenty minutes looking at her wedding ring, realizing she was actually married to the person she loved more than anyone, her best friend, and the most beautiful woman in the world. Suddenly, losing their house and the things that were in it didn't seem like such a tragedy.

❖

The late morning sun peeked through the slit in the heavy curtains.

Claire moaned and moved her leg, turned over, and moaned again. "Oh God, how much did I drink? I'm dying."

Rachel laughed and handed her three Tylenol and a glass of tomato juice.

"Thank you, baby." Claire struggled to sit up but flopped back to her pillow. Rachel helped her sit up and put pillows behind her. She took the pills and drank some of the juice. "My head feels like it got pressed in a vise. What time did we leave the bar?"

"Around one a.m." Rachel handed her a small bag of ice.

"Oh, Rachel, you're an angel." Claire put the ice bag up to the side of her head and slowly moved it over her temple. "I don't even remember leaving. I'm so sorry I blew our wedding night. I'm horrible."

"No, you aren't horrible. That wasn't our wedding night, that was our legal night, and who cares?"

Claire took her hand. "You're so sweet. I married the greatest person in the world."

There was a knock on the door. Rachel leaned down and kissed her forehead, then went to the door, looking through the security opening. Dustin, their security guard, was holding a large bouquet of red roses. She opened the door.

"Ms. Portola, these were sent up to you."

She thanked him as he carried them into the room and set them on the table, the scent of the flowers filling the room.

"And this," he said, holding out a bottle of champagne with a can of ginger ale attached to it.

Rachel laughed and took it, then closed the door as he went out.

She opened the card. *Congratulations, lots of love, Sarah and Ricky.* As soon as she put the card back in the bouquet, there was another knock on the door—it was Dustin again, with more flowers.

"Sorry." He carried the flowers into the room and set them next to the roses. "And this." He set another bottle of champagne on the table.

Rachel went to let him out, but as soon as she opened the door a delivery man was standing in the hallway with flowers and a box of chocolates.

"Ms. Portola?"

"Yes."

"Compliments of The Tribesman." He handed the items to the security guard. "Have a wonderful day."

Dustin put the flowers and chocolates on the table and left. Rachel opened the card from Ilesh. *Love you both, congratulations. I am so sorry to hear about the fire. I'm here if you need me, Ilesh*

A few minutes later there was another knock on the door. Dustin was standing there with an anguished look on his face.

"I don't know what to do, Ms. Portola. There are three more bouquets out here, two more bottles of champagne, and house security just called and said there are reporters asking to come up."

"What do the reporters want?"

"I have no clue."

"Bring the flowers and gifts in, call Jack and tell him we need more security up here, call down and tell house security to help you until you get reinforcements, and I will not talk with any reporters until I know what they want."

As soon as Dustin brought in the flowers and champagne, she shut the door. She called CeCe and Olivia and asked them to come to the suite as soon as possible. She walked into the bedroom. Claire was lying on her back with one arm over her eyes, holding the bag of ice to the top of her head with her other hand.

"What is going on out there?"

"Baby, you need to get up, get dressed, and get out here. Something is going on."

Claire moved her arm off her eyes and looked at her. "What?"

"I have no idea, but something's up."

Rachel walked back into the living room and pulled a card off one of the bouquets: *Congratulations, your friends at the Bellagio.* She pulled another card: *Claire and Rachel, Congratulations, The Shed Crew.*

Another knock at the door. She opened it slightly and peeked out. Dustin handed her three notes. She closed the door and opened them.

Ms. Portola, we would like to interview you regarding your marriage and your house being set on fire, Lewis Connors, WLVN TV.

Ms. Portola, we would like to interview you about the fire and marriage, Sheila M., The NLV Dispatch.

Ms. Davenport need to talk about you and your wife and the fire, Paula, NLVTV Channel 8.

"Claire, you need to get in here."

She picked up her phone and called Jack.

Within thirty minutes the suite was swarming with people. Steve Hathaway, Jack's second-in-command, had experience with public relations and had brought a friend, John Goodwin, who was tasked with managing information flow to the media. Hotel representatives were talking with Jack, and another security guard, who was assigned to assist Dustin outside the suite, was asking David questions. Olivia was trying to order food, and CeCe was asking Claire what she needed. Jack was trying to coordinate security, which was evolving by the minute, and Rachel was getting more nervous by the second. Everyone was talking and phones were ringing.

"What do we do, Rachel? What do we say?" Claire was wide-eyed, wringing her hands.

"I don't know. I don't know what is appropriate or not," Rachel paced, feeling overwhelmed.

Steve stepped forward. "I want Claire, Rachel, Jack, and John with me in the bedroom right now."

They were herded into the bedroom and the door was closed—instant quiet.

She and Claire sat on the bed, looking up at the team.

"I think the media is going to try to make a connection between the fire and you two getting married. Do you think there's a connection?" asked John.

Claire put out her hands. "How can there be? The fire happened two nights ago, and we just got married yesterday afternoon."

John nodded his head, "Good. Now, what do you want to say about the fire?"

"It sucked," said Claire.

John laughed. "Okay. What about your marriage?"

"What about our marriage?" Rachel asked.

"What do you want to say about it?"

"Nothing," said Rachel.

"Do you want to make any comment about it at all?"

"Yes, we don't give a flying monkey's ass what people think about it," Claire said, taking Rachel's hand.

Rachel smiled. "I think what my wife is trying to say is we have no comment. Same-sex marriage is legal in this country. We are residents of the State of Nevada, and we are exercising our rights under the law and hope others will respect our rights and our desire for privacy."

"Excellent. That is a comment, by the way, Rachel, and a good one, and I'm going to quote you. Okay, I'm ready to deal with the media. I suggest you two stay in here while I step out and go down to the lobby. We should be able to wrap this up in about twenty minutes."

Jack stepped forward. "We have to get you two out of here. Do you have anywhere else you want to go?"

They reviewed their option—no to Tilly's, no to Jack's. Rachel called Ilesh, and he offered his house in Tule Springs.

"Tule Springs? A member of your family has a home in Tule Springs?" John asked.

"Yes," said Rachel.

"Go there immediately," John said.

Rachel called Ilesh back and accepted his offer, and arrangements were made to bring CeCe, Olivia, and their security team.

CHAPTER TWENTY-THREE

Ilesh's house was not as big as theirs had been, but it was four thousand square feet of pure beauty, set on several acres with a gate and adequate security. They settled in quickly.

The story of their fire and marriage was carried by local media, but because they'd made clear they felt there was no connection between the two events, it was not picked up by national news.

Two weeks after the fire, they finally caught up with all the people who'd sent them well-wishes or expressed concern. Rachel was sitting by Claire's side when she called Derrick. She hit the button for speakerphone.

"Why haven't you two called me? I've been worried sick about you. Where have you been?"

"Rachel and I were on vacation, and just before we returned, someone burned our home down."

"What? Are you all right?"

"We're fine," Rachel said.

"Where are you?"

"We're at Rachel's cousin's home here in town."

"Do the police know who did it?"

"Not yet," said Rachel.

"Why don't you come up here and stay for a while?"

"Thank you so much for your offer, Derrick, but we're settling in nicely here. Hold on just a second." Claire took the phone off speaker and covered it, whispering to Rachel, "Should we tell him we got married?"

"Sure."

Claire put the phone back on speaker. "Derrick, we've got some exciting news."

"What is it? I'd love to hear it."

"Rachel and I got married two weeks ago." The silence stretched for over a minute. "Derrick?"

"You're right, that's…great news."

He ripped Claire's picture from the wall and started smashing it with the hammer. Blood from a deep cut on the little finger of his left hand ran down the side of his hand and dripped onto the glass. He went into the bathroom and looked into the mirror, seeing his future shattered like Claire's picture. He looked down at his bloody hand gripping the counter.

"Rachel, let's have a party here next weekend. Let's fly Sarah and Ricky down, Tilly can get here, Derrick can come, and we can all be together and have some fun."

"Claire, I'm so glad you're taking this so well. I've been really worried about you. I think that's a great idea. Can we pull it together that quickly?"

"Absolutely."

"We'll need to get some rooms at one of the nicer hotels. We can't accommodate everyone here at the house."

"I agree. We'll get three suites at the Caprice, okay?"

"That's fine. I need to go to the shed for a few hours."

When Rachel returned, Claire told her she had talked with the insurance agent and made arrangements for the cars to be sent to the body shop to be cleaned and detailed.

"They'll be brought back on the Monday after the party. When do you want to have your Viper picked up at Joseph's?"

"Why don't we have someone drive us down on Monday after the party—then we can visit before we come back?"

"Why don't we have someone fly us there Monday afternoon, and then we can spend the night camping and come back Tuesday?"

"Why don't we plan to stay a couple of days, and we can go riding?"

"Oh, I like that idea, but why don't we just go into the bedroom and talk about it some more?" Claire took her hand, led her to their bedroom, and started to undress her. "I missed you this afternoon, wife."

Rachel smiled and kissed her neck as she unbuttoned her blouse. "You smell so good."

They made love into the night and then lay in each other's arms, talking.

"Rachel, I don't know if I want to rebuild the house."

"You know, it's funny you should say that because I've been thinking the same thing. I want to have our own house built. I don't want to buy someone else's home. I wouldn't mind, say, a forty-five-minute commute to the shed, so we could look for property outside of Las Vegas anywhere."

"Rachel, you don't have to be there all the time to do your work. You could work from the house at least part of the time, and if you only went in two or three times a week, we could fly you by helicopter—lots of people do it. And if that's the case, we could pretty much build a home anywhere out here."

"My wife the schemer. What did you have in mind?"

"Well, I've always wanted to live in Arizona, and Ilesh did invite me to exhibit my work in his gallery. I think being able to label my work Arizona-made would be a marketing plus. And living in Arizona would put us that much closer to your property and the reservation, so we can go there more often."

"All great points, my wife."

"So you'll consider it?"

"Yes, definitely, we should consider it."

Claire rolled over on top of her. "Rachel, will you please pinch me, because I can't believe my life."

"How about this instead?" She kissed her. "I'll never get enough of you, Claire."

❖

Tilly finished the song, and the pianist and those standing around the piano applauded. Rachel raised her glass of ginger ale to her and continued to mingle among the one hundred or so guests. Derrick was standing very close to Claire. She looked at Derrick and then Claire, tilting her head slightly, motioning toward their bedroom. Claire excused herself and followed her, closing their bedroom door as they went in.

"You all right? Derrick is awfully close."

"Every time I try to get away to visit someone else or suggest he's being obnoxious, he interrupts me or changes the subject. He keeps staring at my wedding ring and wanting me to go out for a ride with him."

"Is he drunk?"

"He's had quite a bit to drink, but he acted odd when he first got here."

"I'll stay close. If you have any more problems with him, we'll tell him to leave. That's ridiculous. Maybe he had a bad week at work or something. He hasn't said two words to me all night. No *rides*." She kissed her.

"I'll give you a *ride* later tonight." Claire laughed out loud at her own joke and opened the door. "We need to make that band play some good music. Their last set was depressing. I think they're intimidated by Tilly."

As they began to say good night to the guests, Rachel heard Derrick ask Claire one more time to leave with him for a ride. She came up to them and put her arm around Claire's waist. Claire slipped her arm around her back.

"Are you having a good time?" Claire asked her.

"Yes, it's been a great party. Derrick, did you have a good time?"

"Yeah, I guess."

"Did you get to meet MaryAnn, one of Tilly's backup singers? She asked me twice to introduce you, and I couldn't find you." She asked it, knowing he was by Claire the entire night. She saw the irritated expression on his face, almost enjoying it.

"No. I'm not really interested, but you could probably take her in the back bedroom and screw her."

Rachel's and Claire's mouths dropped open.

"What did you say?" demanded Rachel.

"You heard me." Derrick swayed slightly and put his hand up on the wood frame of the kitchen entranceway. "I'm sure she'd be thrilled."

Claire took a step forward. "That is *enough*, Derrick. I don't care if you are drunk."

"What? Don't tell me you're offended." He laughed and looked at Rachel.

She watched as Claire shifted her weight from one foot to the other and her face tensed.

Derrick continued to stare at her. "I've known about the influence you've had over Claire for a long time, and no doubt you talked her into this so-called marriage."

Rachel was ready to kick his ass out the door, but Claire spoke first.

"Actually, Derrick, I was the one who asked Rachel to marry me. Isn't that right?" Claire looked at her.

"Yes, you did." Rachel tightened her arm around her and drew her closer.

Derrick looked at their rings and then glared at Rachel. "I suppose those are your wedding rings. This makes me sick."

"I'm sorry you feel that way, Derrick. I think it would be better if you left." Rachel realized he was almost ready to explode, and it wasn't because of the alcohol.

"Oh, I'll leave. Claire, I'll call you tomorrow."

Rachel felt Claire's back muscles flex against the palm of her hand.

"Don't bother. You've been extremely rude and have acted like a horse's ass all night, and frankly I think it's probably best if we end this friendship on civil terms."

Derrick's hands were visibly shaking when he turned to leave. He looked back at Claire. "I know you'll feel differently in the morning."

They watched in disbelief as he walked out the door.

"What the hell, Rachel?"

"I don't know, but I'm glad he's gone. I don't think you should answer any more of his calls."

"Clearly."

They returned and mingled with the rest of the guests but didn't tell Jack what happened.

Rachel turned out the bedroom lamp. "Claire, I think Derrick has had feelings for you all along and hid them. I just can't get over what he said."

Claire rolled over and put her arm around her. "Don't worry about it. I think he was drunk and just made an ass out of himself, but as far as I'm concerned, our friendship with him is over."

CHAPTER TWENTY-FOUR

Monday morning the body shop delivered the cars at the gate. Rachel watched from the house as the vehicles were waved through by the security guard. But they were followed by a car she didn't recognize, not one of theirs. Their cars made their way to the garage, but the rogue car pulled up near the main door.

Derrick got out, his hands shaking and sweat pouring down his unshaven face. "Claire," he called out. "Claire," he bleated, like a wounded animal.

Rachel was stunned. "What the…Claire, Derrick's here."

Claire came out of the kitchen. "What?"

Rachel looked out the front window again. "I don't like this. You stay in the house. I'm going out to talk with him."

"How did he get on to the property?"

"I don't know. Call the guardhouse and stay inside."

Rachel opened the door and stepped outside onto the front porch.

"Claire," he yelled.

Rachel froze as she watched him raise a gun and point it at her.

"What kind of a sick hold do you have on her, Rachel? She would have chosen me. Why? Why would you do something so evil? You destroyed her life."

Rachel raised her hand. "Derrick, calm down."

He pulled the hammer back on the gun.

"She made her choice. It was me, Rachel—it was me."

He aimed.

Rachel heard Claire scream from inside the house, and then she was there beside her.

"Claire, get back in the house."

"Derrick, no."

Derrick wiped his eyes and brought the gun down to his side.

"Why, Claire? I love you. You're mine, not hers. I bought you a ring. We were going to be married. Why?"

Rachel saw the drivers walking around the corner of the house and the guard coming down the driveway, but just as they got near, Derrick raised his gun hand to wipe the sweat from his forehead and the gun unexpectedly went off. The bullet hit the stone facing on the porch to the right of Claire, ricocheted, and hit Claire in the head. She fell sideways toward Rachel.

Rachel started screaming and caught her, taking her down to the ground as Claire's body went limp, her eyes closed, and blood poured out of the right side of her head. She held her in her arms, crying and screaming, calling out, "Call 9-1-1. Call 9-1-1."

Derrick threw the gun down and started to get into his car to leave, but the three drivers tackled him to the ground.

Olivia came out of the house screaming and knelt beside Rachel, placing a towel on the side of Claire's head. One of the men called 911 as the guard came running toward them.

Rachel checked Claire's pulse but couldn't find any, laid her down, and started CPR. One of the drivers ran over to her and rechecked her pulse as Rachel gave CPR.

"Harder compressions," he told her.

Rachel looked up at him. He moved her quickly away and restarted compressions and mouth-to-mouth resuscitation as she grabbed Claire's shoulder, calling out for her.

The guard ran back to the gate to let the emergency vehicles and the police in. The paramedics brought their equipment and set it down beside Claire, trying to get to her, but Rachel refused to get out of the way. Two of the drivers picked Rachel up and forcibly moved her away from Claire as she tried to reach for her. The paramedics continued CPR, one yelling out, "I have a heartbeat." They loaded Claire into the vehicle and quickly left with the emergency lights and siren on.

More police cruisers arrived. The drivers continued to hold Rachel as she screamed. Olivia came over to her and took her into her arms as she collapsed onto the driveway, the red emergency lights flashing against her blouse, soaked in Claire's blood. Another emergency vehicle arrived, more lights, more sirens.

"We're going to treat you for shock," one of the paramedics told Rachel. She looked up and saw the police handcuff Derrick and put him into the back seat of the cruiser, while more police arrived. She lay in Olivia's arms as the paramedics picked her up, put her on a gurney, and put her into the emergency vehicle. She felt the movement of the vehicle and heard the siren. She tried to reach up to the paramedic, but her arms were strapped down, and her entire body was shaking.

"I have to get to the hospital," she pleaded, trying to speak clearly, but her teeth chattered. "Claire's been shot. I have to go." She tried to stop shaking but couldn't.

The paramedic tried to reassure her. "We're going there right now. We're on our way and going as fast as we can." He looked down at her as he stroked her forehead and pushed her hair out of her face.

She kept trying to get up as he pulled the straps around her arms tighter and covered her with a blanket. He put a small cup of reddish liquid to her lips and told her to drink it as he lifted her head.

"This will help calm your muscles."

The thick reddish liquid tasted bitter. Her body began to calm, and she felt her heart slow as she called out again, feeling like she was in slow motion as the sound of the vehicle's siren began to fade. "I have to get to the hospital. Claire's been shot. I have to get to her."

Lights and noise were a blur as she looked around. She was in the emergency room. A nurse was by her bed, holding her hand, while another nurse wiped blood from her face and hands. *Claire's blood.* She could hear the medical staff working on Claire in the area next to her, calling out orders for procedures and medications. A male voice ordered more units of blood. A few minutes later the area next to her suddenly became quiet. She looked up in terror at the nurses beside her.

"It's all right," the nurse said who was holding her hand. She put her hand on Rachel's shoulder. "They've taken her to surgery."

They sat the head of her bed up and offered her water, but she refused. Suddenly Jack was there, looking at her. She called out his name and he went to her, wrapping his strong comforting arms around her. The nurses left the room as she sobbed in his arms. When she finally stopped, Jack poured water and insisted she drink it. She took the glass with her shaking hand, barely able to raise it up to her lips.

Olivia arrived with a clean change of clothes, her cell phone, and a purse. Rachel picked up the cell phone with her shaking hand. "I have to call Sarah and Tilly and let them know what's happened."

Jack gently took the phone out of her hand. "I'll call them."

She put her head down and continued to sob as Olivia wrapped her arms around her and cried with her.

Jack stepped out of the room to make the calls. While he was gone, a nurse came in and helped Rachel clean up and then discharged her, giving her Claire's wedding ring, her jade and diamond necklace, her watch, and her bloody clothing. Rachel changed clothes and put her bloody clothes into the plastic bag with Claire's, holding the bag out to Olivia.

"Put these away, Olivia, and don't wash them."

She took Claire's wedding ring, necklace, and watch, and put them in her purse.

Jack walked back into the room. "Tilly just landed in Chicago and will be here as soon as she can. Sarah will be here on the next flight from Cleveland Hopkins. The police are outside in the hall and need to get your statement."

"I will stay here at the hospital in case you need something, Ms. Rachel," Olivia told her.

Rachel thanked her and left with Jack to talk with the police.

She felt like she couldn't get enough air as the waves of grief and the images of Claire's bloody matted hair and her pale motionless face burned in her mind. Her head pounded. She walked beside Jack, glancing into the nurses' station, seeing Claire's last name up on the board and the surgical suite she was in. She tried to steady herself. She felt Jack's arm go around her as they walked. Two detectives met them in the hallway outside the automatic doors of the emergency room, introducing themselves and showing her their gold badges. Detectives Baker and some name that started with an R, Richards or Rayburn, she couldn't remember. She looked at them but didn't comprehend what they were saying. She interrupted Detective Baker in mid-sentence and asked if they could wait for her statement until she found out about Claire's surgery. Detective Baker told her they would meet her in the private conference room beside the surgical waiting area. Jack stayed with her as she met with the hospital representative. She sat down in the cushioned chair but didn't remember entering the room. She saw the man's lips moving and finally caught up with him.

"She'll be in surgery for about four hours. A plastic surgeon is with the surgical team. The surgeon will not know the extent of the damage until they actually complete the surgery and then testing. We'll keep you updated, and the surgeon will meet with you as soon as he's done."

Rachel thanked him, and Jack led her out to where the detectives were waiting. They got her something to drink and began the process of piecing together what happened.

Two grueling hours later the detectives left. She and Jack met Olivia in the surgical waiting area—more waiting, more tidal waves of uncertainty, more despair and anguish. She sat in a brown leather chair, staring out into the hallway, watching the elevator...*open, close, open, close*...and when the thoughts and the fear swirled up around her throat and choked her, she folded her arms tightly against her chest for protection and paced.

Through her haze she saw the surgeon walking toward her. He took her into the same room she had been in with the detectives. Jack sat quietly by her side.

"We will not know the full extent of the damage until she begins to recover more fully. Her X-rays and scans look good. Brain activity looks great, but the left side of her body has been affected. The plastic surgeon put a plate in the side of her head and was able to correct the damage done to the exterior part of her scalp and skull."

"What will her recovery be like?"

"I'm hopeful she will gain back most of her function within the next few weeks, and then hopefully make a full recovery within the next three to four months. The faster she recovers, the better the prognosis is for full recovery."

"What problems do you think she might have?"

"She'll probably have some left-sided weakness. It's not uncommon to have some memory loss, especially the events right up to the time of the trauma."

"Could it be permanent?"

"That's a great question, and the answer is we won't know for a while."

"When can I see her?"

"She'll be out of recovery and up in the ICU in a few hours." He took her hand. "She'll be groggy and slow to respond for a few days until she completely wakes, but she did good."

Rachel thanked him, and he left.

When the nurses left, and she found herself alone with Claire in Intensive Care, she maneuvered around her IVs and carefully wrapped her arms around her, then sat quietly holding her hand as she continued to sleep, moaning occasionally. She watched Claire breathing, examined the bandage wrapped around her head, and stared at the fluid dripping into the tubing. Tilly and Sarah arrived, taking turns going in with her while she sat by Claire's bedside.

The long dark hours of the night passed and turned into day. The sunshine streamed into the room, bathing Claire's hospital bed in light. Tilly got up and closed the blinds halfway, blocking the sunshine from the upper part of Claire's bed. Claire drifted in and out of consciousness, thrashing, calling out in moans. In the late evening on the second day, she began to stir and wake fully. Rachel, Tilly, and Sarah were sitting by her bed when she slowly opened her bloodshot eyes and looked at each of them. She surveyed the room, then looked back to Rachel but didn't speak. Rachel took her hand and held it, leaning forward and smiling, calling her name.

"You're in the hospital, Claire," she told her.

Claire looked at her intently, as if studying her. "I have a headache," she said softly. She looked at Tilly and then Sarah. "Tilly, did you drop off that package at the post office like you said you would?"

She closed her eyes and drifted off to sleep, waking again after a few hours. Rachel watched her as she opened her eyes and watched each one of them again.

"How are you feeling, Claire?" Tilly asked.

"My head hurts," Claire said, closing her eyes, "and I feel like I have holes, deep black holes. Did that piece for my potter's wheel come yet? It was supposed to be here yesterday. I have to get that order done." She opened her eyes and looked at Sarah. "I'm sorry, that wasn't right." She closed her eyes. "Tilly, your mom is going to be so mad that you broke her favorite vase."

Tilly reached over and patted her arm. "That happened years ago, sweetie, and she got over it."

Claire smiled. "Oh yes, now I remember. She made you pay for it."

Tilly laughed. "Yes, she did, but I got even."

A faint smile crossed Claire's face as drifted off to sleep again.

Her hand was cold. Rachel rubbed it gently, looking at the IV in her arm. Claire opened her eyes and looked at her, and then looked down at Rachel's left hand at the diamond wedding ring on her finger.

"That's a beautiful ring."

Rachel looked up at her, her worst fear confirmed. "Thank…you." She gently put Claire's hand under the blanket and stood up. "I'll be back in a little while." She walked out of the room and leaned against the wall.

Tilly stayed with Claire as Sarah followed Rachel out into the hallway and put her arms around her.

"It doesn't mean her memory loss is permanent. She has a long way to go. You're exhausted. I'm going to take you home. I want you to get some sleep. Tilly and I can take turns staying with her."

"No, I won't leave her."

"Yes, you need to rest. You won't be able to help her if you collapse from exhaustion."

They went back into Claire's room. Rachel sat back down in the chair and watched her as she slept, refusing to leave her. Three hours later Claire woke again, opened her eyes, and looked at Rachel but didn't speak. She looked over at Sarah and Tilly and smiled.

"Why are you two here?"

Tilly took her hand. "You're in the hospital, sweetheart."

Claire looked at Rachel again. "Are you here to help me?"

Rachel swallowed, forcing the pain and gut-wrenching sadness down. She touched her shoulder. "Yes, Claire, I'm here to help you."

Claire drifted back to sleep.

Rachel stood up, her eyes burning, her head pounding. "I'm ready to go home for a while now, Sarah."

Sarah put her arm around her and walked her out of the room.

Rachel showered, changed clothes, and lay down on their bed. The floral scent of Claire's hair was all around her. She rolled over, clutched Claire's pillow, and held it against her breasts. "Claire, come back to me."

CHAPTER TWENTY-FIVE

Rachel looked down from the stepladder and smiled at Claire, who was struggling but not giving up. "Try it again, Claire. You can do it."

Claire reached for the hook with her left hand and tried to slip it into the Christmas bulb, finally getting it connected. "I did it." She held it up.

"Fantastic job." Rachel took the bulb and hung it on the Christmas tree, and then stepped down from the ladder. "I think it's done—what do you think?" She watched Claire as she looked at the Christmas tree, carefully scrutinizing it.

"Did you know there are 127 bulbs, 400 lights, and 1,248 pieces of tinsel on that tree?"

"How do you know that?"

"I don't know, I just do. Rachel, will you tell me more about our friendship?"

"I will if you promise you'll write in your journal for ten minutes before you go to bed, and you can't stay up late tonight watching movies because you have an appointment with Dr. Crenshaw tomorrow morning."

"Will you take me, or do you have to work?"

"I'm taking you because they want to do more testing, and you'll get the results of your evaluation."

"What day is it today?"

"Today is Tuesday, December 4. How many days and hours has it been since the injury?"

Claire smiled. "That's an easy one." She looked down at her watch. "Forty-seven days or one thousand one hundred and thirty-two hours and twenty-seven minutes. I'm ready now."

Rachel went to the sofa and helped her up, wrapping her arm around her left side. "Get your balance before you step." She walked beside her as Claire slowly made her way to her bedroom.

"I want the red ones tonight."

Rachel helped her change into her red silk pajamas and helped her into bed, sitting in the chair beside her bed. Olivia brought them hot spiced apple cider. Claire reached for it with her right hand.

"Nope, if you want that, you have to take it with your left hand," Rachel told her.

Claire frowned and slowly reached with her left hand, steadying the cup with her right hand.

"Very good, Ms. Claire," Olivia said smiling and started to leave the room.

"Olivia, Merry Christmas, and thank you for all you've done for me."

"Oh, Ms. Claire, it has been an honor to help you."

"It is better, isn't it, Rachel?" Claire switched the cup to her right hand.

Rachel laughed. "Cheater."

She switched back to her left hand. "I love the scent of this cider. It reminds me of Ohio in the fall, don't you think?"

"Claire, did you hear what you just said?"

Claire smiled. "I remember the feelings and scents so well, just like I was there again."

She slapped Rachel a high five, and they continued to sip their delicious hot drinks.

"Rachel, sometimes now I get flashes of memory. I see you riding a horse, or next to me riding in a car. Yesterday, when I was in the kitchen, I had a memory of you laughing, and then I saw you in a small room with pieces of burnt black wood, searching for something. May I tell you everything I think about and remember?"

"Yes, anything and everything." Rachel touched her arm.

She looked at Rachel's wedding ring and then at her own bare finger. "There's something I want to remember, but I don't know what it is. I try so hard, but it's just empty dark space."

Rachel touched her shoulder. "It will come back eventually." But she knew it might not ever come back.

"You've been such a wonderful friend to me. I don't know what I would do without you. Will you have to leave soon to go back to your own family?"

❖

Rachel watched Claire through the two-way mirror as the therapist helped her stretch and bend, then go through her balance exercises. Dr. Crenshaw made more notes.

"She's come a long way these past weeks, physically and cognitively."

"Dr. Crenshaw, she's beginning to have more flashes of memory. How can I help her if she finally has the recall that we're married? How will she take it? What kind of a shock will it be to her?"

"She will recall because her mind is ready to accept the memories. Some will be a shock to her consciousness, and some memories will be so powerful it will be like she is having the experience for the first time all over again. Let them happen naturally. Comfort and support her as she recalls the events. Keep doing things with her that she enjoyed before—take her to familiar places, but also try new things. Her balance and coordination have improved immensely, and she can do more physical things now. Push her to be active because it will only help her. She is way above normal in her visual acuity and sensory perception. For some reasons, unknown to us, she has enhanced those abilities, and her eye-hand coordination is also improving rapidly. As the physical part of her brain recovers more and her memory improves, she will dream more. She will have questions, so answer honestly and simply, but you must be careful to let her remember naturally. Don't tell her—let her remember. It will force her to work harder to get the memories back.

"And Rachel, one last thing is critical for you to remember. Sometimes the subconscious protects our conscious. Claire may not be able to consciously recall her marriage to you because it is a protection by her subconscious."

"I'm sorry, Dr. Crenshaw. I don't quite understand."

"Her memories of her marriage to you may be associated with the shooting and all the myriad of issues connected to it. Even though she may be ready physiologically, she'll need time to subconsciously sort through it all. The human brain is the most complex and astounding organ there is, and as much as we do know, we still know very little about its capabilities and capacities. I'm confident—when her body and mind are ready to face it, she will remember. But it has to be in her own time. She can't be forced. It could cause more trauma if she were told, rather than remembering on her own."

❖

When they all got together for Easter, Rachel, Sarah, and Tilly kept Claire busy and moving.

Tilly walked to the top of the ridge and sat down, gulping her bottle of water. "Painted Desert my ass," she said, wiping the sweat from her forehead.

Rachel laughed as she, Sarah, and Claire came up and sat down beside her.

"This is nothing more than a damn desert—it's dry and hot," Tilly complained.

"It's not hot—it's comfortable, Tilly," said Claire.

"It's friggin' hot, Claire, five days before Easter. The heat was the one thing I could never get used to, living here in Las Vegas, but now that I'm back in Cleveland, my biorhythm is back to normal."

Claire took a drink of her water and looked around. "Have we done this before?"

"Well…" Tilly said.

Rachel stopped Tilly. "What do you remember, Claire?"

"My legs aching and climbing, and a plane."

"We won't hold it against you if you don't remember that," Tilly said, laughing.

Claire stood up. "Trees and cold. It's almost there, but I just can't seem to get it. Damn, it's so frustrating."

Sarah whispered to Rachel, "Let's take her to Lake Mead tonight and have a campfire, see if it triggers anything."

Rachel nodded.

Tilly and Rachel built the fire in the fire ring not far from the lake while Sarah and Claire spread out the blankets.

"Now it's freezing," Tilly complained, looking up at the night sky.

"It's a desert, Tilly," Sarah told her.

They sat around the fire laughing, telling stories about their shared childhood. Claire was able to tell two stories about their childhood in Cleveland. Suddenly she stopped and looked at them.

"Holy crap, it was Alaska, a plane crash, and mountains." She looked at Rachel. "You were hurt, and we were in a cave."

Rachel and the others started clapping and cheering.

"It's foggy, but I can see all of us. Rachel?"

Rachel went next to her and held her hand. "What do you remember, Claire, what do you see?"

"Justin beat me and tied me up."

"You're safe, Claire," said Sarah.

"Let yourself remember, Claire—it's all right," Rachel said. "There's nothing to be afraid of. We got through it."

"The memory is coming so slowly. I'm trying to focus and hold it, but pieces are still missing."

She put her hands to her face and groaned. Rachel put her arm around her. "It's all right, Claire."

"What happened to Justin?"

Rachel didn't want to give Claire all the details if she couldn't remember and didn't want to think about it. "He died, Claire. He can't hurt us anymore."

"What an asshole," Tilly said, stirring the fire with a stick.

"How long ago was it?"

"It's been almost two years," said Rachel.

Tilly handed Claire a stick. "Here, roast a marshmallow and celebrate."

Later in the week, everyone was in the game room. Tommy was playing foosball with his dad, as Jack and Frank watched. Marie, Frank's fiancée, and Jack's latest love, Kelly, were playing Five Crowns at the game table with Rachel, Claire, Sarah, and Tilly.

"Come on Tilly, there's at least five queens left, play already," said Claire.

"How do you know what I need, and how do you know how many are left in the deck?"

"Trust me," said Rachel. "She just does."

"How's your pool game coming, Claire?" Tilly chided. "Are you ready to lose?"

Rachel smiled. "I'll bet you one hundred dollars she beats you."

"Oh, you're so on," said Tilly, smiling.

"I want a piece of that—Tilly is good," said Sarah.

"Okay, I'll cover each of you for one hundred, but if she wins, Tilly, you have to sing us a song, just Claire and me, for two nights."

Claire smiled.

Tilly nodded to Sarah.

"Bet," said Sarah.

They finished the game and walked over to the pool table.

"Each player gets to warm up. Then they'll roll closest to the break line to see who breaks, agreed?" asked Sarah.

Rachel nodded. "I need to talk with my player for a minute." She walked Claire over by the bookcases and whispered to her, "Only beat her by two balls, or she won't play you again."

"Is she any good?"

"I don't know—you've never played her before. You've never played anyone but me. Don't get more than two balls ahead of her."

Ricky and Tommy continued to play foosball as Tilly and Claire started the pool game, but Tommy stopped to watch them when Tilly put a solid and a stripe ball in on the break.

"Go, Aunt Tilly," he cheered.

They began watching the game.

Tilly put another solid in, declared solids, and then missed her next shot.

Rachel watched Claire chalk her stick, put one striped ball in, and then purposely miss the next shot. They continued to take turns until Claire had two balls left, and Tilly was shooting the eight ball but missed the side pocket. Claire looked over at Rachel and winked at her, then put both of her balls in and called the eight ball in the corner pocket before putting it in.

"Aw man, that was just luck," Tilly complained. "Let's play one more game."

"What's the bet?" Rachel asked.

Tilly and Sarah conferred.

"My player and I propose five hundred dollars, and the losers have to caddie for the winners at the golf game on Monday," Sarah said with confidence.

Claire and Rachel huddled.

"Claire, how much should we take them for?"

"Make 'em pay for it."

"That's my girl. We propose one thousand and caddie." She and Claire slapped a high five.

"Well, hell, if you're going to get greedy about it, why not two thousand?" Tilly said.

Claire and Rachel looked at each other and smiled.

"Okay, you have a bet." Rachel turned to Claire. "Sting her."

Claire let Tilly break. Tilly put two striped balls in on the break, then three more, and then missed. Claire stepped up and ran the table, called the eight ball in the corner pocket, and hopped Tilly's ball to get it in.

"Holy shit," said Tilly.

Sarah's mouth dropped open as the rest of the group applauded.

Claire walked up to Tilly. "We don't want your money, but you will have to caddie for us."

That night, when the house was quiet, Rachel passed Claire's bedroom door and saw her still awake. She stepped backward and peeked in through the bedroom doorway.

"Why are you still up?"

"Come in here for a minute, Rachel." Claire turned on the lamp.

Rachel came in and sat down on the bed beside her. "Are you all right?"

"Rachel, let me see your wedding ring." Rachel gave Claire her hand. "That is such a beautiful ring. I had a dream about a wedding ring, only it was pear shaped, and it was in a fire."

Rachel wondered if this was the moment she'd been waiting for.

"When did we start living together?"

"Right after the mess from the plane crash."

"When did we move from Cleveland to here?"

"About a year ago."

"When did you get married?"

She looked at Claire for a long time, trying to decide if she should tell her, but remembered what Dr. Crenshaw had told her and decided against it. "I don't want to talk about that."

Claire looked up at her and then traced her ring with a finger. "I'm sorry. I didn't mean to upset you. You have beautiful hands—they are kind and loving, and gentle." She looked into Rachel's eyes. "I feel like I'm trying to put a picture puzzle together, and I can almost see it, but some of the major pieces are missing, and as hard as I try, I can't get it. There was a fire, wasn't there?"

"Yes, right before you were shot."

"Did Derrick love me?"

"Yes, I think he did, but he was confused. He was sick and got lost in his own feelings and forgot what love is about."

"What do you think love is about?"

Rachel held her hand. "That's a great question. People have debated that since the beginning of time. I think love is about the one you love, not about yourself."

Claire touched her face. "You are so beautiful. I feel like I can talk to you about anything. Were we engaged?"

Rachel hesitated. She wasn't sure if she was asking about Derrick or her. "No, Claire, you were not engaged to Derrick."

"How long have we been in this house?"

"We leased this house October 31 at one p.m., right before you came out of the hospital. How many hours ago was that?"

Claire continued to hold her hand, not letting it go.

"You all right?"

"Rachel, when will you have to go back to your family?"

She stroked the side of Claire's face with the back of her hand, trying to calm her, but her own frustration at not knowing how much she should tell her began to surface, and the million-dollar question raised its head again. *Will the shock of our marriage be too much for her to handle?* She held Claire's face in her hand. "I don't want you to worry about it. I'll stay as long as I can help you. Now, get some sleep."

She made her lie down and turned her light out.

"Good night," said Claire, and then she called out to her, using a Native American word. "Rachel, what does that mean? It just came to me."

Rachel thought it was good that it was dark. She tried to stop the tears as she turned to leave. "It means *Beloved* in my tribe's language."

Claire called out to her again. "Moon Shadow. You are Moon Shadow, aren't you? It's your Indian name, isn't it?"

Rachel could hardly speak. "Yes."

She heard Claire whisper as she left her room. "It's a beautiful name."

She went to her bedroom, not knowing how many more days of separation and uncertainty she could endure.

❖

Claire slid down in her bed and fluffed her pillow. Flashes of a teepee and beautiful sunsets flooded her mind. She tried to piece it together. How did it fit into her past? Frustration filled her heart. All she could reason was that Rachel was a major piece.

CHAPTER TWENTY-SIX

Tilly talked the adults into playing Texas Hold'em for a fifty dollar per person buy-in pot. After two hours, everyone was out of the game and watching, except Rachel, Jack, and Claire. Rachel went all-in on a pair of kings before the flop, but Jack put her out of the game with three queens.

Three hands later, after the flop, Jack bet ten thousand dollars in chips.

Claire looked up. "Jack, I'm going all-in and have you beat. You should fold and give me the pot."

"What kind of trash talk is that, Claire?" He laughed and looked over the cards on the table again. "I'll call you."

Rachel watched as they flipped their cards over. Jack held a pair of queens, Claire held the ten and nine of hearts, and the cards on the table gave Jack a full house, and a possible straight flush for Claire.

Tilly, who was dealing, flopped the next card, a two of spades, no help to either Jack or Claire. She looked over the cards on the table. "All right, here it is, you two. Claire, you better get something because Jack has you beat with a full house, and you've got about as much of a chance at getting your card for a straight flush as I do at getting a Grammy."

Everyone laughed.

Claire looked at the cards and then at Jack. "Tilly, before you flop the river card, Jack, one last chance. I'll split the winnings with you if you fold right now."

Jack smiled. "You have got some kind of balls, Claire. I have you beat right now, and there is only one card in the entire deck that could turn up that would beat me, and that's the jack of hearts. I have just as much of a chance to get the fourth queen, so no thanks, I'll take my chances with the river card."

Tilly flopped the card. It was a jack of hearts—Claire won.

Jack's mouth dropped open, and Claire winked at Rachel.

That night when Rachel came to Claire's bedroom to say good night, she sat down on the bed. "You saw the cards, didn't you?"

"Yes, I saw them as clear as day. They fanned out in front of me and stopped, and then floated down onto the table. How do you think I did that?"

"I think you subconsciously saw Tilly shuffle the cards, and somehow that amazing brain of yours put it together."

"Do you think this thing is going to go away eventually?"

"I don't know. Dr. Crenshaw seems to think it's just something that happens. He is always saying, *The brain will do what it's going to do.*"

Claire smiled as she repeated it with her.

"How would you like to come to the shed with me and help test a program I'm working on?"

"Yes, I would love it, when?"

"Next week."

❖

Rachel brought Claire to the shed, where they were met by Frank, who slapped Claire a high five.

"Everything's ready," he said.

Jack motioned from his office window for Claire and Rachel to come in. Steve Hathaway was seated in one of the office chairs and stood up when they entered, shaking hands with both of them.

Rachel could see the anxious expression on his face through his smile.

"Are you ready, Claire?" Steve asked.

"Yes. It's going to be fun—don't worry, I've got this."

Rachel watched Jack shuffle papers and Steve shift his weight from one foot to the other. "She is ready. You two should calm down. We've only invested over seven million dollars in this program."

"Well, when you put it that way," Jack said. "What in the hell were we thinking?"

Rachel tried to reassure him. "Jack, it's going to be great. I know you're nervous. Just relax."

Everyone who was involved in the test sat in the chairs surrounding the table in the main conference room. Rachel could sense the excitement and anticipation in the room as she booted up the computer.

"Claire, let's go over this one more time before we start," she told her.

Claire nodded, watching her.

"Once the equipment is in place, you and José will leave for the test area. Each command given must be initiated quickly. Any deviation from the planned test will take a few seconds to adjust, so give me some time to catch up with you, okay?"

"What if I miss a test point?"

"Don't worry about it. It's just a preliminary test, and I don't expect you to get all of the test points the first time out. Are you ready?"

She gave a thumbs-up. Rachel could see she was nervous but excited.

José picked up the small earphone and placed it in Claire's right ear, snapped the attachment in place behind her head, and then put the other earpiece into her left ear, adjusting it to make sure it fit snugly. He placed the special lubricating liquid into her left eye and inserted the contact with the microchip.

She blinked as the microchip slipped perfectly in place. Rachel watched her carefully.

"You act like your eye is irritated—are you okay?" she asked.

"It feels a little heavy in my eye."

"Let's give your eye a minute to adjust."

Claire nodded.

Everyone in the room watched Claire intently as she sat quietly.

"Stop looking at me. You all are making me nervous."

Rachel watched the group as they nervously laughed. Kathrine sat with her hands tightly together, her knuckles white, and Frank's face was so tense you could have bounced a quarter off his cheek.

"I'm telling you, it's going to be fine," Claire said. "All of you, quit worrying. It feels okay now, good to go."

Rachel nodded. "Okay, I'm switching on the program. Get ready to feel a little surge in your eye, your ears, and at the back of your skull."

Rachel hit the key on the computer. The screen on the wall went momentarily blank as she watched Claire, trying to see any difference in her when she felt the surge. "You okay?"

She gave a thumbs-up.

The wall screen suddenly lit up with the images Claire was seeing. Everyone started clapping and cheering.

"Phase one, test one complete," Rachel told Jack. "Claire, like we practiced, reach up on the right earpiece and press the button once."

When Claire reached up and pressed the button, the images on the screen zoomed in as Rachel's computer screen was enhanced with her sight images.

"Now left earphone button, once."

Rachel's computer screen went blank.

"Blink your left eye three times."

"Does it matter if I also blink my right eye at the same time?"

Rachel smiled. "No, not at all."

She blinked three times, and the computer screen came back on.

"Phase one, test two complete," Rachel announced. "Program off.

Claire reached up and pressed the left button and the program went off.

Jack walked over and stood over her. "Put your right arm up on the table and relax it as much as you can, deep breaths."

Rachel looked at her and then Jack. "Are you sure this is necessary?"

"She will now be the most valuable asset we have. We have to monitor her. Claire, I'm sorry."

Frank left and returned with the medical box, took out the injector, loaded the tracker, and then swabbed her right forearm with the alcohol pad. "This one is good for eight months and satellite-capable of tracking within a hundred meters, but X-ray will disable it for about forty-five minutes, always remember that, Ms. Davenport, especially if you are going through airport security."

"Good to know," Claire said, looking up at him.

Frank pushed the injector against her arm, held her arm firmly, and then pulled the trigger.

"Ouch," she said when the microchip went into her arm.

Rachel winced and activated another part of the computer program as Claire's tracking data came up in a small box in the right upper corner of her screen.

"Phase one, final test completed," she announced. "All right, everyone, go to your positions, phase two is beginning."

Everyone wished Claire good luck and left for their assigned points on the test route, leaving Rachel alone with her, except for the support staff in the main office.

Claire went around the conference table to Rachel and sat on the table beside her computer. Rachel reached up and took her hand.

"How's your arm? You all right?"

"Never better."

"No headaches or anything?"

"Nope, I feel great."

Rachel looked at her watch. "Okay, we have five minutes. Turn on your program, woman, and hit the road and make history."

"Today is just a walk in the park. Your program is going to blow the competition away, and Jack is going to have the most powerful secure investigative system in the world."

"That may be true, Claire, but it doesn't work fully without you attached to the other end of it. Without you, it's just another very cool camera system. Go do your magic, and don't forget to put your sunglasses on when you get outside."

Claire waved as she walked to the door.

"And don't forget to make sure your sunglasses are clean. I won't be able to see through your dirty glasses."

Claire shook her head, opened the door, and left to meet José.

Rachel watched her computer screen, put in her earphone, and heard Claire start the car.

She spoke quietly to her. "Claire, remember, the human brain processes much more quickly than my computer can, so don't show off."

"Quit worrying—your program is perfect." She blinked three times.

Rachel's computer screen and the wall screen came to life with the images Claire saw. She tracked her movement on the screen, listening as José gave her instructions.

"Coming up on test number one. On your ten o'clock in three-two-one-now," José said.

Claire looked to her left at the ten o'clock position. Rachel recorded the images and watched her screen as Claire looked back in front of her while she continued to drive.

Rachel spoke to her in the microphone. "The images are a little dark. Tap the top right frame of your sunglasses." The tint of Claire's sunglasses become slightly lighter. "That's better for me—can you still see all right in the sun?"

"Yes, it's still okay for me."

José instructed her, "Get ready, coming up on test two at your three o'clock in three-two-one-now."

Rachel watched the images as Claire looked right at three o'clock, looking inside the small corner store. The images showed Kathrine, standing by the aisle just inside, and then Claire looked straight ahead again.

Rachel continued the testing, and then Claire returned to the shed, and Rachel sent José to help her remove the equipment. All the members of the team gathered in the conference room for the results of the tests. Claire sat down beside her, putting her arm around her and hugging her.

"You did great," Rachel whispered.

"I want everyone in this room to remember that everything you see and hear is classified. You are not to talk about it outside this conference room, and that means with anyone, including significant others and spouses. You all signed confidentiality agreements. Am I making myself clear about this?" Jack stopped speaking and looked around the room at each member of the team.

They all nodded.

"Okay, Rachel, what do you have for us?"

"First of all, we will have to adjust Claire's sunglasses more. The images are a little darker than I would like, and we have missed some details."

She put the recording up on the screen, forwarding to test two, and everyone gasped as they watched.

They could see Kathrine and every detail of what she was wearing, the two people beside her, the prices of the boxes of cereal she was standing by, and even the products in the cooler to her left.

The room was quiet as everyone sat staring at the images on the screen.

Rachel reviewed the results with the team.

"Here's the immediate problem I see." She took the laser pen and circled the area to Kathrine's bottom right. "The degraded images here"—Rachel moved the pen to the images on the left—"and here. Claire's vision is so acute that our system cannot pick up what she sees there, and that's a major problem because we could lose something invaluable during an investigation. We have to find a way for the computer to catch up with what she sees."

Everyone in the room was still speechless.

David finally spoke. "Claire, since you gained this amazing visual acuity, what's it like to see that much all at once?"

"My brain, like the computer, stores most of it, and I usually don't see it all until I go to sleep, and it floats around in my head all night, but if I try, I can remember lots of what I saw after I have had some time to process it. It's not much fun to play card games anymore because if I watch the shuffle, I know the order of the cards, and then everyone's hand."

The group laughed.

"It's not really something I think about—it's just there."

Kathrine asked the next question. "Is it ever going to go away, or is it permanent?"

"No one seems to have the answer to that question. It slowly came to me as the weeks went by after my head injury, and so far, it seems to remain, but I can't be sure if it will stay with me. I refuse to have any more testing done at the neurological center, so I'll just use it while I've got it."

Jack stood up and dismissed the group, and Rachel stood with Claire as each team member came up, congratulating them as they left the room.

Once they all left, Jack faded the glass and hit the soundproof mechanism.

"Wow," he said, looking at them, shaking his head, smiling. "We are going to kick ass with this program."

Frank knocked on the door and came in, holding a small flashlight and other equipment and sat down beside Claire. "I need to do a quick exam on her," he told them. Claire turned around and sat toward him as he began to examine her. "I see some redness in that eye, but nothing else out of the ordinary." He looked in her ears with an otoscope and then carefully checked the outside of her ears and the back of her head, reaching up and gently touching the deep scar above her right ear from the bullet wound. "Any extra sensitivity?"

"No, everything feels good."

"Well done, both of you." He took his equipment and left.

"Rachel, we'll talk money later next week," Jack said.

Rachel nodded and then she and Claire left to go home.

Chapter Twenty-seven

Rachel stared out the window at the early morning rain. She was alone, more alone than she had ever been in her life. Today was their first-year anniversary. She rolled over in the bed, looking at the extra pillow beside her. She pulled it to her and wrapped her arms around it, pressing it to her breasts, aching for the comfort of Claire next to her, but the feeling was empty and cold. She threw the pillow onto the floor. A thousand memories of their life together flooded her mind. A year ago, they were on the reservation. She could smell the earth, see the sunsets, and feel Claire next to her. She could feel their love and want and need for each other. More than anything, she missed the intimacy. If everything had been different, what a day it would be today. They would have a party in the house they would have built, and it would be filled with their family and friends. They would have celebrated the entire week, not just today.

Claire was at the breakfast bar drinking coffee with Olivia when she walked into the kitchen. Olivia looked at her as if to say, *I know what today is.*

Claire looked over and smiled. "Good morning, Rachel."

Olivia handed her a bagel with egg. She looked down at her food, avoiding Claire's gaze, and mumbled a greeting.

"Are you not well?" Claire asked, sipping her coffee.

"I'm fine." She took a bite of her food and then pushed the plate away. "I'm going for a swim."

She stopped in the middle of the lap and dived under the water, screaming as loud as she could. She pushed herself up, breaking the surface, gulping for air, startled to see Claire bent over the side of the pool watching her.

"Rachel, what's wrong?"

She wiped the water from her eyes and swam to the side, put her arms on the edge, and looked up. "What makes you think there's something wrong?"

"Well, first of all you're moping around the house, now you're screaming under the water, you haven't said two words to me this morning, and you aren't eating. It doesn't take a rocket scientist to see there's something bothering you."

She pushed back from the side and backstroked to the middle of the pool, getting as much distance as she could from Claire.

"I'm fine. I'm just having a bad morning."

She avoided Claire the rest of the day, staying in her office, trying to focus on work. She promised herself they would celebrate someday.

Claire could no longer keep her concern to herself and called Sarah. "I think Rachel wants to leave."

"What makes you say that?"

"She's acting distant. She's moody, and she's been avoiding me all day."

"Oh, I doubt she wants to leave."

"When are you coming to see me?"

"I can't for a while. We're short-staffed at the hospital, and I used up all my vacation time."

Claire was barely listening, preoccupied with Rachel's odd behavior.

"Claire, you still there?...Claire?"

"I'm going to talk with Rachel. I'll call you later."

She headed to Rachel's office, knocked on the door, and entered at Rachel's acknowledgment. She sat down heavily on the sofa across from Rachel's desk and folded her arms against her chest. "Rachel, why are you avoiding me?"

"I'm not avoiding you."

"Bullshit."

Rachel placed her hands on the desk and looked at her. *Is she ready to know? Should I tell her or let her figure it out for herself? Will it traumatize her?*

"You can leave if you want. You don't have to stay here. I don't understand why you've stayed all this time in the first place. It's a little odd that you don't want to go back to your family. If I were you, I'd want to go back." Claire unfolded her arms and leaned forward, looking at her and then down at her wedding ring.

Here it comes.

"You left your husband, didn't you? And now you're hiding out here, using me as an excuse. Only you're tired of being here, and now you don't have anywhere else to go."

"That's not true, Claire."

"Well, then what the hell is it?"

Rachel leaned back in the chair and looked at Claire. Strands of her short hair were clinging to the side of her face, her eyes a vivid green, her jaw muscles tight.

They were at a standstill. She remained quiet and didn't speak. The birds outside the window chirped loudly, as if trying to add their two cents to the conversation.

"I'm here because I want to be here with you."

Claire put her arm on the end of the sofa and looked out the window then back at her. "What is everyone not telling me?"

"Do you really want to know?"

Claire leaned forward. The intensity of her gaze shot through her. "Yes. I do."

"I'm not married to a man."

Claire leaned back. Her gaze still fixed on her. "You...you're married to a *woman*?"

"Yes." *Come on, Claire, you can figure this out.*

Claire pushed the hair back from her face, ran her hand through the side of it, and then looked out the window again.

The birds warbled louder...*figure it out...figure it out...figure it out...*

"Are you separated?"

Rachel took a deep breath and hung her head. The birds were suddenly quiet. The decision was hers to make. She pushed back farther into the chair. She knew she wouldn't be able to take it back once she said it, and if she did say it and Claire wasn't ready to hear it, she could be traumatized. She needed to stretch out the moments, give Claire more time.

"Not exactly."

"What do you mean *not exactly*?"

The tension and anxiety were so thick you could have smeared it on the wall with your fingertips. Her heart pounded in her chest. She couldn't breathe.

"Claire, you are my wife."

"I'm sorry?"

"You are my wife. You and I are married."

Claire shot up out of her seat and leaned over the desk. "No, that's ridiculous. That can't be true. We're just friends. You're here because of our friendship. You're playing some kind of joke."

"It's true, Claire."

"No. It's not true." She turned and stormed out of the office.

The doctors had warned Rachel, but she didn't listen. It was a mistake, and now she couldn't take it back. Not only could she not take it back, she didn't know what to do.

Claire slammed her bedroom door shut and locked it. She held her arms tight against her chest and paced. She sat on the bed, put her face in her hands, and rocked back and forth. *It's not true. It can't be true.* She strained so hard for the memories to prove it was a lie that she felt like her head was going to explode. *I'm divorced—how can I be married to her.* She threw herself onto the bed and curled up in a ball. She sat up and inhaled as deeply as she could, and screamed out to Rachel, "I'm not your wife."

Rachel jumped up when she heard her scream. It took a second for it the register what she was screaming. She sat back down and stared out the window. What must it be like for her? No memories of their life together, only glimpses, nothing sure, nothing solid, nothing to reach for. She remembered how Claire had struggled with her feelings for her at the very beginning, but she had no memory of it now, no memories to compare, no remembered experiences, just darkness and emptiness. She had to go to her.

She knocked on her bedroom door and tried to turn the handle, surprised it was locked.

"Go away."

She knocked again.

"I said *go the hell away.*"

"Claire, please talk to me. I know you'll feel better. Let me in?"

"I don't want to talk to you."

Rachel walked away from the door and went down the hall to call Sarah.

"Well, did she find out?"

"That's an understatement."

"Oh God, what happened?"

"I told her, Sarah, and she had a meltdown. Now she's locked herself in her room and won't talk to me."

"Rachel, she's in love with you, she just can't remember. For her to move forward, she is either going to have to remember or fall in love with you all over again."

"She acted like I lied to her or made it up."

"Which is she more upset about, the fact that she's married to you or that she can't remember?"

"I have no clue."

"Well, you need to find out, or you won't be able to help her work through it."

"I think she needs to talk with you."

"No, she needs to lean on you, not me. Start rebuilding your marriage right now. Break the door down if you have to. Break all the doors down if you have to."

❖

"Claire, open the door."

"Go to hell."

"I've been in hell since you got shot and lost your memory of our marriage—now open the damn door."

Nothing but silence on the other side.

"I'm not leaving until you open the door."

Still silence.

She looked down and saw the handle move, and then the door opened.

She stepped in as Claire walked back to the bed and sat down. She walked over and sat down in the chair beside the bed.

Claire rubbed her hands together and stared at the carpet.

"Thank you for letting me in. I know that wasn't easy for you." Silence. "It would be a lot easier if you would talk to me."

Claire's knuckles were red from the strain of pressing her hands so tightly together.

Rachel reached over and touched her shoulder.

Claire jerked away. "Don't touch me."

She held up her hand and moved it back from Claire. "Talk to me."

Claire turned and looked at her. "Am I really married to you, or is it just some bullshit story?"

"I would never mislead you about something like that."

"How long have we been married?"

"Today is our first-year anniversary."

"That explains a lot."

"It's been a hard day."

Claire half laughed. "No shit. Why did we get married? All of my memories of you are as friends."

"We are best friends, and we're in love. We got married because we couldn't live without each other."

"I have no memories of having sex with you." Claire looked at her, surveying her body. "Even if you are beautiful."

"Claire, let's take this very slow. I know this is a shock for you."

"Shock? You think this is a shock? Do you have any idea what it's like to hear something like that? How would you feel if someone walked up to you and said, "Oh, by the way, you have a daughter who's twenty years old, and you raised her, and oh yeah, she's standing at your door to say hello? I have no memories of you as my wife, none. How did we end up getting married?"

"What do you mean?"

"I mean how was the decision made?"

"Claire, you asked me."

Claire stood up and started to pace again.

"But we were both excited about it," Rachel added.

Claire walked over to her nightstand and opened the bottle of Xanax and took one, then sat down on the bed. "I'd like you to go. I don't want to talk about this any more tonight."

"Claire, I'm so sorry. I can't bear you being in pain. What can I do to make this easier for you?"

"I'm not ready to find out anything else. From now on I don't want to be told anything unless I ask."

"I asked you if you were ready to hear it, and you said you were."

"I wasn't ready to hear *that*."

"Obviously, and it was a mistake to tell you. I'm sorry."

Claire watched her. She could feel her looking at every part of her, like she was being inspected and would later be graded and stamped with the results.

Claire put her hands to her face again. "I'm afraid to know anything else."

"There is nothing in your past you need to fear. You are a wonderful person, and you have lived a good life. You have nothing to be afraid of."

Claire threw herself back on the bed. "Just go."

Rachel got up from the chair. "Good night."

❖

Jack walked into Rachel's office and slouched down into the chair across from her. She looked up from her computer. "What is wrong with you? You look awful."

"I just got a call from the state prison about Derrick."

"What's happened?"

"Derrick hanged himself in his cell last night."

"Oh God, that's horrible!" She put her hand to her mouth and started to get sick to her stomach. Jack walked over and put his arm around her.

"There are two lawyers who want to talk with Claire. Evidently he changed his will and left almost his entire estate to her."

"What? Why did they call you?"

"They didn't—the head of prison security called me and gave me a heads-up. We're friends."

Thirty minutes later Rachel's cell phone rang. It was the law firm representing Derrick's estate, wanting to know how to get ahold of Claire. She refused to give them Claire's cell number but set up an appointment for Claire and her to meet with them in three days at their offices in Seattle.

She called their attorney and then told Jack she would need to take a few days off.

❖

Rachel sat in silence, picking at the asparagus on her plate with her fork, trying to decide how to tell Claire and how to keep it uncomplicated. She took her hand. "Claire, there's something I need to tell you."

Claire pulled away. "I told you, no more revelations about my life unless I ask."

"This is something you have to know, and there's just no easy way to say this. Derrick hanged himself in his cell last night."

Claire put her hand up to her mouth. Her face turned pale and her hands began to tremble.

"I'm so sorry I had to tell you that news."

"Is it my fault?"

"What?"

"Did I cause it?"

Rachel put her hand on her arm. "No, of course not. You had nothing to do with it."

"Yes, I did. He was in prison because of me."

"No, absolutely not. He was in prison because he was a psychopath and showed up at our house with a gun."

"I feel like somehow it's my fault. Maybe I didn't always treat him like I should have. If I would have treated him differently, perhaps he would not have done what he did."

"It's not your fault in any way, Claire."

"I don't have many memories of Derrick, just some faint thoughts about when you were in the hospital in Juneau when you were hurt, and when I think about him, I get an anxious feeling. The only thing I remember of the day of the shooting is seeing you look out the window."

"You shouldn't feel any guilt. You did nothing wrong. He was the one who did something wrong. I'm glad you don't have any memory of that day—it was a horrible, horrible day, the worst day of my life. I'm sorry, but there is something else."

"Is this never going to end?" An anxious expression crossed Claire's face.

"Evidently Derrick made some changes in his will, and he left almost his entire estate to you."

Claire gasped, shaking her head. "No, absolutely not. I don't want his money. It's blood money." She stood up, a look of panic on her face.

Rachel stood up with her, putting her arms around her. "It's okay."

She pushed her away. "No, I won't take that money. I won't do it." She started to collapse.

Rachel grabbed her and walked her to the living room, sitting her down on the sofa. She poured her a shot of whiskey. Claire took a drink, holding the glass with both hands, staring off as Rachel sat down beside her. She took another drink, slowly shaking her head.

The wind beat against the windowpane. The rhythmic ticking of the Windsor cherrywood grandfather clock in the hallway, with its polished brass finished dials sparkling in the light, marked the silent seconds.

"I don't think Derrick left you his money to hurt you. I think it was his way of trying to make things right for what he did. He did not shoot you on purpose. It was an accident."

"Tell me what happened that day."

"Are you absolutely sure you want to hear it?"

"Yes, but just that day, nothing else."

Rachel didn't want to talk about it, but she knew Claire needed to hear it, and she felt confident that this time she was ready to hear about her life.

After she told her, she sat quietly, feeling nauseated.

"What did he do after it happened?"

"I don't remember," Rachel admitted. "I was too focused on you to worry about him, but I do know the police arrested him there at the house, and later he pled guilty."

Claire finished her drink and set the glass down on the end table. "Poor Derrick."

"Don't feel sorry for him. He was a psychopath, and he ruined our lives."

"I can't remember that day, so all I remember about him is that he was nice to us and was your surgeon in Alaska. I'm glad nothing more happened, and you weren't hurt."

"It could have turned out so much worse."

They sat together on the sofa. Rachel felt it was a good start.

"I don't understand why Derrick was so upset with me. What horrible things did I do to him that he wanted to kill me?"

"Claire, he didn't want to kill you—at least, I don't think he did. It was an accident."

"Yes, but he showed up with a gun."

"You weren't interested in him romantically, and he just couldn't deal with it. Love can make you go crazy."

"That doesn't sound like love to me. Was I good to him, or did I use him and lead him on? I know I did that to someone when I was younger, and it caused a lot of problems."

Rachel tried to be careful with her answer. "Derrick had some serious mental issues."

Claire sat looking out the window, not asking any more questions.

CHAPTER TWENTY-EIGHT

The female assistant led Claire, Rachel, and their lawyer, Michael Waverly, to the conference room of Shultz, Hess, and Walters, on the fifth floor of the Maritime Building in Seattle.

Claire sat cross-legged, breathing deeply. Rachel could see that the half a Xanax she had taken twenty minutes before finally kicked in. Mr. Hess thanked them for coming, introduced himself and his aide, shook hands, and then offered them something to drink, which was declined by all parties.

After a few minutes of small talk, Hess got down to business, stating the formalities. Then he addressed Claire. "Ms. Davenport, Dr. Morris left you a substantial about of money and a few items. I want you to know that I visited with him in prison many times, and every single time I was with him, he expressed great remorse for what he did. I also want to inform you that two of his extended family members have already contested the will..."

Rachel tuned out his long ambiguous ramblings, focusing on Claire. Would she break down? Would someone say something about their marriage? If they did, how would she react? She tried to make herself concentrate as Mr. Hess continued.

"The estate was probated in compliance with the laws of the State of Nevada, and all state and federal debts and obligations were paid, all court costs, fines, legal fees, penalties, and financial obligations have been settled in toto. The amount of money willed to you is..."

Rachel watched Claire's face.

"Three hundred twenty-seven million dollars."

Claire turned almost an opaque green. Her hands and knees started to tremble.

"Would you please get her some water," Rachel asked an assistant, who quickly brought back a pitcher of ice water with glasses on a tray.

Rachel poured the water for Claire and handed it to her.

She took the glass with her shaking hand, sipped slowly, and then set the glass down, looking at the table.

Mr. Hess continued, "There is a stipulation in his will that the following statement be read—"

Rachel looked over at Michael, who stopped Mr. Hess, saying, "Due to the nature of this will and the extreme stress caused to my client, it is in the best interest of my client that I review the written statement prior to its being read aloud."

"Of course."

Mr. Hess handed the paper to Michael, who read the statement, nodded to Rachel, and handed it back to Mr. Hess.

"The following statement was written by Derrick John Morris of his own free will and choice at the Nevada State Prison: *Claire, I know I will never be able to repair the damage I have done to your life. I want you to know I am eternally sorry for what I did, and I ask for your forgiveness. Please accept this money in consequence of the heartache and pain I have caused you. Derrick.*"

Claire put her hands to her face. Rachel put her arm around her.

Michael looked at Mr. Hess. "Would you excuse us for a few minutes?"

Mr. Hess stood up. "Of course." He and his assistant left the room, closing the door.

"He helped us at a time when we desperately needed it, Rachel. He saved your life in Juneau. I know he made some terrible, violent choices, but I'm trying to forgive him, and I hope you will also."

"I'm trying, Claire."

Claire grabbed her hand.

"I'm so sorry, Michael," Claire said.

He placed his hand on her shoulder. "It's quite all right, Claire. Would you like something stronger to drink?"

"No, I'll be okay in a minute."

After ten minutes, Michael left the room and returned a few minutes later with Derrick's attorney and his team.

"May I get you something else, Ms. Davenport?" Mr. Hess asked.

Claire cleared her throat. "No, thank you, I'm fine."

By the time all the papers and forms were signed, she and Claire were exhausted.

"We'll work with your legal counsel to resolve the contest. I imagine it won't take too long, given the circumstances and situation. The family members have already expressed a desire to settle quickly. Dr. Morris's wishes were clear, and all of his legal documents are in proper order," said Mr. Hess.

When they arrived home, Claire followed Rachel to her bedroom and sat down on the bed beside her. "I'm sorry I was such a bitch to you."

Rachel felt the stirrings of want and need spread throughout her body as she watched Claire looking at her.

Claire continued, "Who wouldn't want to be married to you? You're gorgeous. But what I don't remember is that I'm a lesbian."

"Claire, don't label yourself. You told me the day we picked out our wedding rings that I needed to not be ashamed of loving you and not worry about what others thought. I believe the words you said were *I don't give a flying monkey's ass what anyone else thinks.*"

❖

Rachel got out of the pool and soaked in the hot shower. When she came out of her bathroom, Claire was in her room. "You all right?"

"I had a dream last night about you and me. We were riding horses at sunset on a mountain somewhere. We were holding hands and there was a teepee. Tell me?"

"It was when we were on the reservation, after seeing my cousin Joseph. We stayed a week in a teepee." She looked at Claire and moved a step closer to her. "It was a few days before we got married here in Las Vegas. We made love and lay naked under the stars."

Claire closed her eyes.

It was so still Rachel could hear the residual drips of water from her shower in her bathroom.

"For God's sake, tell me we didn't get married by an Elvis impersonator."

Rachel laughed out loud. It felt good—she hadn't laughed that loud or that hard in a long, long time.

"I don't want you to go away," Claire said.

"I'm not going anywhere."

Before Rachel could do anything, Claire moved closer to her and kissed her.

Rachel couldn't stop herself. She hungrily returned her kiss, moving into her, feeling the deep familiar warmth, tasting the wet and softness of her mouth once more, longing, starting to fall into her. She somehow managed to make herself hold back, straining to not rip Claire's clothes off and ravish her body, forcing herself to let her take the lead.

Claire whispered after they kissed, "I knew you would be wonderful, but I shouldn't have done that."

Rachel put her arm around her. "It's perfectly all right. You have every right to kiss me."

Claire moved slightly away and looked at her. "I wish I could remember. I want to so badly."

Rachel couldn't stop herself. She leaned in and kissed her again, feeling Claire respond, moving her mouth gently against hers, the deep longing and need penetrating into her body. She withdrew and looked at Claire, hoping that somehow she would remember. She tried to let go of the sexual want and need building up, but she knew it was only going to get stronger.

"Rachel, I've wanted to kiss you for so long. I just wouldn't admit it to myself. Every night when you came into my room, I wanted to take you in my arms and kiss you."

Rachel put her hand up to Claire's face, trying not to break down and let go. "Do you remember anything about us?"

Claire looked intently at her, as if searching. "Just a few images. Was it good?"

Every muscle in Rachel's body tensed, sending flashes of throbbing heat down into her core. "It was wonderful." And at that moment she realized the memories caused the feelings—and Claire didn't have them.

"Do you want to pick up where we left off?" Claire asked.

"More than you can possibly know, but I think we should wait until you get your memory back." She forced herself not to take her into her arms. It wouldn't be the same for Claire, not without her memories.

Claire frowned.

Rachel felt herself gain a little more control. "Seriously, Claire, I think we should wait until you can remember."

Claire sighed heavily. Rachel felt her searching, straining to remember.

"Maybe if we make love, I'll remember."

"Maybe, but maybe you won't remember. Will you still want to be with me in the morning?"

Claire smiled. "I've wanted to be with you for a long time."

Rachel could feel the desire pulsing, raging, but the familiar pain of holding back began to haunt her, and what the doctor had told her echoed in her mind. She forced herself to say the words. "I think we should wait until you get your memory back about us."

"Why can't you just tell me? *You* be my memory. I trust you. I know you wouldn't lie to me. Tell me, please tell me."

"You have to remember on your own, Claire. I'm sorry."

"Bullshit." Claire stomped out of the room.

Well, at least she didn't slap me. Damn doctors.

Claire woke in the middle of the night, sweating, her heart pounding from a dream. She sat up and reached for the water on the nightstand, then picked up her cell phone and called Sarah.

"What is it, Claire?"

"I'm having dreams, and they're horrible."

"What kind of dreams?"

"I'm running, but I can't tell if it's to something or away from something. I'm afraid and anxious and full of dread. And I think about Rachel…"

"What do you remember about Rachel?"

She strained to remember, trying to focus. "She's always watched over me, starting in college. In Alaska she helped us, kept us alive, protected me, got hurt. I have seen flashes of us together laughing, doing things together. I see her face close to me, her deep hazel eyes."

"What kinds of feelings do you get when you think of her?"

Claire closed her eyes. "I feel security and safety and…" Her palms were sweaty. "Sarah, she told me we're married. I kissed her. I have had sexual thoughts about her, strong vivid sexual thoughts. I've wanted to be with her. I know I was attracted to women when I was younger."

"Honestly, I have never seen a stronger deeper love than you and Rachel had."

"Had?"

"Well, yes, *had*…you can't remember it."

"When did it start?"

"When do you think it started?"

"I don't know. I get the feeling she was married, but I don't have a memory. It's just a feeling. Was she married when we had the affair?"

"She was married to Alex right after college, but he was killed in a car accident."

Claire put her knees up and wrapped her arms around them. "She is so beautiful, but I can't believe I would have had an affair with her when she was married. Damn it, I wish I could remember." She closed her eyes again, searching, trying to remember. "Sarah, it all just feels so empty and gray. I get nothing. I want to go back to Cleveland with you. I don't want to stay here in Las Vegas anymore—there's nothing here. Why did I come here in the first place? I want to go home, Sarah."

"Claire, you haven't lived in Cleveland for a long time. There's nothing here for you. You sold your house. You probably feel displaced now because you aren't in the house you bought. You are living in a rented house."

"The only real memories I have of Rachel are when we were in college, and pieces of Alaska, and just fragments. I can't take this anymore."

Rachel sat in Jack's office, her knees crossed, swinging her leg. The anticipation of using her program on a case was so strong she thought she wouldn't be able to stay in her chair.

He leaned in. "Do you know what a redirect server is?"

The anticipation burst like someone popped a balloon. She leaned back. "Sure, it's used in high-level security to redirect confidential information in order to avoid detection, but that's classified information."

Jack grinned and folded his hands on his desk.

Her excitement inflated the balloon again. He had something, and she was going to get to use her program. "You have a case, don't you?"

"Let's put it this way, something stinks at the Cuyahoga Valley Hospital in Cleveland, and it's not the fish sticks or the cabbage rolls in the cafeteria. I'll let Frank and Kathrine do the initial snoop, and we'll go from there. We have a pretty full caseload right now, but I'll have them work it into their schedule."

When she got home, she walked into the kitchen and saw Claire looking in the refrigerator. She walked up behind her and called her name, not wanting to startle her. Claire stood up and turned around with two plastic containers of food in her hands.

"I'm so glad you're back. I was just getting something out to warm up. Are you hungry?"

"I'm starving—Claire, we're starting a new case, and I don't know how big it's going to be."

"Are you going to be away a lot?"

"I'm sure more than I want to be."

Claire smiled.

She could see Claire's desire for her growing stronger. She was making more eye contact and stood closer to her, as if wanting to linger with her just a few more seconds.

Claire warmed their food, and when they finished eating, she took their plates and set them down in the sink and then turned to her. "Rachel, would you like to go Red Rock Canyon?"

They drove the winding road, stopping at the far end of the park, then walked the trails along the foot of the mountains as the sun cast its shadows into the rust-colored face of the canyon.

"I like spending time with you. I feel content and at peace when I'm with you," Claire said.

It was all Rachel could do to restrain herself.

Rachel watched through the glass office window as Jack ended the call and set his cell phone down on his desk, looking out at her. She looked at Claire, who continued to talk with Kathrine, laughing about something she had said. It had been almost a month since Derrick's death, and it was good to see Claire beginning to interact with everyone again. Jack motioned for her to join him.

"How's Claire doing?" he asked.

She sat down in the chair across from him. "She's doing great. She's sleeping better and laughing more. It's not been easy for her."

"I know it's not been easy for you either. I have some news about the case we talked about."

Rachel looked at him, watching his expression, trying to read his face, but he was like a stone. "Okay, what news?"

"It looks like some type of insurance billing fraud. From what we can uncover, whoever is doing this has taken over a million dollars from this particular hospital network."

"So did you turn it over to the FBI?"

"Well, not exactly."

"What do you mean, *not exactly?*"

"The president of the hospital network doesn't want to go to the police yet because of all the publicity and possible recoil on his hospitals. He's worried that confidence, image, and investments may take a huge dive. He wants us to try to handle it first, but I can't do it without you."

Rachel sat back.

"I want to run what's called the domino effect. We'll go in, get whoever is doing this, set them up, take them down, and get back what was stolen."

"You mean push one domino over and watch the rest fall, that kind of effect?"

"No, someone has already pushed the first domino. I mean find out where and how many dominoes to pull out in order to stop the rest from falling."

"I promised Claire when we got married that I would not do anything dangerous until I talked with her first. I won't break that promise just because she can't remember we're married."

"Talk with her, and let me know right away. We have to start this as soon as possible."

"Don't tell me I have to go back to Cleveland if I choose to do this. It's twenty-two degrees there right now. Plus it's only a couple of weeks before Christmas."

He looked at her and frowned. "We can't wait."

"Cleveland?"

❖

"Claire, I need to—"

Claire immediately turned off the movie. "I know. You're leaving for a job. I watched you and Jack when you went into his office this afternoon. I know he asked you to do something, and I know it's dangerous because I watched your body language and his facial expressions, and I'm getting very good at lip reading. Remember, I can see everything. What's the domino effect?"

Rachel forgot she could see them through Jack's office window. She told her about the case.

"If you're going to do this case with Jack, do you think it would be all right if I went with you and stayed at Sarah's while you're in Cleveland? Tilly is going to be at Sarah's in a couple of days and plans to stay over Christmas."

"I think that's a great idea."

"Maybe, if I go there, I can get some memories back."

"That would be wonderful. Maybe you can buy some memories downtown."

Claire shoved her shoulder.

CHAPTER TWENTY-NINE

The team met in Jack's hotel room in Cleveland.
"Let's review. After spending days going over every process, protocol, and procedure in their finances, and investigating their personnel, we got shit," Jack said, disgusted.

Rachel looked at him. "We at least figured out which hospitals it's coming from and that it's being siphoned from the main hub, but we have to get in and figure out how these people are doing this. I can't do it from the outside looking in. I have to get deep into the programs. It's an inside job. They are not taking the money by pirating the program. They are actually physically going into the program and somehow rerouting the funds. It's in their billing protocol or online transfer of funds somewhere."

"I don't want you going in, Rachel. They already killed one person," Jack said, running his hand through his hair. "I don't want to say this, but this may be the job that is over our heads."

Kathrine protested. "I don't think so, Jack. These are crooks who are smart, but I think we can do this, and Frank and I can go in as service employees and watch over Rachel. No one gives a flying fig about the maintenance staff."

Frank laughed. "That's true."

"All right, Rachel and I will meet with the president of the company tomorrow and set up for you all to go in as employees," Jack said.

"Jack, has the president been cautioned not to talk to anyone about this, including his executive staff?" Frank asked.

"Yes, and he is scared, so he's been very cautious," said Jack.

"We have to be careful. If whoever is doing this suspects that someone is on to them, they are going to pull out and we'll never catch them," said Rachel.

"How long until you can spot the problem on the inside, Rachel?" asked Jack.

"I'm hoping not more than a day."

"I suggest we do one more thing," said Frank. "I suggest we get Claire in there and let her do a walk-through in the finance department. We can wire her up, send her in, and take a close look. She can go in as maintenance and slowly walk through, pushing a trash container or something. No one will suspect, and she can get a real good look at the employees, everyone's desks, and the area, including the supervisors' desks, but we are going to have to dress her down. No one will believe she is maintenance unless we do."

Everyone looked at Rachel.

"I don't think so. I want to use the program but not on this case, not with Claire. It's too dangerous. Let's set up video cameras."

"Video setup will take too long, and we won't be able to capture the information Claire can get us," said Frank.

"All she has to do is go in and look, and then get out, right?" Rachel confirmed.

Everyone smiled.

❖

When Rachel opened her hotel room door at the knock, Claire stepped in with an overnight bag and quickly closed the door.

"Rachel. This is so exciting. It's my first case. I feel like a spy or something."

Rachel laughed.

"Do you want to go down to the bar for drinks? I'm spending the night with you."

"Drinks yes, spending the night no."

Claire frowned. "Please?"

"What do you remember?"

Claire got a disgusted look on her face. "It would be better if I stayed the night. I can save time driving here in the morning, and you can prep me on the case. I already found out from Kathrine that it's at the hospital, and we're a lot closer from here than from Sarah's, and besides that there's nothing to do at Sarah's tonight because she's still working, and Ricky and Tommy went to some sort of male-bonding thing. And I can tell by the way you act, you really want me to stay, so you can quit pretending."

Rachel smiled. "Well, look at you, getting all Sherlocky Holmes."

Before Rachel could say anything more, Claire came in and sat on the sofa. "Rachel, come sit down by me. I have some things I need to say to you."

Rachel went to the sofa and sat next to her.

"I've constantly thought about the day you told me we were married, and all the confusion and feelings I had. But after getting to know you and being around you, I can see why we're married. You are a wonderful person. You are gentle and kind, and you are certainly beautiful, and I know you love me because I feel it every time you're around me. I've tried so hard to remember. I want you to know that I want to remember, but the memories just aren't there, and I want to get on with my life. I think about it all the time. I don't know what to do to help them come back."

Rachel could see the stress in her face and the concern in her eyes. She took her hand. "I think you should just try to relax and not think about it so much. There's no schedule for this. I hope—oh, how I hope—you will get your memories back, but if you never do, Claire, we'll just have to deal with it. Your doctors have told me it's best that your memories come back naturally, and that I not tell you. We both saw what happened when I told you we were married. I regret that I did it because it caused you pain. Your brain is full of the memories of us, but they are also lumped together with the memories of the shooting and everything that happened. I think the best thing is to just take it slow and let things happen, not force them."

"I want to be with you, Rachel."

"But is it out of curiosity, or hope, or lust? I want it to be because you are my wife, and you are in love with me and all the implications of that."

Claire put her hand over hers. "But that may never happen. I may never get those memories back. Can't we start from here, in this moment?"

"Yes, we can, but I think for now sex should not be a part of it."

"But don't you want to be with me?"

"Oh, Claire. I think about it every day and night, but I believe it will hurt you more than it will help you for right now."

"I need a drink."

❖

Rachel snapped the strap behind Claire's head and adjusted the right earpiece. She placed the lubrication liquid in her left eye and put the contact in. Claire looked out the hotel window as the snow fell, then scanned the room. She put the blond wig on over the strap. Rachel fluffed it over her ears and adjusted it slightly.

"Perfect, you can't see a thing." She sat down at the computer and ran diagnostics with Claire.

"Good to go," she told Jack.

"Okay, Frank, take her in. Now remember, Claire, act natural and take your time. Frank will be watching you and the people around you as you do your walk-through."

Claire and Frank left for the hospital. David, Kathrine, Jack, and Rachel remained in the hotel suite. Rachel turned on the program again, listening to Claire as she and Frank talked. When Claire walked into the hospital, Rachel told her, "Blink three times."

Claire blinked and began her walk-through, the images coming onto the computer as Rachel recorded everything. Rachel and Kathrine saw it at the same time.

Rachel whispered, "Claire, stop. Go back to the last cubicle and pan left."

Claire stopped pushing the trash can and slowly pulled it back, going into the cubicle like she was emptying the trash. The man sitting at the cubicle looked up at her.

"Excuse me," she told him, "I thought I saw a piece of trash under your desk."

He rolled his office chair back and looked under the desk. "Nope, nothing there," he told her.

Claire scanned his desk one more time, concentrating on the left side. She smiled and left.

"We got it," Rachel told her.

When Claire and Frank returned to the hotel room, he helped her remove her equipment, and the team gathered around Rachel as Kathrine and Rachel slapped a high-five.

Rachel smiled because she knew Claire put it together "Here's what we have. Claire, what was the reoccurring piece of information?"

"It's the temporary employment agency," Claire said, a big smile on her face.

Jack got up. "Great work, Claire. Okay, let's set the trap and work out the plan. We now know pieces of who and how, but we have to find out where the money is."

"We follow that employee," Rachel said, pointing to her computer screen and pausing the video of the man with the small dark birthmark on the left side of his chin, sitting in the cubicle.

"Let's get his address and stake him out. I want his house wired, and I want to know everything about this guy," he told Frank.

Frank took Kathrine and David and went off to formulate the plan.

CHAPTER THIRTY

"A bsolutely not," said Rachel, "it's too much of a risk."
Claire stood defiant. "Wait a minute. Let me get this straight. It's okay if you and Kathrine and everyone else goes out and risks your lives, but I'm not supposed to go out with the team? I stopped by here to tell you as a courtesy. I wasn't asking your permission." She stood in Rachel's hotel room, her hands on her hips, glaring at her. "What's the point of all the training, if I can only use my skills to walk through a hospital, pushing a trash can?"

"It's more dangerous than you know."

"I'm a legitimate member of this team. I can do what I want and go where I damn well please, and you can't stop me."

Rachel clenched her fists. She didn't know what to say. Claire had never spoken to her like that before. "It's dangerous, and Jack should never have asked you to do this."

"Well, that's the nature of this business, isn't it?"

"You have no idea what you're getting into."

"I'm going, and you aren't stopping me. I'll see you when you get to DC, and I hope you'll be in a better mood."

Claire walked out of the hotel room.

Rachel watched out the window as she got into the taxi with Kathrine. Her stomach churned, and she seethed and mumbled under her breath, "Son of a bitch, this has got to stop. I can't take this anymore."

❖

Claire watched Kathrine move the hotel curtain slightly, looking across the street at the darkened corner. After a moment, Kathrine let go of the curtain and looked at her.

"I can't see a damn thing."

Claire cautiously moved the curtain. She could see the men's breath as they exhaled against the cold night air, their dark heavy winter coats barely visible as they stood near the building, the brick wall announcing discount dry cleaning for men's suits in faded black and yellow lettering.

She spoke quietly into the microphone. "There's two men to the left of the building." She described them in detail.

Jack instructed, "When you leave the hotel, you two evade and meet me in the parking lot of King George's Steak House, east on Madison Street, toward downtown DC, about two miles on your right. I'll be in a silver SUV, headlights on."

She and Kathrine managed to get out of the hotel without being seen and hailed a taxi, taking it to the restaurant as instructed, and then got into Jack's SUV.

Jack immediately went out into traffic.

"What's going on?" asked Kathrine.

"I messed up. This case is much bigger than I initially thought. Frank, Rachel, and David are waiting for us at a safe house. If anything goes wrong, you two get back to that point and wait for instructions."

Rachel's words of how dangerous the assignment was suddenly echoed in Claire's ears.

Jack pulled into a narrow driveway. The dingy two-story framed house had peeling white paint and two missing shutters on the first floor. The team members were waiting, equipment in place, anxious expressions on their faces. She saw Rachel breathe a sigh of relief when they came through the door.

"No one followed us—I'm positive," Frank assured the group.

"Okay, here's the situation," said Jack. "We have been approved to run the black op, but if this involves anyone more than an agency head, we are to immediately turn it over to the FBI."

"Wait a minute," Frank said. "You mean if we do all the work, take all the risks, and find out a congressmen or senator is involved, we have to turn it over and give it up?"

"Yes, exactly."

"I say we let the FBI handle this—let them take all the risks and get their hands dirty for a change," said David.

"I agree," said Jack, "but I'm under the American Defense Council director's orders to run the black op first. I know it sucks, but that's the way it has to be. Claire, you'll do a walk-through like before, only this time you'll be going in as an auditor. Make sure before you start your walk-through that Frank has you in sight at all times."

Claire nodded.

"Rachel, are you sure the program will automatically record Claire?"

"Yes. It's all set and ready to go." She pointed to the laptop on the desk.

"Rachel, you'll be in the basement directly below Health and Human Services. You will be able to access all the mainframe information." He handed her the flash drive with the code she needed. "This will get you into the system. Once you're in, the rest is up to you."

Rachel secured the flash drive.

"When we drain the accounts, the money will go into a holding fund. Make sure you have a handle on the accounts, no mistakes."

"We'll have to move fast. Once we infiltrate the accounts, they'll be on to us within four minutes," said Rachel.

Everyone separated and went to their designated positions.

CHAPTER THIRTY-ONE

Claire stood on the corner watching Rachel and Kathrine run through the exit door as they made their way across the street to her.

"Go, go, go," Kathrine yelled, motioning toward the SUV. Rachel jerked open the passenger side door as Claire jumped into the back seat. Kathrine slammed the gear in place and squealed off, reaching the Beltway in a matter of minutes, then began weaving in and out of traffic.

Claire gripped the headrest of Rachel's seat. "What happened?"

Kathrine pounded her hand into the steering wheel. "I don't know—somehow they knew."

Rachel zipped her computer case the rest of the way and laid it down beside her feet. "What now?"

"As soon as we're sure we aren't being followed, we go back to the safe house." She looked in the rearview mirror. "Hold on. We're being followed." She accelerated and changed lanes again.

Rachel pushed her hand against the dash and looked back through the rear window. "How is that possible?"

"Oh God, I know how they found us so quickly." Claire held up her right arm. "My tracker, somehow they have the signal."

"Shit. We have to disable it right now or we'll never lose them," said Kathrine.

Claire saw a spark, and then the driver's side mirror splintered.

Kathrine swerved. "Hang on, they're shooting at us."

Claire leaned forward. "Airport, get to the airport. We can disable the tracker there."

Kathrine's fingers gripped the steering wheel tighter. "No, no good, they're too close. We'll never lose them."

Claire looked out the front windshield and saw the hospital sign in the distance. "Get off the exit up ahead, and turn right to the hospital."

Rachel looked out the side window. "No, we won't lose them that way either. Stay on the Beltway—I have an idea." She undid her seat belt and climbed into the back seat with Claire and looked at her.

As soon as Claire realized what she was going to do, she pulled back and turned away, covering her arm. "No, Rachel. I can't do it. Please don't make me do that."

"It's the only way. We'll never lose them if we don't."

She saw Kathrine glance at her through the rearview mirror, grimacing. "She's right, Claire. It's the only chance we have. You have to do it."

Another shot hit the SUV, shattering the passenger side mirror. Kathrine swerved and continued to weave in and out of traffic.

"I'm so sorry, but it's the only way." Rachel reached behind her and pulled out her knife. "I need something to use as a tourniquet." She searched frantically but didn't finding anything. "Damn it, I don't have anything." Claire pointed to Rachel's blouse. She reached down and cut the lower part of it and then ripped off a strip. "I can't see."

"Here." Claire turned on her cell phone flashlight.

Suddenly, Kathrine swerved again, and Rachel bumped into Claire.

"Kathrine, you have to drive straight or I can't do this. Hold up your arm for few seconds, Claire. It will slow the bleeding down."

The headlights went off.

"Hurry, we're coming up on an exit, and they're back far enough that they can't see us."

"I'm sorry, Claire." Rachel brought her arm down, wrapped the strip tightly, and guided the knife where the microchip had been inserted. She pushed the blade. The blood oozed.

Claire cried out and gritted her teeth.

She made the cut deeper, then probed with her fingers, finally pulling out the microchip and laying it in Claire's hand. She untied the tourniquet and wrapped her arm.

"Throw it out the window," yelled Kathrine.

"No." Rachel motioned out the window at the black pickup truck with the right blinker on. "Pull up as close as you can to that truck before it gets onto the exit ramp."

Kathrine drove faster and maneuvered beside the black truck, almost touching it.

Rachel lowered the window.

"Dump the cell phones too, just in case," Kathrine told her.

She jammed the microchip into one of the cell phones and threw them in quick succession out the window, landing them in the truck bed as the truck went down the exit ramp. Kathrine slipped back into traffic.

Claire looked out the back window, straining to see, holding her arm. "They didn't get back on the entrance ramp."

"Are you sure?" asked Kathrine.

"Positive."

"I'm so sorry, Claire," said Rachel.

"Don't talk to me. I'm really angry right now." She continued to hold her arm. "Damn it, that hurts, and thanks to you I'm going to have another scar, shit."

"We have to get off the Beltway," Kathrine mumbled.

Claire could see Kathrine's pale face in the freeway lights. "There's blood on your right shoulder." When she saw the bullet hole in the driver's seat, she looked back and saw the hole in the rear window.

Rachel reached over and put the palm of her hand directly over the wound in Kathrine's shoulder and pushed. Kathrine moaned.

"We've got to get you to a hospital—you're bleeding badly. Get off the next exit," said Rachel.

They helped her into the back seat. Claire placed her coat on the wound while Rachel drove to the ER.

❖

Kathrine was taken for surgery. The ER doctor finished suturing Claire's arm and dressed it. "Four stitches," he told her. "Ibuprofen should help with the discomfort."

She glared at Rachel, but was glad she didn't have to stay for observation. She and Rachel returned to the safe house.

Jack stood in the middle of the living room, watching Claire. "Pretty exciting stuff," he said.

Claire was in a mood and not amused.

"Okay, here's the way it's going to go. Kathrine will be joining us by tomorrow afternoon. Claire, you and Kathrine will be leaving to go back to Cleveland tomorrow on the eight p.m. flight with extra security. Rachel and I have agreed it would be best to have you and Kathrine at the hotel with security until this is all over, if that's okay with you?"

"Do I have a choice?"

"Not really. We'll regroup later this evening. I want everyone to destress and get a few hours' rest. When they went after you three, they tipped their hand, and we now have what we need to wrap up this case. Frank, let's talk in the den."

Claire left the group and went to her assigned bedroom to lie down. She was exhausted. Rachel came in a few minutes later and sat on the bed next to her.

"Claire, please don't be mad at me. I'm so sorry."

Claire put her hand on Rachel's arm. "I can't stay mad at you. I know you probably saved our lives, and I know it was hard for you, but I just don't want to have any more scars."

"Four stitches will not leave much of a scar. What about Kathrine's scar?"

Claire took a deep breath and looked at her. "I want you to come back with me. I don't want you to stay here. You were right."

"I can't do that. I have to stay here and finish this."

"Damn it, I don't want to do this. This is it for me, I mean it. I'm not going to go through this stress one more time."

"Claire, you're upset. This is not a good time to talk about this."

"You're damn right I'm upset. I don't like this tension and stress. I have money and I don't need to be doing this. I want some peace in my life. And I'm not going to a hotel either, I'm going to Sarah's, and Jack can kiss my ass if he doesn't like it. He can't do a damn thing about it."

"I see your defiance and stubbornness have come back."

Rachel took her hand, but she pulled it away.

"I'm not kidding, Rachel. This is going to stop. I'm tired and I want to rest. Please leave me alone."

Rachel left the room, closing the door behind her.

Claire cussed and threw a pillow at the door.

CHAPTER THIRTY-TWO

The entire team, including Claire, sat in the back of the Cleveland hotel bar, drinks in hand.

Jack raised his glass. "One hell of a job, all of you."

Everyone raised their glasses to Jack and drank.

"Claire, great job." He raised his glass to her.

She didn't care if he did toast her, she wasn't going to work with them anymore. They would have to find someone else. She raised her glass.

Jack raised his glass to Rachel. "Rachel, no words, baby, you are the best."

When he finished his drink, he and Frank said good-bye and left for the airport.

Rachel, Claire, and Kathrine took a taxi from the hotel to Sarah's house and arrived just in time for a late supper.

"Aunt Rachel," Tommy yelled and gave her a hug when they came through the door.

"Tommy, you have grown at least a foot since I last saw you."

"You are all staying for Christmas Eve, Christmas Day, and the day after, and there is no discussion about it," said Sarah. "Tilly is singing tonight at Troy's downtown and won't be home for a while."

Ricky came in and hugged Rachel, and then introduced himself to Kathrine. Tommy and Ricky took their luggage to their assigned bedrooms, and then they all sat down and had supper.

"I'll see you tomorrow," Tommy said. "I'm going tobogganing with some friends, and then we're spending the night at the Roof Top." Tommy looked at his dad. "With some of the parents." He told them good night and left.

"Wow. He sure turned out to be one terrific kid," said Rachel.

Sarah and Ricky beamed.

After supper Ricky went into the den to watch TV and they went into the living room.

"So Kathrine, I want to hear about you. Where did you grow up, and what did you do before you worked for Jack?" asked Sarah.

"I'm originally from Denver, Colorado. My folks own an art studio downtown. My mom is an artist, and my dad was a general contractor but retired and built Mother a studio and became her greatest fan and helper. He makes all of her frames and does special orders for frames. I went into the military right after college and served six years and then went to work for Jack."

The front door opened and Tilly walked in. She went straight to the liquor cabinet. "No one is drinking—why not?"

"We already drank at the hotel bar earlier," said Claire.

Tilly poured herself a drink and sat down next to Claire and Rachel on the couch. "What are we talking about?"

"Kathrine just told us about her family," said Rachel.

"Did she tell you she was in the 2010 Winter Olympics in Canada?" asked Tilly.

"No," said Claire, looking at Kathrine.

Kathrine's face turned slightly red as she smiled.

"Oh, yeah. Bronze medal, downhill skiing."

"Wow, impressive," said Rachel.

Kathrine's face turned even more red.

"But that's not the most impressive thing. She has a silver medal from the Summer Olympics in the United Kingdom 2012. Pistol at twenty-five meters."

Claire looked at Kathrine. "Now I am really impressed."

Rachel leaned forward. "So am I, Kathrine. Congratulations, that is quite the feat."

"Thank you."

"Wait a minute," said Claire. "Tilly, how do you know that?"

Everyone was quiet and looked at each other, not knowing what to say.

"Let's play cards," said Tilly, ignoring her question.

Claire felt even more confused. "Stop. Tilly, how do you know Kathrine?"

Tilly and Kathrine looked at each other.

"I met Tilly at a party at Lil' Nell's last year," said Kathrine.

Claire saw Tilly look at her out of the corner of her eye. She didn't say anything more.

"Kathrine, I like to play a game called hossy—it's double deck euchre. Have you ever played euchre?" asked Tilly.

"Actually, I played it in the army all the time when we had downtime. We used to have tournaments."

"Now we're talkin'."

"I think I'll pass tonight," said Rachel. "I'm going to bed."

"I'll play," said Claire.

"I will also," said Sarah.

"What's the sleeping arrangements for everyone tonight?" Claire asked. She was hoping sleeping accommodations would be limited, and Rachel would want her in with her.

Sarah looked at Rachel and then at her. "You and Tilly are in Tilly's room, Kathrine is down here in the den, and Rachel is upstairs in the other guest room."

Claire nodded, trying not to look disappointed.

"This card game is not a fair match," said Tilly. "Claire's going to cheat."

"Stop your complaining," said Claire. "I am not."

"You'll have to excuse them, Kathrine. We all fight like sisters," said Sarah.

After she and Sarah blew Kathrine and Tilly away, three games straight, Claire said she was going to bed.

Sarah walked Kathrine to her room, and then she, Tilly, and Claire went up to their rooms. Claire climbed in bed next to Tilly. She lay in bed wondering about Rachel and what was going to happen.

"Tilly, you awake?"

"Barely."

"Do you have to sing tonight or Christmas?"

"No. I don't have any more commitments but rehearsals until New Year's Eve."

"Tilly."

"What?"

"I…I think I'm in love."

Tilly immediately sat up in bed and turned on the lamp.

Claire saw the worried expression on her face. "Why are you looking at me like that?"

"Claire, Rachel loves you so much. It would break her heart."

"You're an idiot."

❖

Rachel woke in the morning when Claire came into her room and got in bed with her, putting her cold feet against her legs.

"Good morning. I'm sorry I was so mean to you in Washington." Rachel wanted to kiss her but didn't. "It's all right. I know you were stressed. Today is Christmas Eve, and all of our gifts for each other are in Las Vegas. Can we go shopping this morning and get a few gifts for each other and for Kathrine? The gifts we shipped a couple of weeks ago for Sarah and her family and Tilly arrived, didn't they?"

The smell of bacon and the rattle of pots and pans drifted up into the room.

"Yes, their gifts arrived last week. Let's do that—maybe the others would like to go with us." Claire took her hand. "Merry Christmas. I'm so glad you're here."

"Merry Christmas." *Another Christmas with Claire, but not with my wife.* Her entire body ached—her arms ached to hold her, her fingers ached to touch her, her heart ached to express the words of love. She felt Claire's absence in every nerve and fiber—the pain was almost unbearable.

Claire looked over on the dresser at a picture of her and Rachel with Sarah and Tilly. "When was that picture taken?"

She looked at the picture. "I think that was here in Cleveland, before Tilly moved to Las Vegas." She watched Claire as her face strained. "Do you remember?"

Claire sighed and shook her head slowly. "No, I feel like it's on the edge somewhere, but I just can't grab it. It's so frustrating. I remember some of it. It feels so familiar, but I can't get the important memories to put the pieces together."

She put her arms around Claire and held her. "Try to relax about it, and don't worry so much." *Please try, try harder to remember. I miss you so much.*

Claire stayed with her for a long time, talking and laughing, and then left her bed and went to the bathroom to shower.

Rachel dressed and went downstairs to the kitchen.

Claire came down and picked up a piece of bacon off her plate.

"Hey, I was eating that."

Claire touched her face as she walked by and smiled. She put scrambled eggs on a plate, grabbed a piece of replacement bacon for

Rachel, and sat down beside her at the table, opposite Sarah and Ricky. "Tilly isn't up yet?"

"No, you know her—she's definitely not a morning person. She is so used to it because of staying up all night at the clubs."

Claire laughed. "Remember when she used to be up before any of us at those sleepovers and wake everyone up and whine because no one wanted to do anything?"

Sarah laughed. "Do you remember Kitty Chamber's thirteenth birthday party?"

Claire started laughing. "Oh my gosh, Rachel, you should have seen Tilly. She let Kitty cut her hair. What a hoot that was, and she..." Claire suddenly stopped and got quiet.

Rachel's heart skipped a beat and her breath caught in her throat. She grabbed her arm. "What is it? Are you all right?"

Claire looked at her and then at Sarah. "I remember so clearly—there's no fog or covering over that memory. It's just there." She put her arms around Rachel and hugged her. "What a wonderful Christmas present."

Sarah came over and hugged her. "Merry Christmas, sweetheart."

"Merry Christmas, Sarah."

"This is a wonderful Christmas. Everyone is healthy and strong," said Sarah.

"We want to go get a few Christmas presents this morning. Would you like to go with us?" Rachel asked.

"Yes," Sarah lowered her voice, "I need to get a gift for Kathrine."

"Ricky, what are you doing today?" Claire asked.

"I'm finishing up my home-made Christmas presents," he announced, proudly.

"I'm so impressed," said Claire.

Downtown Cleveland was packed with last-minute Christmas shoppers. Rachel remembered that even though she didn't particularly like Cleveland, no city dressed up finer for Christmas. All the stores had festive red, green, and white Christmas lights, and people smiled and wished each other Merry Christmas.

Their gifts were purchased and wrapped in colorful Christmas paper and ribbons, and then they walked downtown past the stores, ready to catch a cab to go home.

"Stop," yelled Claire.

Rachel and Sarah immediately stopped.

"That store back there is being robbed."

Rachel looked around for a police officer but there was none to be found, no cruisers or officers on horseback. "I don't have a weapon on me."

"Wait here," said Claire. She walked into the small corner grocery store and came back a few seconds later with three cans of peaches. She walked back toward the building and told them to follow her.

"When I tell you, both of you throw those as hard as you can toward whoever comes out of that door there." She pointed to the door in the building as she watched through the corner window. She kept her eyes on the window. "Okay, get ready."

They drew back their cans of peaches.

"What if we hit somebody else?" asked Sarah.

"We won't...Now!"

They threw their cans of peaches as hard as they could.

The man came out of the store and was hit in the head by the can Claire threw and blasted in the shoulder and stomach by the other two cans. He staggered and went down to the sidewalk.

"The police are just around the corner and are walking toward him," Claire warned. "Run."

They took off running for a taxi, hailed it down, and got in, throwing their packages on the seats.

Rachel told the driver to go up past the building. When he drove by, the police were handcuffing the man, and the store owner was yelling in his face.

"Wow, you are the hero of the day, Claire," she said.

The taxi driver slowed. "I saw what you did—you threw cans at that man. He is very bad. You ladies ride free anywhere today."

"Well, aren't you just the sweetest cab driver in Cleveland," said Claire.

He drove them home, and before they got out, Claire reached into her purse and pulled out two hundred-dollar bills. "Here, this is for you, a tip. Merry Christmas."

He got out of his cab and walked around to her and hugged her. "And you, Merry Christmas to you and your family. You are beautiful." He also hugged Sarah and Rachel.

They went into the house laughing and put the presents near the tree.

Tilly and Kathrine were sitting in the living room, listening to Christmas carols and visiting.

Claire plopped down on the couch between them. "Merry Christmas," she said laughing. "You are beautiful."

Sarah and Rachel laughed.

Tilly looked at Claire and then at Rachel. "Is she drunk?"

Rachel shook her head. "You had to be there to get that one, Tilly."

Sarah came over and sat down in the chair. "You two are sitting next to a bona fide hero."

Claire laughed.

"I mean it, Claire was a hero today."

"What happened?" asked Tilly.

Sarah told the entire story, and when she was finished, Tilly's mouth was open.

Kathrine applauded. "Well done, you."

"It was a team effort," said Claire.

The evening was spent celebrating the love they all felt for each other and expressing gratefulness for their blessings. Tommy arrived home with gifts and put them under the tree.

"Mom, is it okay if I have a couple of guests tomorrow for dinner?"

"Sure, who is it?"

"I met someone a couple of weeks ago, and we've been talking. Her name is Sheryl. She's from Mentor. Her mom and dad are divorced and she's with her dad this week."

Sarah gave a mom look to the others. "Great."

He insisted they test his Aunt Claire's skills.

"All right, you get five seconds to look, and then you have to tell me everything you saw." He held up the flash card with a picture of multiple kitchen items. "Ready, go."

Rachel laughed as she watched him try to trip her up. He counted out loud to distract her, and then whipped the card behind his back after the five seconds.

"Okay what did you see? Aunt Rachel, check them off."

Claire named every single item on the card, plus two smudge marks and a small ink dot in the upper right-hand corner of the card.

"No way," he said. "One more." He held up a card with a picture of items found in a garage. "There is no way you are going to get all of these." He turned the card toward her and counted off the five seconds and then gave the card to Tilly. "Aunt Tilly, check them off."

Claire once again named all the items.

He stood up. "No way! How do you do that?"

Claire smiled and shrugged her shoulders.

Rachel laughed. "You think that's impressive, watch this." She took the deck of cards and held them out in front of Claire, shuffled twice, and then set them in front of her. "All right, Tommy, hold each card up without showing your Aunt Claire, and she'll tell you what the card is."

Claire told him every card before he showed it.

"You cheated. I know you did."

Rachel laughed. "No, she didn't cheat. She's just gifted."

"Okay, enough for the night," said Sarah. "Big day tomorrow."

Sarah looked at Tilly. "Are you up to singing one Christmas song for us before we go to bed, Till?"

"Of course, I'd love to." Tilly stood up and sang Sarah's favorite Christmas song as Sarah got tears in her eyes.

When she was done, they all hugged and wished each other Merry Christmas and went to bed. Rachel hid her tears and the lonely ache for Claire deep inside.

CHAPTER THIRTY-THREE

Claire woke, seeing the numbers to the combination safe rolling around in her head. She shook Tilly.

"Tilly, wake up. I have to go back to Las Vegas right away."

Tilly rolled over and looked at the clock. "Are you nuts, it's twelve thirty at night. Go back to sleep."

She shook her again. "Tilly, I'm serious. I have to go home right away."

Tilly sat up and turned on the lamp, covering her eyes. "What is wrong with you, Claire? There are no flights leaving Hopkins this late, and it is now officially Christmas Day. Go back to sleep."

Claire sat up and got out her cell phone. "Then I'll charter a private jet."

"Oh my God, Claire—you have finally lost your mind."

Tilly tried to take the phone away from her, but she ripped it back out of her hand.

"I'm going."

Tilly grabbed the phone again, and she grabbed it back.

"Stop it, Tilly, I'm going."

"Why? What is so damned important that you have to fly home Christmas Day?"

"There's something in the safe, and I have to see it."

Tilly looked at her. "You're starting to remember, aren't you?"

"I can't remember what it is just yet, but I know it's important."

"All right, I'll go with you."

"No, stay here. I don't want you to miss Christmas. I'll be back as soon as I can."

"You are not flying to Vegas by yourself in the middle of the night on Christmas Day. We can be back by early afternoon if we get a flight right away."

"Okay, let's go."

As soon as she got into the house, she went to the pantry where the safe was and turned on the light, knelt down and dialed the numbers, turned the handle, and slowly pulled the heavy cast iron door open. She sat down on the floor and took three envelopes and several jewelry cases out of the safe, and then started to look through the envelopes, fanning the contents. There were two sets of key life documents for her and for Rachel, and the last envelope held the insurance papers and lease for the house. She laid them down beside her.

The first jewelry case contained a beautiful jade and diamond necklace. She took it out of the case and held it in her hand, studying it. She closed her eyes and could see Rachel holding the necklace in front of her, and then she felt her close to her, the sweet scent of her hair, and the warmth of her body. She kissed the necklace and put it back into its case.

She picked up the second case with a matching smaller case. The larger case contained a diamond necklace surrounded by opals encased in gold, and the smaller case contained the matching earrings. She tried to get the memory, but all she saw was Rachel close to her, kissing her. She could feel the sensual pleasure of her hands on her body. She closed the cases and set them down, picking up another case with two diamond and gold wedding bands. She touched them with her finger, and in her mind she saw a picture of the courthouse steps and everyone raising their glasses at a party. The images were vivid and clear.

She took out the remaining small black velvet case, her hands shaking as she held it for a long time, moving her finger slowly over the soft cover, realizing what was in it before she opened it, sensing its sparkle, beauty, and shape. She opened the lid slowly, reached in, and took out the pear-cut diamond ring, holding it securely in her hand. Before she put it on her left ring finger, she knew it would fit perfectly. She slipped it on her finger, gazing at it, desperately searching in her mind for the memories she wanted and needed, and then she reached farther into the safe and pulled out the last folder and opened it—their wedding certificate.

The needed pieces of the puzzle floated into place. She brought the ring up to her lips as she saw Rachel's face, Cleveland in the fall, Rachel lying naked next to her, Tilly's house, the bedroom with Rachel, Rachel's scars, and their struggle to overcome her fears. She saw herself looking into her eyes, and their nights of love in Arizona. She trembled as she took the ring off her finger and closed the case. She put the envelopes and jewelry back into the safe, and then their marriage certificate and the empty case. She closed the safe and locked it. She went back to her room, clutching the diamond ring in her hand. She buried her face in her pillow, relieved, wanting Rachel, needing her, loving her.

Tilly came into her bedroom and got on the bed beside her.

"All this time, Tilly. Why, why wouldn't any of you tell me?"

Tilly wrapped her arms around her. "Because you needed to remember, not to be told."

Her body ached and throbbed. "I have to get to Rachel."

"I know. Let's get out of here."

On the way to the airport, Claire formulated her plan.

Tilly called the best hotel on Cleveland Square and made a reservation in Claire's name for one of their most expensive suites for three nights, and then called Sarah and told her the plan.

Tilly hugged her before she took a taxi to Sarah's. "We'll get her there, don't worry."

Claire heard the knock on the hotel door and answered it in nothing but her turquoise silk negligee.

Rachel's grin almost exceeded her facial capacity. "Wow, you look fabulous. I was worried. Where have you been?"

Claire took her by the hand and led her into the room, sitting down with her on the cream-colored brocade sofa.

"Are you all right?" Rachel asked.

"Yes, very much all right. I needed to talk with you without anyone around."

She watched the color drain from Rachel's face.

"Claire, you've been alone, haven't you?"

She reached out and took her hand, looking into her deep hazel eyes, seeing the momentary glimpse of apprehension, a shudder of disquiet that seemed to form in the iris and then slowly recede.

"Yes, I've been alone."

Rachel breathed out a sigh.

Suddenly, as if a door had been thrown open in a darkened room and the sunshine burst in, the shadows disappeared, and she could see it—Rachel had been holding back so she would have the best chance to remember. She watched her as the thick wet snowflakes floated down on the Cleveland skyline. She saw her hands tremble. She saw her longing and need, her pain and desperation after over a year of grief and separation.

"You look so sad, Rachel. What's wrong?"

"Nothing, nothing of importance." Rachel turned away, withdrawing.

"Will you tell me a story about us?"

The pain seeped down her face as she slowly shook her head. "No, I can't."

How painful it must have been for you, to remember and know, to be alone where I couldn't go and be with you.

"Why not?"

She watched Rachel, knowing she was trying to hold back the floodgates of pain and tears. She saw how much she was suffering, her agony, her loneliness and despair from not knowing if Claire's memories would ever return. It was etched in her face.

"I just can't."

Claire reached up and touched Rachel's face, looking into her—it was time. "I'll tell you a story. I remember the first time I saw you, standing in the doorway of the art department lecture room, and I knew my life would never be the same. We loved each other from the moment we met, and we fought our love and desire through the depths of hell and back, but through it all, our love just grew stronger." She leaned toward her and rested her hand on her waist. "Rachel, my love, my heart—my wife—I remember...I remember everything."

She pulled her to her and wrapped her arms around her as Rachel collapsed into her arms. She held her, comforting, assuring. She kissed her hair and stroked her head, then kissed her face. There were so many tears she couldn't tell where Rachel's ended and hers began.

She cradled Rachel in her arms. "You feel so wonderful to be in my arms again." She touched her face, seeing her notice her ring.

Rachel wrapped her arms tightly around her, burying her face in her neck. "I thought I lost you, Claire. I thought our life together was over."

"No, Rachel, just a momentary separation, and if I would have never remembered, I know I would have fallen in love with you all over again. I already did." She stood up and took her hand, lifting her up, leading her to the bed. "I need to feel you next to me."

They lay down on the bed and held each other.

Claire stroked her face. "No words we speak will ever be enough, but I will say this to you, Rachel. I will be with you each morning when you wake for the rest of our lives. Are you really mine, or was it just a dream I had long ago?"

Rachel held on to her. "Yes, I'm yours."

"I remember our lovemaking, but it feels like a fog and that it was so long ago. I want to make new memories. I don't want to think about the past."

"We have the rest of our lives—we can take our time."

Claire moved closer against her and began to kiss her face, and then kissed her, deeply entering her mouth, feeling her respond as consuming desire and hunger swept over her. She reached up and ran her fingers through Rachel's hair and then began to unbutton her blouse, kissing her neck. "I don't want to wait, Rachel. We've both waited long enough. I need to touch you."

She moaned and throbbed as Rachel kissed her, wanton need rising. "Was it always like this for us? I can hardly breathe I want you so badly."

Rachel brushed her fingertips over her waist and up to her breasts. Claire could feel Rachel's desire and need pulsing, merging with hers.

"Yes, we've always wanted each other."

Claire moved on top of her, looking down into her face, seeing the radiant flecks of amber in her eyes. She breathed out Rachel's name and kissed her more deeply, the soft and wet and warmth of their kiss full of love and hope for their future.

"You are my breath and soul. Have I ever told you my life is nothing without you? Rachel, you are my wife."

"And you are mine—come to me."

About the Author

Suzie was born in a small town in Northeast Ohio, a middle child with three brothers, which explains a lot. It was hard to be heard as the only girl in a family of three rowdy boys, and since no one listened to her anyway, she started making stuff up—and has been doing it ever since. She was given a journal at the age of twelve, and it started her on the adventure of writing. She spent part of her childhood in Florida, where she acquired a love of all things Southern. When she is not writing she can be found with her family, enjoying the outdoors, backpacking, golfing, or just being in nature.

Books Available From Bold Strokes Books

Secret Agent by Michelle Larkin. CIA Agent Peyton North embarks on a global chase to apprehend rogue agent Zoey Blackwood, but her commitment to the mission is tested as the sparks between them ignite and their sizzling attraction approaches a point of no return. (978-1-63555-753-4)

Journey to Cash by Ashley Bartlett. Cash Braddock thought everything was great, but it looks like her history is about to become her right now. Which is a real bummer. (978-1-63555-464-9)

Liberty Bay by Karis Walsh. Wren Lindley's life is mired in tradition and untouched by trends until social media star Gina Strickland introduces an irresistible electricity into her off-the-grid world. (978-1-63555-816-6)

Scent by Kris Bryant. Nico Marshall has been burned by women in the past wanting her for her money. This time, she's determined to win Sophia Sweet over with her charm. (978-1-63555-780-0)

Shadows of Steel by Suzie Clarke. As their worlds collide and their choices come back to haunt them, Rachel and Claire must figure out how to stay together and, most of all, stay alive. (978-1-63555-810-4)

The Clinch by Nicole Disney. Eden Bauer overcame a difficult past to become a world champion mixed martial artist, but now rising star and dreamy bad girl Brooklyn Shaw is a threat both to Eden's title and her heart. (978-1-63555-820-3)

The Last First Kiss by Julie Cannon. Kelly Newsome is so ready for a tropical island vacation, but she never expects to meet the woman who could give her her last first kiss. (978-1-63555-768-8)

The Mandolin Lunch by Missouri Vaun. Despite their immediate attraction, everything about Garet Allen says short-term, and Tess Hill refuses to consider anything less than forever. (978-1-63555-566-0)

Thor: Daughter of Asgard by Genevieve McCluer. When Hannah Olsen finds out she's the reincarnation of Thor, she's thrown into a world of magic and intrigue, unexpected attraction, and a mystery she's got to unravel. (978-1-63555-814-2)

Veterinary Technician by Nancy Wheelton. When a stable of horses is threatened, Val and Ronnie must work together against the odds to save them and maybe even themselves along the way. (978-1-63555-839-5)

16 Steps to Forever by Georgia Beers. Can Brooke Sullivan and Macy Carr find themselves by finding each other? (978-1-63555-762-6)

All I Want for Christmas by Georgia Beers, Maggie Cummings & Fiona Riley. The Christmas season sparks passion and love in these stories by award-winning authors Georgia Beers, Maggie Cummings, and Fiona Riley. (978-1-63555-764-0)

From the Woods by Charlotte Greene. When Fiona goes backpacking in a protected wilderness, the last thing she expects is to be fighting for her life. (978-1-63555-793-0)

Heart of the Storm by Nicole Stiling. For Juliet Mitchell and Sienna Bennett a forbidden attraction definitely isn't worth upending the life they've worked so hard for. Is it? (978-1-63555-789-3)

If You Dare by Sandy Lowe. For Lauren West and Emma Prescott, following their passions is easy. Following their hearts, though? That's almost impossible. (978-1-63555-654-4)

Love Changes Everything by Jaime Maddox. For Samantha Brooks and Kirby Fielding, no matter how careful their plans, love will change everything. (978-1-63555-835-7)

Not This Time by MA Binfield. Flung back into each other's lives, can former bandmates Sophia and Madison have a second chance at romance? (978-1-63555-798-5)

The Found Jar by Jaycie Morrison. Fear keeps Emily Harris trapped in her emotionally vacant life; can she find the courage to let Beck Reynolds guide her toward love? (978-1-63555-825-8)

Aurora by Emma L McGeown. After a traumatic accident, Elena Ricci is stricken with amnesia, leaving her with no recollection of the last eight years, including her wife and son. (978-1-63555-824-1)

Avenging Avery by Sheri Lewis Wohl. Revenge against a vengeful vampire unites Isa Meyer and Jeni Denton, but it's love that heals them. (978-1-63555-622-3)

Bulletproof by Maggie Cummings. For Dylan Prescott and Briana Logan, the complicated NYC criminal justice system doesn't leave room for love, but where the heart is concerned, no one is bulletproof. (978-1-63555-771-8)

Her Lady to Love by Jane Walsh. A shy wallflower joins forces with the most popular woman in Regency London on a quest to catch a husband, only to discover a wild passion for each other that far eclipses their interest for the Marriage Mart. (978-1-63555-809-8)

No Regrets by Joy Argento. For Jodi and Beth, the possibility of losing their future will force them to decide what is really important. (978-1-63555-751-0)

The Holiday Treatment by Elle Spencer. Who doesn't want a gay Christmas movie? Holly Hudson asks herself that question and discovers that happy endings aren't only for the movies. (978-1-63555-660-5)

Too Good to be True by Leigh Hays. Can the promise of love survive the realities of life for Madison and Jen, or is it too good to be true? (978-1-63555-715-2)

Treacherous Seas by Radclyffe. When the choice comes down to the lives of her officers against the promise she made to her wife, Reese Conlon puts everything she cares about on the line. (978-1-63555-778-7)

Two to Tangle by Melissa Brayden. Ryan Jacks has been a player all her life, but the new chef at Tangle Valley Vineyard changes everything. If only she wasn't off the menu. (978-1-63555-747-3)

When Sparks Fly by Annie McDonald. Will the devastating incident that first brought Dr. Daniella Waveny and hockey coach Luca McCaffrey together on frozen ice now force them apart, or will their secrets and fears thaw enough for them to create sparks? (978-1-63555-782-4)

Best Practice by Carsen Taite. When attorney Grace Maldonado agrees to mentor her best friend's little sister, she's prepared to confront Perry's rebellious nature, but she isn't prepared to fall in love. Legal Affairs: one law firm, three best friends, three chances to fall in love. (978-1-63555-361-1)

Home by Kris Bryant. Natalie and Sarah discover that anything is possible when love takes the long way home. (978-1-63555-853-1)

Keeper by Sydney Quinne. With a new charge under her reluctant wing—feisty, highly intelligent math wizard Isabelle Templeton—Keeper Andy Bouchard has to prevent a murder or die trying. (978-1-63555-852-4)

One More Chance by Ali Vali. Harry Basantes planned a future with Desi Thompson until the day Desi disappeared without a word, only to walk back into her life sixteen years later. (978-1-63555-536-3)

Renegade's War by Gun Brooke. Freedom fighter Aurelia DeCallum regrets saving the woman called Blue. She fears it will jeopardize her mission, and secretly, Blue might end up breaking Aurelia's heart. (978-1-63555-484-7)

The Other Women by Erin Zak. What happens in Vegas should stay in Vegas, but what do you do when the love you find in Vegas changes your life forever? (978-1-63555-741-1)

The Sea Within by Missouri Vaun. Time is running out for Dr. Elle Graham to convince Captain Jackson Drake that the only thing that can save future Earth resides in the past, and rescue her broken heart in the process. (978-1-63555-568-4)

To Sleep With Reindeer Justine Saracen. In Norway under Nazi occupation, Maarit, an Indigenous woman, and Kirsten, a Norwegian resister, join forces to stop the development of an atomic weapon. (978-1-63555-735-0)

Twice Shy by Aurora Rey. Having an ex with benefits isn't all it's cracked up to be. Will Amanda Russo learn that lesson in time to take a chance on love with Quinn Sullivan? (978-1-63555-737-4)

Z-Town by Eden Darry. Forced to work together to stay alive, Meg and Lane must find the centuries-old treasure before the zombies find them first. (978-1-63555-743-5